"THE WEAPON THE ENEMY HAS FORGED AGAINST YOU . . . AIN'T EVEN REAL," PASTOR KING DECLARED.

Charity listened intently to his sermon.

"Quit getting upset when he throws something at you, quit getting distracted, quit giving up . . . When he throws a weapon at you, he's giving you ammunition to use against him. Every time he messes with your children, your finances, your car, your spouse, and you speak the Word out of your mouth, it becomes as sharp as any two-edged sword."

Charity was pleased she had received a word of encouragement. She didn't want to talk to anyone; she wanted to go home and reclaim her house. She realized she'd been living in fear and expecting something bad to happen since the incident with her patient. She directed her thoughts toward the devil. *You want a fight, you just picked one, and I ain't backing down this time . . .*

"Fiction for the faithful."
 —Black Issues Book Review

"Need a little good news in your novels? Look no futher."
 —Essence

GOOD TO ME

LaTonya Mason

Walk Worthy Press

West Bloomfield, Michigan

WARNER BOOKS

NEW YORK   BOSTON

Published by Warner Books with Walk Worthy Press™

Warner Books

Time Warner Book Group
1271 Avenue of the Americas, New York, NY 10020

Walk Worthy Press 33290 West Fourteen Mile Road, #482, West Bloomfield, MI 48322

Visit our Web sites at www.twbookmark.com and www.walkworthypress.net.

Printed in the United States of America

First Edition: October 2005
10 9 8 7 6 5 4 3 2 1

Library of Congress Cataloging-in-Publication Data
Mason, LaTonya.
    Good to me / LaTonya Mason.— 1st ed.
        p. cm.
    Summary: "The life of an accomplished single mother who juggles her responsibilities as a therapist at her counseling firm and a minister at her church"—Provided by publisher.
        ISBN 0-446-69645-5
    1. Working mothers—Fiction.   2. Single mothers—Fiction.   3. Women clergy—Fiction.
I. Title.
        PS3613 .A8174G66 2005
        813'. 6—dc22

                                                    2005010567

Book design and text composition by L&G McRee
Cover design and illustration: TRUE (www.trueart.biz)

This book is dedicated to my Heavenly Father as firstfruit, for being faithful to His promises. Thanks, Daddy.

Acknowledgments

So many people to thank and so little space.

I first thank my children, Floyd Jr., Isaiah, and Destiny for toler-ating all of my "I'm sorry, Mommy's working" shoo-aways and for taking care of one another. I thank God for each of you. What a great inheritance you are to me.

I bless my parents Charles and Lorraine for accepting God's assignment to raise me, and for pushing me to rise above my obsta-cles (and for permission to use their names in my book). Kiss, kiss. I honor my younger sisters and brother, Tasha, Charles, and Adrienne for humbly accepting me, always supporting me, and believing in me. I am proud of each of you. To my niece and nephew, Jasmine and Anthony, thanks for letting me aggravate the mess out of you. "Who wants some Auntie love?" To all of my aunts, uncles, cousins, and grandparents, thanks for your hand in raising me.

To my biological parents, Gibran and Brenda, I wouldn't be here without you. Thanks for genetically imparting your talents to me—writing, singing, drawing, and the ability to survive anything. Daddy, thanks for sending me a newspaper clipping on Walk Worthy Press years before I dared to write this novel. I love you both.

Hugs and kisses to my church family at Chappell Memorial Bap-tist Church for all of your prayers and support. A big shout-out to the intercessory prayer team for putting thousands of demons to flight on my behalf—BJ, Wanda, Keila, Velma, Vonne, and Jeneen. I praise God for my spiritual father, Reverend Norman Kerry, for your spiritual leadership and guidance. May God pour back into you all you've poured into me. I send love to First Lady Phette, Mackenzie, Madison, Tre, and Mother Kerry.

To the best girlfriends on this side of heaven, Lavonne Sadler, April Thompson, and Kim Mayhew. Y'all are the biggity bomb! What would I do without you? I love you.

Blessings to Sha-Lai, Koren, Regina, Kim, and Lavonne for reading draft after draft of this book when it was in its infancy. Thanks Toots for letting me use your names.

A big shout-out to my coworkers at Presbyterian Behavioral Health for picking up my slack on the days I left early to write. I found the greatest encouragement through your words and prayers.

To Floyd Sr., Shirley, Tabitha, Jeremy, Jarvis, Madear, Geraldine, and Mel. Thanks for your unreserved support and love.

I blow a kiss to Victoria Christopher Murray for encouraging me to write. If it wasn't for your admonishment, this book would still be in my belly. I also thank Andrea Michele Bowen for encouragement at one of your book signings in Charlotte, NC.

A hug to Tara Godfrey for allowing me to be your first client and taking my photographs for this book. May your photography business grow and grow.

Denise Stinson, you're a breath of fresh air to the book publishing industry. You've ministered to me in so many ways. I've learned a lot about writing, publishing, discipleship, and myself through you. One Scripture comes to mind when I think of you, He who wins souls is wise (Proverbs 11:30). Grace to you and everyone at Walk Worthy. Frances Jalet-Miller, you're an awesome editor and teacher. You've been a blessing to me. Thanks for tirelessly editing my manuscript, even when I was tired of it.

I bless each and every reader. May God make His grace abound unto you so that in all things, at all times, you'll have all that you need and you'll abound in every good work (2 Corinthians 9:8). Thanks.

Prologue

JOSEPH WAITED ANXIOUSLY FOR THE OLD MAN TO ARRIVE. Even though Chaplain Nesbit had become a father away from home to him, the chaplain was sometimes difficult to talk to. Joseph's heart was heavy and he needed to talk without being judged. Not that Chaplain Nesbit was judgmental. He was such a "live by faith and not by sight" man that he refused to hear about feelings of discouragement, anger, or anything that sounded like lack of trust in God.

They met more than two years earlier when the chaplain came to visit the prison's inmates to do weekly Bible studies in the common area of their dormitories. During their first meeting, the chaplain embarrassed Joseph so bad that he considered not going to any more of his sessions. Out of all the men in the Bible study that day, the old man chose to pick on Joseph.

"The third thang Hannah did is in chapter one, verse 12 of first Samuel," Joseph remembered the chaplain preaching. "'Member the first thang she did was stood up. That means she changed her position. Secondly, she prayed. And the third thang is . . . she continued to pray. She didn't stop prayin' 'cause she didn't see 'mediate results. She kept on prayin'. She didn't get caught up in the rules and reg'lations of religion that say if you pray mo' than once you don't have faith in God. She kept on prayin'. But you wanna pray one time and if God doesn't honor your lil' microwaved prayer, you retta give up. But not Hannah, she pushed. You know what that means, don't you?" he asked, looking over the top of his round gold-rimmed glasses that hung on the tip of his wide brown nose. The prisoners were attentive to the old man as he stood among them at the raggedy wooden podium. His small frame was a contradiction to the confidence he exuded. His gray mustache matched his small uncombed Afro and the tiny hairs that protruded from his ears. "Young man," Chaplain Nesbit called to Joseph. "You know what it means to push, don't you?"

"Uhm, yes, sir," he stammered. "Uhm, to push means to, uhm, apply pressure to something."

"You a dictionary or something, boy?" Chaplain Nesbit laughed, and started a roar of laughter as the other men laughed too. Joseph had a reputation for being a know-it-all. It was not uncommon to find him somewhere studying the Bible with a dictionary, concordance, a commentary, and a Greek and Hebrew parallel Bible. His peers called him "Brother Word." "Y'all young people thank you know everything. To push, p-u-s-h stands for praying till sumpin' happens. Hannah pushed. When do a woman in labor starts pushin', boy?"

"When she feels contractions?" he asked, thinking this was another trick question.

"That's right, a woman in labor don't start pushin' till she feel contractions, some pain. That's when you oughta start pushin'. When you feel some resistance, some pain, start pushin'. What'chu say, boy? Start 'plyin' some pressure. That's what Hannah did—she 'plied some pressure with the fervency of her prayer."

Before Chaplain Nesbit could give the benediction good, Joseph was already at the back door of the common area. He stopped in his tracks when he heard the chaplain yell, "Boy, I need to see you." Joseph thought the night would never end, but he was pleasantly surprised when the chaplain formally introduced himself and carried on a decent conversation with Joseph.

Ever since then they'd become good friends. Especially after Chaplain Nesbit's wife died and he retired from visiting the men. Joseph reached out to him and became his biggest source of support. They'd become so close that when Joseph felt led to become a minister, Chaplain Nesbit arranged for the Virginia General Baptist Association to license him. Just reminiscing over how much of a blessing Chaplain Nesbit has been to him made Joseph smile. When he looked up and saw his spiritual father walking over to him, his smile broadened.

"Hey, Pop, it's good to see you," he said, standing to hug him.

"You looking good, boy," the old man said, pushing his glasses up on his nose and stepping back to get a full view of Joseph's almost six-foot, thin, but newly muscular frame. "I see you've been takin' care of y'self. Liftin' weights?"

"Well," Joseph said, blushing and flexing his right arm. "You never know when Jesus will show up in the flesh presenting Himself as my bride. And a brother gots to be ready."

"Boy, you just as crazy as you was the last time I seen you."

"What'd you expect? That was just six months ago."

"Seems like yesterday. Time flyin' ain't it?"

Joseph looked down. "That's kinda along the lines of what I wanted to talk to you about. I'm kinda getting weary here and I need your help in getting refocused." He looked back up at his mentor. "Pop, I've been here for more than two years. Two years! I didn't plan on being here this long. I just knew I would've been shipped back home by now. I feel like I've fulfilled my purpose here. I gave my life to God the very first day I walked up in here and I serve Him wholeheartedly. I humbly accept my calling as a minister of the Gospel. Why am I still here?"

"Well, son—"

"I mean, I'm not complaining," Joseph said, remembering the last one-hour lecture he got the last time for complaining. "If God hadn't orchestrated my coming here, I would've still been out there womanizing, drinking, and partying. I would've never taken the opportunity to sit at the feet of great men and women of God. My time here has been blessed, but I miss my parents and my daughter. I miss the civilian lifestyle. You understand?"

"Yeah, I—"

"I don't mean to cut you off, but I've been holding this in for so long that if I don't get it out I feel like I'mma get angry at God and I know good and well that He's not the problem. I've done everything I know to do—I pray, I study, I fast, I confess the Word, I give sacrificially . . . I don't know what else to do." Joseph knew he was rambling on and on, but he figured he might as well finish what he'd already started.

Joseph was glad to see the old man smile, and was surprised to see him nod for him to go on talking. "I know what you're thinking, and you are right. I know God has a plan for me being here. I'm just ready to go home. I'm ready to settle down and remarry. I'm ready to be the father I should've been. I'm ready to pastor the church God will give me. I think ministering here has prepared me for that, don't you?"

"Is that a r'torical question or a cue for me to speak?" he chuckled. "Ever since I've known you, you've been tryin' to tell God how to be God. He's faithful to His promises, not yours." The chaplain slowed his voice down, "I see—"

"You see? See what?" Joseph asked, thinking he was about to receive a prophetic revelation of some sort.

"I see that you becomin' puffed up and proud. All you do is talk about yourself . . . about what you've done. You done fasted. You done prayed. You, you, you. Maybe that's why you're still here."

Joseph dropped his head.

"Look, son. I'm trying to help you here. If I ain't learned nothing else 'bout God in all my years, I've learned this one thang. If He ain't answerin' you, if He's ignorin' you, leave Him alone. It's for your own good. Ever had somebody gettin' on your nerves and you kept ignoring them 'cause you knew if you opened your mouth, you'd regret it?" Joseph nodded. "That's what I'm talkin' 'bout. God sees your work. The Bible says 'be not weary in well doing.' Don't faint now. Keep doing well. Keep confessing, serving, praying, and fastin'. You gone be rewarded. You of all people should know that a miracle don't happen based on what a situation looks like. Your change could come t'morrow. And if it did, you'd find that you ain't as ready as you think you is."

Joseph returned the old man's smile. "It's tight but it's right. What you've said is true. God doesn't owe me anything and I need to quit acting like He does. I know I'm going home soon. I'mma just wait on the Lord and let Him renew my strength."

"Now that's the man of God I know. Waitin' is only hard when you need to 'velop patience. And as a pastor-to-be, believe you me, you gone need a lot of it. 'Velop it now. God know what He doin'. Just thank, God could've used anything to exercise your faith . . . financial troubles, troubled marriage . . . anything. I ain't sayin' He puts those thangs on us, but He does allow 'em to happen and He works 'em out for our good."

"I've never thought of it that way." Joseph looked as if a light-bulb came on in his head. "I *can* count this one with all joy then."

"Absolutely. In due season, you'll obtain favor if you faint not."

"You mean reap if I faint not."

"Same thang."

"Not quite. That Scripture says, 'let us not be weary in well doing; for in due season we shall reap, if we faint not.' Now over in Proverbs it says, 'whoso findeth a wife findeth a good thing and obtaineth favor from the Lord.' Now I'm looking to obtain favor in that way, are you speaking prophetically?"

"Boy, you always lookin' for a prophecy. Let's finish this over lunch," the old man chuckled. "One thang's for sho." He stood to face Joseph. "When He does send you a wife, you gonna be pleased. 'Cause you done gone from being a ladies' man to a man after God's own heart. Everything you learnin' 'bout Him and 'speriencin' with Him, He gone make sho you 'sperience it on earth through her. She gone be the 'stension of His arms, His heart, Himself. The moment God started working on you two years ago, He started working on her. She gone be a mighty woman of God."

Joseph confessed aloud, "I receive her in the name of Jesus," and he walked with Chaplain Nesbit to the canteen.

Chapter 1

"*MAGNIFIQUE! MAGNIFIQUE!*" CHARITY EXCLAIMED, blowing kisses with both hands to her two staff people, Iesha and Harmony. "This place looks wonderful," she said, looking around the suite and admiring the purple and black balloons, decorations, and the sign that read, WELCOME TO HORIZONS CHRISTIAN COUNSELING CENTER. "You guys have done a wonderful job setting up. This open house is going to be the bomb."

"The bomb?" Iesha, her administrative assistant, asked with her head cocked back and her hand on her hip. "Sistergirl, you need to leave the slang to me. It doesn't become you at all. One minute you speaking French and the next you talking Westside. I believe they call that a *faux pas.*"

Iesha and Harmony erupted in laughter. Charity laughed too.

Imitating Iesha, Charity put her hand on her hip and swung her shoulder-length bobbed hair. "*Excusez-moi, mademoiselle.* Let's get one thing straight. I might be your big sister, but in this place, I'm your boss. You'll want to leave the shot-calling to me."

"My bad, Boss. Well since you handling things around here, tell me where you put the music so we can get this party started right."

"Oh shoot!" Charity said, stamping her foot on the carpet. "I knew I was forgetting something. Do either of you have music we can use?"

"I have a sounds of nature CD in my office," Harmony offered slowly.

"Pst!" Iesha sucked her teeth. "Don't nobody wanna listen to no birds or thunderstorms. Cherry, I got some Missy Elliott, Jay-Z, Nelly, R. Kelly—"

"Iesha, sweetie, this is an open house for a Christian counseling center, not the grand opening for Club 2000."

"I was just trying to help you out."

"Good," Charity said, walking toward her office to get her purse. "It'd help me out if you would go to my car and get the Fred Hammond, Kirk Franklin, and Israel and New Breed CDs."

"All right, then. I see how you want to be."

Charity handed her keys to her sister. "And please remember to call me Charity at work."

Iesha took the keys and playfully rolled her eyes as she spun around on her heels, away from Charity. Charity shook her head, trying to make light of the situation in front of Harmony, whom she'd met two years ago at a counselors' workshop. Charity was excited about working with her, a woman in her fifties who was always patient with insightful things to say. But the most important quality to Charity was that Harmony was a born-again believer. She hoped that Harmony wasn't offended by Iesha's comment. "Harmony, you'll have to pray for her. She's not yet come in under the Blood." Charity was glad to see Harmony smile. "Keep your CD on standby in case folks get tired of hearing mine, okay?"

"I will."

"Would you mind greeting guests and having them sign the guest book at the entryway?"

"No, I don't mind. What a wonderful opportunity to be a blessing, and to bless each and every person that comes through the door."

Charity smiled. That's why she recruited Harmony to work

with her. She had such a sweet spirit and was so pleasant to be around. "Please do. I have some special people coming tonight, including my pastor, Reverend King from Damascus Road Baptist Church."

"Yeah. I've heard of him. I went to a revival he did a few years back. He was good. I'm sure I'll recognize him while I'm hosting. By the way, I'm an excellent hostess. You know I used to be a waitress in my former life."

Charity glanced at her watch, hoping it would mask the scowl that appeared across her face. "Oh, look at the time," she tried not to sound so obvious. "Guests should be here any minute, you'd better make your way downstairs. I'll make sure everything is all right up here."

Charity watched Harmony walk toward the entryway. She was relieved that Harmony wasn't offended by Iesha's insensitivity, but she took offense at Harmony's *former life* comment. *I bind up that reincarnation mess, in the name of Jesus.* She was a stickler for listening to the words that people spoke. Even though Harmony may not have meant anything by what she said, Charity knew that since she had spoken it, a door had been opened. And if a door had been opened, Charity would see to it that it be closed.

"Harmony," Charity called. "Two things. One, if you see Iesha while you're down there tell her I said she'll be guiding tours tonight. And two, remind me to bring up communication at our first staff meeting."

"Okay."

Charity made a mental note to speak with Iesha about how to talk to people and to remind Harmony to be careful about what she says.

Iesha glanced at her watch. It was 4:50 p.m. The open house would begin in ten minutes. But more important, at 5:00 the building would come alive with men getting off work. She sashayed her way through Present Day Office Park in case any of them might leave their office suites early.

Present Day Office Park was located within Charlotte Executive Park, a community of five high-tower office buildings. Of the entire park, Present Day was the only building that was black owned. The other buildings had professional names. Dead smack in the middle of Park Abbey, Gateway Village, Lincoln Heights, and Wendover Towers sat Present Day. Aside from the name and the owners—Doris and David Humphries—the building was a nice place.

She stopped by the building's directory just to see how many men she would have access to. The names were countless. Dr. John Webber, Ophthalmologist, Suite 303. *I think I need my eyes checked.* She grinned at the thought. Wallace Austin, Financial Planner, Suite 201. *It's about time I start working on one of those Y2K or whatever those retirement plans are called.* Davis, Watson, and Blalock, Attorneys at Law, Suite 203. *Now, if that's an office full of men I see a bad check charge in my future.* That thought made her laugh out loud. Dr. Donald Moore, Dentistry, Suite 412. *I got a sweet tooth for men that needs—*

"Ma'am, do you need some help?" a male voice came from behind her.

"Nah, I was just . . ." her voice trailed off as she spun around to meet face-to-face with a hazel-eyed redbone in black slacks, a white shirt *that had to be dry-cleaned because can't nobody iron like that*, and a tie with zebra stripes. "I was just looking," she said, referring to him more than the directory.

"I saw you over here talking to yourself," he grinned. "And I was going to direct you to the fifth floor where that new counseling center is. I hear they're having an open house at five. You'd be right on time."

"I know," she said, looking down. She was impressed that his patent leather shoes had a suede zebra print on top that matched his tie. "Exactly what I was looking for," she said, looking up. "The counseling center, I mean."

His grin faded. "Oh ma'am. I didn't mean any harm," he apologized. "I'm very sorry. My name is Wallace Austin, my office is upstairs." He extended his hand to her.

"I'm Iesha." She noticed that his hands were soft and moist. His nails looked manicured and there wasn't a wedding band in sight. "I work at the new counseling center you were going to refer me to. I was just looking to see if we'd been added to this directory yet."

"Whew, what a relief," he exhaled. "For a minute there I thought you were a client. I was getting ready to be gone."

"And now?"

"Girl, don't start nothing, won't be nothing, with'cho fine self," he said, admiring the full-figured cocoa beauty. It felt like he was eyeing her down with x-ray vision, but she didn't mind. Those birth control injections she used to get blew her up in all the right places. Her legs and waist were still small, but her breasts, thighs, and behind were men's eye candy.

"Iesha! Iesha!"

Looking around and seeing Harmony coming toward her felt like someone pouring a glass of water over hot charcoal embers. She didn't know what it was about Harmony that she didn't like, but she sure took the fire of pleasure out of working for her sister. And the last thing she wanted to do was to be seen with her. She turned to Wallace and said, "I'm supposed to be getting something out of my car. I'll see you around?"

"You bet," he said slyly.

Iesha walked away slowly. She knew where his eyes were. She walked toward the door so that Harmony would follow her outside. *No need to be seen with her in public.* They met at the door and as she impatiently received Charity's message from her, she looked back at Wallace to see if he was still watching her. *A lil' trick I learned from Loretta Devine in* Waiting to Exhale. When she saw him still standing by the signboard with a mesmerized look on his face, she knew what that look meant. She smiled, *this is going to be my year after all.*

"Will you be okay with that?" Iesha heard Harmony ask.

This chile just messes up my groove. "Yes, Harmony. I'll be the tour guide. Now gone." Iesha shooed her away. She knew she should respect her elders and she hated to be rude, but *dang!* Iesha walked to her sister's Ford Explorer and opened the door with the remote. It was something about Harmony that made Iesha not want to be around her long. *I can't put my finger on it.* Iesha checked her thoughts. She realized she felt the same way about the Humphries, the people who owned Present Day. *Either they're a little shifty or I'm just paranoid. Either that or Charity's losing her touch. She used to be able to read people up and down.*

"Where's that girl at?" Charity asked, looking at the clock hanging in the waiting area. "She should've been back here by now." She walked out to the mezzanine and saw Iesha coming back into the building. *Talking about some Missy Elliott and R. Kelly.* Charity walked back into the suite. *If I had known she was going to show up looking like a hoochie from a video, I would've told her earlier she was working an open house and not a grand opening.* Charity shook her head and walked out of the waiting area. She gave it a nod of approval, as everything was in its place and ready for the event.

She had to admit it, Iesha was *wearing* that outfit. Those suede tan-and-brown patchwork boots set off her brown cowneck sweater dress just right. The thigh-high split didn't hurt it either. She even had a matching patchwork purse. *You go, girl!* Charity didn't have to look at her sister's nails to know they were manicured and perfectly polished. Only Iesha could pull off wearing the auburn Afro puffs she was sporting. Charity chuckled to herself, wondering how long Iesha's hair really was. It was hard to tell because Iesha was always doing something to it—weaving it, braiding it, tucking a piece in it. *The lifestyle of the bling, bling,* she mocked Iesha. "Thank You, Lord," Charity said aloud, remembering how God transformed her from her hoochie mama days. "God, if You did it for me, You'll do it for my sister."

She continued walking through the office, making sure things were in place. Before she knew it she was thinking back on the other things God had delivered her from, including a hellacious marriage. There was nothing that would make Charity turn her back on God. He'd faithfully provided for her since she came to Him two years ago.

She remembered the exact day, time, and place she cried out to Him. "Lord, this man has put his hands on me for the last time," she had prayed. She didn't know how God was going to do it, she just held on to a promise she found in the Bible about God providing a way of escape. She knew it wouldn't be easy. The only places her ex-husband, Emmitt, would permit her to go without him were to church and work. The Sunday after she made her vow, she and their four-year-old son, Xavier, went to church. She was inspired and comforted by Pastor King's sermon, "Get Out of the Boat." She left church determined that she was going to do something different. And sure enough, she found herself in the parking lot of the battered women's shelter. She sat in the car for an hour, crying and cradling Xavier. "I'm sorry, I'm so sorry," she apologized to him. She wasn't sure if she was apologizing for leaving Emmitt, or not leaving sooner than she did.

"Thank You, Jesus," she whispered, bringing her mind back to the present moment. "You work all things out for the good of them who love You, and have been called according to Your purpose."

When Charity turned the corner past her and Harmony's offices, she could hear the buzz of several voices. She stepped into the foyer and was greeted by a crowd of people. She shivered as a feeling of peace washed over her. *Thank You, Father.* She knew that it was only the hand of God that moved so many people to support her. When she sent out the invitations to as many pastors, physicians, judges, and mental health providers as she could think of, she assumed that they'd all be too busy or too tired to attend an after-hours event. But, she daily confessed Proverbs 16:3, "I will commit my works unto the Lord and my thoughts will be established." God had honored His Word. Charity made her way through the crowd, greeting people. By the looks of it, most of the invited had come. The suite was almost full, and when Charity made it to the entryway, she saw people coming in through the mezzanine, and pockets of people were socializing everywhere.

Charity spotted Iesha leading a line of people on a tour on the other side of the room. She knew she'd have to relieve her soon, because Iesha was walking like her high-heeled boots were getting the best of her. Between shaking people's hands and making small talk, Charity looked around for Harmony. She found her walking over to the food tables, where it looked like the crowd was getting pushy. Charity took that as a cue to get started.

Charity shouted as loudly as she could so that she could be heard over the buzz of conversations. "May I have your attention, please?! May I have your attention?"

Yelling at the top of her lungs didn't make the slightest bit of difference. But when a man yelled, "Listen up, everybody," the noise was hushed instantly like someone'd stuck a bottle in a hollering baby's mouth. *Lord, if I had known You were going to show out like this, I would've rented a sound system.* Charity smiled and nodded at the man.

"Good evening, everyone," she said, greeting the attendees with a smile. "I'm Charity Phillips, and it's so good to look out over this crowd and see so many familiar faces. I want to personally thank each and every one of you for your support and kind words. Your being here tonight means so much to me and the staff. Thank you all for sacrificing and taking time out of your busy schedules to come by and be with us on a Friday evening. I was told that an all-black counseling center wasn't necessary. Naysayers said that we have enough things separating us as it is. But when I started practicing as a therapist six years ago, I became aware of the divisive devices they spoke of and have desired ever since to do something about them . . ." Charity stopped speaking to allow the applause that erupted through the crowd. "Thank you. The word 'horizon' refers to the line that forms the boundary between the earth and sky. That's what we'll strive to do for each person you refer to us. We want to help them realize that the line, the boundary, the barrier that stands between where they are and where they want to be is a thin one. It can be over-stepped, overdrawn, and overcome. Horizons is a place where our people will be encouraged to come for help, a place where we will be validated, and a place where we can learn about ourselves and be challenged to grow." The applause grew more thunderous than before.

"At this time, I would like to introduce two very special people." She scanned the room. "Iesha and Harmony, will you come forward and say hello?"

Charity saw two places in the crowd open up as people stepped back to allow Harmony and Iesha through. Harmony, whose light skin radiated in an African-printed frock, walked toward Charity. It looked like her dreadlocks had been half dipped in gray paint. The black part was secured at the nape of her neck with a thick, red rubber band, and the rest looked like gray cords resting on her back as she slowly made her way to the front of the room where Charity stood. To allow Iesha the extra time she needed to sashay through the crowd, she motioned for Harmony to introduce herself.

"Good evening," she said slowly as if she was concentrating on the articulation of her words. "My name is Harmony Scott. I am an adolescent and family counselor. I have more than ten years' experience and am excited to be working with Charity. I share her vision for Horizons and appreciate the referrals you will send to us. For the people you send, we hope to help guide them back to their spiritual source and help them open up their hearts and minds as they are challenged by large and small difficulties. We hope to help them find sacred footing on ordinary ground, and experience miracles every day. Thank you," she said, bowing.

Charity clapped along with the audience, ignoring the scowling expression on Iesha's face once she saw Harmony bowing. Hoping that no one else would notice Iesha's bad man-ners, Charity motioned for Iesha to introduce herself.

"Hey, everybody, I'm Iesha," she said plainly. "I'mma be the voice on the other end of the phone when you call. I'm the secretary."

Administrative assistant!

"I'm excited about the center, too. Thanks for coming out." She shrugged, letting Charity know she couldn't think of anything else to say.

"Staff, let's give everyone a hand for coming out tonight," Charity rescued her. The three of them clapped together. "Everyone, let's give the staff a hand in advance for all the hard work, long hours, and sacrifices they'll put in to make Horizons the best counseling center in Charlotte." After the applause, Charity thanked her attendees again and invited them to take some of her promotional pens, pads, and business cards on their way out.

The three Horizons staff members escorted people out of the building. As Charity walked and talked with a small crowd, she felt a tap on her shoulder.

"Hello, Judge Fulton," she said, turning around to hug the juvenile court judge she'd befriended years ago when she worked as an adolescent counselor. She hated being subpoenaed to court by her clients' probation officers, but she took a liking to Judge Fulton because it was obvious that she cared for the kids in her courtroom. Charity watched judges sentence kids to detention centers and boot camps without asking any questions. Judge Fulton always asked questions. She'd talk to the family members who were present and would counsel adolescents right there in her courtroom. She was well-known for ordering family counseling, drug treatment, and community service at an orphanage, children's hospital, or homeless or battered-women's shelter. Charity would be subpoenaed time after time to testify against repeat offenders sentenced by the other judges, but Judge Fulton's kids rarely came back through the system. It was Judge Fulton who encouraged Charity to open her own practice. "Long time no see. How are you?"

"I'm well. I can see that you are."

"Oh yes, God is good. You know this wouldn't have been possible without your prayers and support."

"Glory to God. I'm proud of you. You're a young woman and you've got so much ahead of you. You're opening the way for many others who'll come behind you."

"Aaaawww." Charity hugged her again. "We'll have to do lunch soon and catch up. I've got to run. The Humphries lock up at eight o'clock sharp. That gives me less than an hour to clean. I'd hate to be locked up in here."

"I know that's right. Speaking of the Humphries, there was some talk in the courthouse about Present Day closing because of some financial or legal troubles or something. Is that true?"

"I hate to think." Charity frowned. "The black Taj Mahal closing? And I just gave them my whole life savings. That best be just a rumor."

"That's what I said when I heard it. I'll keep my eyes and ears open. If I hear anything, you'll be the first to know it."

Even though Charity felt the information about Present Day's closing was false, she had the same sinking feeling in her stomach that she'd felt when Harmony made mention of her former life.

Chapter 2

She barely locked the doors behind her before she had half of her clothes off. The only thing Charity wanted to do was to soak in a long, hot bath surrounded by candlelight. It had been one of those days. She had had her share of smiling, entertaining, and pretending to be interested in other people's opinions. She just wanted to relax and go to bed. Since now-six-year-old Xavier was with his father for the weekend, she planned to do just that.

She hung her purse on the coatrack by the door, then kicked off her navy high-heeled sling backs and carried them to her room. She placed them in the shoe rack on the floor of her walk-in closet and hung her navy wool blazer and skirt up behind other winter suits. She pulled her silk, pink-blush blouse over her head and hung it between the shirts and blouses in the front of the closet. Leaning back on the edge of the bed, she extended her legs in the air and rolled her thigh-high hose off as if she were in a commercial shoot.

Having a restful sleep was essential tonight. Charity looked for the one gown she knew would make that easy to accomplish. She went through two drawers of clothes to find the long, thin white cotton gown with pink embroidered flowers on the bodice and wide shoulder straps. She draped it over her shoulder and went to the bathroom to draw her bathwater. As the water filled the tub, she lit a jasmine-scented candle on an adjacent black wrought-iron stand. The only thing missing was a cup of hot tea. She left the tub running and went to the kitchen to boil a small pot of water.

When she noticed the blinking red light on the wall phone, she picked up her cordless and dialed the number to check her messages.

Welcome to the message center. Two new messages are in your mailbox. First message, today, three thirty-one p.m. "Helllllooo, this Emmitt. Just calling to let you know I picked Lil' Man up from school. Hold on, he wants to say something. Tell your momma hey."

"Hey, Mommy."

"She not there, we leaving a message. Tell her you love her."

"I love you, Mommy."

"All right, tell her bye."

"Bye, bye."

"Like I said, we was just calling. Call us when you get in. Bye."

To save this message, press two, to erase—

She pressed "two." She knew it wouldn't be long before she'd start missing her son and would want to hear his voice again. It made no sense for her to call him, because it would make him want to come home. And the last thing she wanted was to hear him cry. Especially while he was with his father. That would make things harder for them both.

Charity walked back to the bathroom to check on her bathwater.

Message saved. Second message, today six p.m.

"Cherry. It's Mom. Y'all must still be at work. I ain't heard from Esha yet either, she supposed to bring the kids by. I was calling to find out how she did on her first day at work. Hope you ain't had to fire her already. Take it easy on her, you know she ain't never worked a day in her life. I don't know where she get that from 'cause I ain't raise her to be like that. What you do with

Zavey if y'all still at work? Lord, this his weekend with his daddy, ain't it? They better not mistreat my baby down there or I'll go down there myself and . . . Hello? Hello? See, God don't like ugly, your answering machine trying to cut me off. What Esha say? 'They better recognize, they better ask somebody.' Let me get off this phone, I cracks myself up. Call me later, Cherry. Love ya, bye."

To save this message—

"Definitely erase this one," she chuckled, and pressed "three." She ran her hand through the bathwater to make sure it was hot. "Just right." She dried her hand on a nearby towel and dialed Emmitt's phone number.

Lord, set a guard over my mouth and keep watch over the door of my lips.

"Joe's Pool Room," Emmitt answered.

There used to be a time when Charity thought his dry sense of humor was cute. But after they married it irritated her that he would answer like that. It didn't matter to him that she was a professional woman, that important people from her job or church called the house. There was no telling how many opportunities they missed from people who hung up thinking they'd really dialed Pizza Hut, The House of Blues, or Psychic Friends Network.

"It's a good thing I'm not Ed McMahon calling to tell you you've won the Publishers Clearing House Sweepstakes," she said, forcing laughter into her voice.

"Well, are you?"

"Emmitt, it's Charity. How are you?" She hoped she didn't sound too agitated.

"I'm hanging in there. How 'bout you?"

"Really tired, but I wanted to return your call and see how Zavey is."

"He's out like a light. I knew he was sleepy around seven 'cause he started whining."

"Umph," was the only thing she could think of to say. She

knew he was getting ready to go into his spiel about boys crying like little punks.

"He must've forgotten where he was 'cause he know I don't play that whining mess. It might work when he's with you 'cause you let him have his way. But I done told him, whining don't get you nowhere."

She attempted to appease him. "You're right about that. Whining won't get you anywhere. Well, I just wanted to return your—"

"I'm just saying, sweetie . . ."

Charity straightened her back like she was bracing herself. She knew that he only called her pet names when he wanted something.

"The boy six years old whining like a little girl," Emmitt continued. "You need to nip that in the bud. It ain't cute no more. He too old for that."

"Okay, I will." Charity fought back frustration and worked hard to keep her voice even. She didn't want to raise her voice or let any choice words slip out of her mouth. In the past she'd given him plenty of reasons to accuse her of not being Christian-like, and she didn't want to add this to his repertoire. She'd grown tired of his sarcastic remarks about not believing that she was *really* a minister.

"I ain't fussing at you. You're doing a good job with him, but all that whining ain't necessary for a boy. People gone think he a punk. He's already small for his age and I know the little boys are gone tease him. I've been there, I know. You used to work with kids, you know that too."

She could still hear him talking even though she'd taken the phone away from her ear. Every now and then she'd put the phone up to her ear and mouth to say, "Uhm hum."

"All right, Emmitt. It was good talking to you. You have a nice night and kiss Zavey for me."

"I will. Just think about what I said."

"Okay, good night." She hung up the phone before he could respond.

She grabbed the Bible she kept in the bathroom on the shelf above the toilet. She could feel her emotions rise up on the inside of her like boiling hot lava in an erupting volcano. She was either going to cry or vomit if she did not calm down. She hated feeling like this—like a scared child who could not stand up for herself. No one could make her as angry as she allowed Emmitt to. She turned her Bible to Ephesians 6. But she kept going back and repeating verse 12 over and over. "For we wrestle not against flesh and blood," she read aloud. "But against principalities, against powers, against the rulers of the darkness of this age, against spiritual hosts of wickedness in the heavenly places." She meditated on that Scripture until the strong grip of her anger was loosened.

She ran more hot water into the tub and relaxed every part of her body easing into the water. She wondered if Calgon could really take her away.

Iesha was glad to get those boots off her feet. It felt as if she'd already spent the night on the dance floor and she hadn't even left the house. She figured that if she soaked her feet for a few minutes and wore her bedroom shoes for awhile, her feet would be rested by the time her friends arrived to pick her up for the club.

"Raquan, what'chu in there whining about?" she yelled from her room to her son.

"Sha-Lai hit me, Momma," he whined.

"Sha-Lai, get your fast tail somewhere and sit down 'fore I come in there and sit you down. I done told you, you ain't nobody's momma. You ain't got no chaps to be hitting. Is your stuff packed?"

"Yes, ma'am."

"Quan, you done packed your bag?"

"Almost."

"Get y'all stuff together so I can drop y'all off at Momma's. Y'all getting on my nerves and we ain't been home but fifteen minutes."

Raquan walked into her room carrying the cordless phone.

"Telephone, Momma." She'd been yelling so loudly that she hadn't heard the phone ring. "She got it, Sha-Lai," he said into the telephone, "hang up that other phone."

Iesha snatched the phone from him. "Hello?"

"Hey E, what you up to?"

"Nothing, girl. Hollering at these hard-headed chaps of mine. Wait a minute, Mercedes, hold on a minute." She covered the mouthpiece with her hand and yelled, "Sha-Lai, put some water in my foot spa and bring it here since you need something to do with your hands besides hitting people." She took her hand away from the phone and continued her conversation with one of her best friends, Mercedes. "I'm back, girl. These chaps getting on my nerves. Sha-Lai is nine, going on nineteen. And Quan seven acting like he two. They're getting ready to go to Momma's."

"You late. Mine are already gone. Why yours still there?"

"You know I started working today."

"That's right. E is a working woman now. How ya like it?"

"It's all right, I guess. I don't think I'mma like working for Cherry and all her uppity, super-Christian friends," she said, plopping her feet into the bubbling foot spa. "She got this one chick working for her who be talking in proverbs like Gandhi or somebody. We had to introduce ourselves tonight and she gave a freaking speech. And then had a nerve to bow. I think something wrong with her, myself. She ain't quite right if you ask me. She weird and I don't fit in with them and I ain't gonna try."

"That's right. Keep it real. West siiii-eeed," Mercedes chanted.

"Girl, you stupid. There is a lot of plus sides though."

"Like what?"

"For one, her office is in the black Taj Mahal."

"You lying? Your sister got an office in Present Day? She is uppity, ain't she?"

"Watch your mouth. Can't nobody talk about my sister but me."

"My bad."

They laughed together. "Girl, the biggest plus is all the BMWs they got in there. It's black men working in there everywhere. Doctors, lawyers, you name it. I even met one today."

"Whaaaaaat?"

"Yep, a businessman. His name is Wallace and the boy got it going on. You hear me? He gotta body like a man fresh out of prison," she laughed. "Ya'll gone have to come and eat lunch with me in the courtyard one day."

"You ain't said nothing but a word. How 'bout Monday?"

"Long as you don't come looking as desperate as you sound. What time ya'll gone get here tonight?"

"I don't know why I'm still your friend with all the junk I let you talk to me."

"'Cause you know I love you."

"Nah, it must be because I love you. It's almost eight-thirty. What time you gone take the kids to your mom's?"

"As soon as I get off the phone with you, I'm out the door."

"Well, I'mma pick Traci up and we'll stop by the ABC store and then head on over to your place. You want anything in particular?"

"Nah, the usual will be fine."

"All right then, I'll see you in a bit."

"Peace out."

Iesha carried Raquan into her mother's house. He had already fallen asleep during the fifteen-minute drive.

"Hey, Ma," she said, opening the door with her own key.

"Hey, Mah Mah," Sha-Lai sang as she wrapped her arms around as much of her grandmother's wide waist as she could. It was unmistakable that Iesha got her looks from Mama Lorraine. They were both the same cocoa complexion, same height of five-foot-seven, and had the same body type. Mama Lorraine looked young for her age and was always mistaken to be Charity's and Iesha's sister.

"Hey, Tootie," she reached down to return her granddaughter's hug. She kissed Iesha on the cheek, "That boy already sleep? Go lay him across the bed in the back." Iesha left the kitchen but she heard her mother tell Sha-Lai, "I guess we'll have to watch *The Son of the Mask* and eat this popcorn and peanut butter chocolate chip cookies all by ourselves."

"Ma, ya'll still buying those bootleg videos?" Iesha called from the back room. "I thought Daddy said he wasn't going to buy any more of them tapes since the last ones were messed up?"

"Chile, Willie gave him his money back and let him trade them tapes. Your daddy's been a faithful customer ever since." When Iesha walked back into the room, Mama Lorraine pointed to the long cabinet drawers on the bottom of the entertainment center. "Look down there. We got *Mudear Goes to Jail, Man of the House,* and *Diary of a Mad Black Woman.*"

"Ya'll wrong. Ya'll still Christians ain't you?"

Mama Lorraine laughed. "Where in the Bible does it say we can't buy bootleg tapes?"

"Ooooh, Ma. You know you're wrong for that. Your Bible does say 'thou shalt not steal,' don't it?"

"Since when you know what the Bible says, Ms. Lady-of-the-night? If I'dda known it was only going to take one day for Cherry to rub off on you, I would've prayed about this sooner than I did."

Iesha raised her eyebrows. "Cherry ain't rubbed off on me. I ain't nothing like her and never will be."

"You say that like it's a bad thing to be like her."

"I don't mean it like that—"

"I was gone say, 'cause the girl doing good. She done gone to college and got not one, but two degrees. She has her own business and got you working in it. She in church every Sunday, not to mention that she's a preacher. And, she doing a good job raising that boy all by herself without so much as a penny from that sorry ex-husband of hers who still living with his momma. What you see that's so bad about that?"

"Nothing Momma," Iesha said, figuring she'd better quit while she was ahead. Mama Lorraine was not the type of mother to lose an argument. At least not without a fight. Iesha still remembered the whipping Mama Lorraine put on her when she was thirteen. She recalled sneaking out of the house after Mama Lorraine changed her mind about letting her go to the mall with friends. When she returned, Mama Lorraine didn't let her get in the door before she pinned her to the floor. If her father hadn't pulled her off Iesha, Momma would probably still have her hands around Iesha's neck. If she didn't know it before, she learned it then that Mama Lorraine doesn't play. "Cherry never could do no wrong in your eyes anyway," she heard herself say before it registered in her brain.

"What'chu say?"

Oh Lord. Iesha didn't say anything, for fear that she'd already said too much.

"I said, what did you say?"

"I was just saying, Momma, you always call me on my mess but you don't never say nothing to Cherry when she mess up."

"Girl, I'll slap the tastebuds out your mouth, accusing me of treating y'all differently. As hard as I work not to give one of y'all more than the other. You been whining about I love Cherry more than you ever since she became a part of our family. I love that girl like she my own flesh and blood and here you is acting like the adopted one. Girrrrrrrl," she growled.

Iesha grabbed her purse. "Ma, I did not come over here to argue with you. I just wished you'd realize Cherry and I are two totally different people and be okay with that." She turned her back on her mother to walk to the door. She just knew Mama Lorraine would snatch her back.

"I am okay with it, you're the one that's got a problem with it."

"Okay, Ma. I gotta go."

"See, there you go. You're always running when you get uncomfortable with something."

"No, I don't want to keep Mercedes and Traci waiting. They're probably already at the house," she said, trying to sound like she wasn't lying.

"All right then. I expect we'll finish this over dinner on Sunday.

That way your daddy and Cherry will be involved. I wanna get this out in the open. Should've done this a long time ago. You go on. I'll see you tomorrow. What time you coming to pick up the kids?"

"About noon."

"All right, I'll see you then."

When Iesha got outside she couldn't do anything but thank God because she knew it was only Him that kept her mother off of her. She sat in the car for almost ten minutes, to think more than to warm up the car. *Maybe Momma's right. Maybe I am the one with the problem not being like Charity.*

Chapter 3

It had to be all of six o'clock in the morning. The bedroom was enveloped in total darkness. Emmitt raised up high enough to look at his alarm clock.

"Boy, you better go back to bed," he said, lying down again. Xavier was on his knees bouncing up and down on the foot of his father's bed.

"Is it time to eat, Daddy?"

"Time to eat? Xavier, it's six twenty-seven. Go back to bed."

"Six twenty-seven in the day or at night?"

"Xavier Ahmad, it is early in the morning. You need to go to your room before you get a whooping."

"Ooookay, Daddy," he whined, crawling backward off of the bed. "Can I sleep in your bed?"

"Only if you gone sleep."

Xavier climbed back onto the bed and snuggled so close to his father that he felt like a second layer of skin. He and Emmitt lay on their sides, and he fell asleep with his head under Emmitt's chin and his back against his chest. Emmitt secured his son in position with his arm over him. He wished it could be like this always. He hated that Charity had left him. *Talking about she didn't want a divorce, she just wanted to separate for a while. She could've at least left Xavier*. Emmitt smiled before he drifted off to sleep, remembering how hurt she was when she received the divorce papers in the mail. That was a move she never expected him to make.

"Aaahhh . . . ain't that sweet?" Emmitt's mother sang as she watched them sleep from the doorway.

"Can a man get some sleep around here?" he joked as he yawned and stretched, waking himself up. "Lil' Man came in here ready to play at six this morning. I thought I was gonna have to whoop his behind to make him go back to bed."

"He probably used to waking up that time of morning since he's in school now."

"I know he tired." Emmitt smoothed Xavier's hair with his hand. "Always running with Charity—she got a meeting on this day, working out that day, church services this, and prayer meeting that. The boy be up from six in the morning to about seven thirty at night. That ain't good for a little boy. I bet that's why he so hyper."

"Now, don't you go worrying yourself about that girl and what she do. All that matters is our baby is here. And, if we gonna spend some quality time with him, y'all might wanna get up soon. You know how fast the weekend goes. Breakfast will be ready in a few minutes. We can talk then about what we gonna do with the baby today."

He was so focused on what it would be like if he had custody of Xavier full-time that he did not hear his mother invite herself to the things he planned to do with his son for the weekend. And he had gotten on her about calling him a baby, let alone treating him like one. "That's why I wish I had custody of him. If I could take my son I'd . . ." He stopped when he realized that his mother was the last person with whom he wanted to have this type of conversation. Anytime he made it known that he wanted something, she did not stop until she made sure he received it. It was like she owed him something, like she was guilty for something.

And he had no idea of what. Besides, he was not sure he was serious about what he was saying.

"Why don't you?"

"Why don't I what? Take him?"

"No! Well, not like *that*. You know we got one of them pre-paid legal plans? Call one of them lawyers and see if we can get the baby."

"Ma," he whined. "We've already been to court one time. I don't wanna go back through that. And I don't wanna set Charity off. The last thing I need is for her to not let me see my son. If I lose him again I don't know what I'll do . . ."

"Don't talk like that," she held up her hand to silence him. "I done lost one son. I'll be a dead monkey's uncle before I lose you."

He knew talk of his younger brother, Greg Jr., made her sad. It made him sad too. Greg had been incarcerated for selling drugs. There's no way he would let ten years slip by without his son.

His mother was still talking, sounding like she was angry now. "You should've listened to me in the first place. I told you not to marry that little soddity heifer. She was always running around here thinking she was better than everybody else. Got my grand-baby talking like a little white boy. You better call them people. You're a different man than you was two years ago—"

"Ma, calm down before you get a migraine. Things ain't that bad the way they is now. I just love my son."

"That's why you should call them people. It sure would be nice to have that boy around here all the time. He something else," she smiled. "And greedy. Just like you was when you was that age. Always begging for something to eat."

"That's what he was talking about when he came in here at six this morning, talking about 'is it time to eat?' I'll think about what you said, Ma. I didn't listen to you when you told me not to marry Charity. I see where that got me. I think I need to listen to you this time."

• • •

It was too much stimulation for him. There were too many kids, too many people, too much noise, and too many colors. They had been there an hour too long as far as Emmitt was concerned. He and his best friend, James, decided to spend Saturday afternoon with their sons at Chuck E. Cheese's. Xavier and James's son, Brandon, were running through the place and going from game to game. They stopped by the table long enough to get more tokens, or to leave the tickets they won from playing games, or to sip on their drinks.

James looked around the establishment and back at Emmitt. "Man, are you sure you could do this full-time? We've only been here for an hour and you look like you're about to jump out of your skin."

"I can't take this place full-time," he laughed. "But being a full-time daddy, that much I'm sure about. I'm all right. Me and my moms got into it before I left. I told her I wanted to spend the day with Xavier alone and she went off. You'dda thought I slapped her or something she was so mad. I don't know why that woman act like that."

"Because she's a grandma. That's how they are, man. When I was little, my momma would tear my behind up for messing with the figurines on her coffee table. Last year, Brandon ran crying because he broke her ceramic praying hands. He just knew she was gone beat the black off of his behind. Instead of whooping him, she gave the boy a piece of cake and some ice cream to calm him down. They're crazy about their grandkids."

"I can understand that. That's normal. But what I'm going through with my mom ain't normal. This some Jerry Springer mess here. I mean, I feel like my momma's husband. I live with her, pay her bills, give her spending money, grocery shop with her, and I gotta fight with her to spend time with my own son. That ain't right, now is it?"

"My name is Bennett and I ain't in it."

"You know it ain't right, that's why you ain't saying nothing."

"So, what are you going to do?"

"I'mma have to talk to her."

"Not about her, what are you going to do about Xavier?"

"I don't know. Charity is a good mother, and it ain't nothing wrong with the way things are now, except that I'm a part-time daddy. Before I married Charity, I made her promise me she'd never leave because I told her I wasn't gonna be no part-time daddy. I was either gone be his daddy full-time or not at all. I meant it then and even though that's the grounds she won the child custody case on, I still feel the same way now. Her attorney argued that she was in an abusive marriage and that was just one of the ways I controlled her."

"What? Man, why didn't you tell me this before?"

"For what? It wasn't going to change nothing." When James didn't respond, Emmitt looked around to make sure the boys were not close by. "When Charity woke me up that morning and she and Xavier kissed me good-bye, I had a feeling she wasn't coming back. I don't know how I knew, but I had this feeling. Matter of fact, I expected it for a while because I started taking the baby's car seat out of the car and hiding it from her. Like she wouldn't leave without it. There were times I would think she was gonna leave and I'd call my mom to drive two and a half hours to get Xavier in the middle of the night while Charity was asleep."

"And your mom would come?"

"Happily."

"That's cold, man. No wonder she left."

Emmitt cocked his head back.

"I mean with all of that going on. How could you think she would stay?"

"Oh, I forgot who I was talking to. You were the one who liked her in the first place. If you think you could've done a better job with her, you should've married her."

"Come on, man, you know better than that. Bygones are bygones." Emmitt watched James fidget in his seat. "So, what you're saying is that if Charity had left Xavier with you, you would've been fine?"

"And you know it. I knew she was gonna leave anyway, so I just shut down emotionally. It's still the only way I can deal with her."

"That's gotta be hard."

"I've been doing it so long I don't even know I'm doing it."

"Is your home girl . . . uhm, uhm . . ." James was snapping his fingers trying to recall Emmitt's girlfriend's name.

"Shawanda?"

"Yeah, Shawanda. Is she okay with all this?"

"What I got to tell her for? I don't see no ring on her finger."

James smacked himself on the forehead. "What was I thinking? If you didn't love your own wife, and the mother of your child, then how could you possibly give a hoot about a girlfriend?" he asked facetiously.

"I like Shawanda. She accepts me for who I am and I feel comfortable with her."

"Hel-lo," James sang. "That's 'cause she young and . . ." He looked up at the ceiling, trying to think of the word. "Inexperienced would be nicer than what I want to say. She don't know no better. She just glad to have somebody. She's one of them desperate single mothers."

Emmitt looked at him crossly.

"All I'm saying, man, is if you want to be a full-time dad, go get your wife back."

Emmitt stood up and stretched. He reached for his and Xavier's coat. "I ain't the only one this place has gotten to. You sound like you need some rest."

"All right. Have it your way," James said, tidying the table and getting his belongings. "You know you still love the girl. I just hate that this is gonna tear her up."

Emmitt's eyes narrowed. "Then she'd know how I felt when she just up and took my son from me. She made me out to be the biggest devil, and my life's been a living hell ever since. I think it's time she felt some of the heat."

CHAPTER 4

"MINISTER PHILLIPS, THANK YOU FOR THAT WORD," Koren, said approaching Charity to give her a hug. "You always break the Sunday school lessons down in a way I can understand them. But this morning, I'd swear you've been listening to my phone conversations. You talked about everything I'm struggling with. And you're right, I've turned away from my first love."

Even though Charity needed to hear the encouragement, she did not believe what she was hearing. She knew she had done a terrible job with the Sunday school lesson. She'd been too preoccupied with Horizons' open house to prepare for the lesson. She felt so unprepared and scattered. What she had in her head did not come out of her mouth. The students were unusually silent, which meant to her that they were confused, bored, or convicted.

"Bless you, Sister Koren," she said in her ear as they hugged. "Thank you so much for your kind words. I'll keep you lifted up in prayer concerning the situations you're facing, okay?"

"Please do, I need all the prayers I can get."

"If you need a prayer partner, call me," she said still holding Koren's hands.

"I will," she said, initiating another hug. "Let me get on down here so I can be on time for praise and worship. I'll see you later."

"All right, you take care of yourself."

Charity pondered her words in her heart as she packed up her belongings. She believed that Koren felt sorry for her and wanted to make up for the lack of response from the class. She knew she did a terrible job and felt there was no one or nothing that could prove her wrong. She walked slowly downstairs to the pastor's study. She was feeling so inadequate and unequipped as a minister, the last thing she wanted to do was to be around her pastor or fellow ministers. *I will bless the Lord at all times, His praise shall continually be in my mouth. My soul will make her boast in the Lord.*

"Good morning, Minister Phillips," Pastor King said heartily as he stood when she entered the study. He had not yet put on his robe, which was draped over the back of his chair. The room's lighting was so dark it was hard to tell the color of his suit, and his light complexion appeared two shades darker. His natural curly hair looked different today. Maybe he'd had a haircut, she mused. He was an attractive man in his early fifties, who was a little weightier than when he had first come to the church.

That was none of her business. Pastor King was happily married. His wife was a former fashion model in New York. She still looked and carried herself like she was on the runway. Charity still felt goose bumps whenever she thought about how the Kings met. Pastor King saw his future bride featured in an *Ebony* magazine as a Fashion Fair model. He cut out her picture and claimed her as his wife. He carried that picture around in his Bible for months. One Sunday, he was sitting in his father's pulpit and guess who walked into the church? In the middle of the service, he pulled her picture out of his Bible to compare the faces. He thought he would fall out of the chair. After the service he talked with her and learned that she was in Charlotte for a special event hosted by *Ebony* and Fashion Fair. He has told the congregation that story many times. Especially in his sermons on faith and hope. And the rest is history. Pastor King married her on one Sunday and he preached his first sermon as pastor of Damascus Road Baptist Church the next. That was fourteen years ago.

Pastor King's desk was closest to the door, so she went over to him and gave him a quick hug before she greeted the other associate ministers in the room. "Good morning Pastor. Is all well?"

"All is well, Minister. How are you?"

"I'm blessed," she said as enthusiastically as she could. "And highly favored."

"Good, good. It's good to see you. Have a seat."

Pastor King loved antiques. An old oak floor-model cabinet displayed his collection of miniature automobiles. Glass end tables matched the cabinet. An aluminum knight in the corner behind his desk held a shield in one hand and a sword in the other. Pastor King said it was his reminder to get dressed in the whole armor of God. The oldest members of the ministerial staff, Reverends Charles Hubbard and Walter Johnson, occupied the two chairs facing his desk.

"Good morning Reverends," she said, extending her hand to them individually to shake. Neither of them stood and they barely returned her greeting. She walked over to the newly ordained Reverend Tim Miller, who sat in a chair diagonal to the pastor's desk. "Good morning, Reverend." He stayed seated but he firmly shook her hand. The other three ministers sat on the two love seats in the back of the room. They were young ministers, in age and in years of ministry served. Ministers Richard Dukes and Joshua Sadler were in their mid-thirties. Charity used to be the youngest until Minister Michael Adams came on board last year. He was the church's minister of music. The three ministers stood as she approached them.

"Hello, everyone," she smiled, making her way around the circle they formed to hug each of them. Ministers Adams and Dukes made room for her to sit with them on the couch. She sat at the end of the couch beside Minister Dukes, away from Minister Adams. She didn't know how long she could keep her best friend April's crush on him a secret.

"Good morning, everyone," Pastor King said in greeting to get their attention. "It's good to see you all. I pray peace and prosperity upon you and your households. Does anyone have anything that should claim my attention?"

Everyone sat quietly, looking around the room.

"All right then. I want to congratulate Minister Phillips. She came to me some time ago to let me know that God had put it on her heart to open an all-black counseling firm. She had her open house on Friday and the place was packed. People were lined up out there like the government was giving away free cheese." When the laughter died down, he asked Charity, "What's the name of your office?"

"Horizons," she answered shyly.

"Let's keep her in our prayers. You know she's got her work cut out for her. It's hard to work with black folks, let alone those of us who are a little touched in the head." He grinned. "I'm just playing with you, Minister Phillips." Then he turned to the other ministers. "All of us need a little help every now and then, even us men and women of God. It's important to keep a balance between the natural and spiritual. Amen?"

"Amen," the seven agreed.

"Minister Phillips, since the Lord is blessing you so much, I want you to lead the call to worship this morning."

Everyone fell silent. One of the older reverends had always led the beginning part of worship services. Before she could open her mouth, one of them spoke up.

"Pastor, did you say 'call to worship'?" Reverend Hubbard asked.

"Yes, I'd like Minister Phillips to do the call to worship. Minister Dukes to do Scripture and Minister Sadler to do prayer." Charity looked around the room. Pastor King didn't concern himself with the ministers' blank stares and dropped mouths. "Reverend Miller, will you do the tithe and offering appeal?"

"Pastor, with all due respect," Reverend Hubbard persisted. "Reverend Adams and I have always led the call to worship. Reverend Miller hasn't even had a chance to do it yet, and you're gonna let Minister Phillips do it? That's out of order, Pastor, don't you think?"

Pastor King sat quietly for a minute. He looked like he was thinking of a way to respond tactfully. Ever since last week's end-of-the-year meeting, the church had been in an uproar. The older charter members of the church were most perturbed with the changes Pastor King talked about making.

Charity remembered how he had started the church meeting with a brief sermonette on Joshua and how God commissioned him to break out of Moses' mold because he was now dead. "Following tradition will keep you out of the Promised Land," he said. He admonished the church to get prayed up because God was "getting ready to send Damascus Road Baptist Church on a Damascus Road experience.

"We can't continue to do thangs the way Momma, Grand-momma, and Big Momma 'nem did 'em," he'd joked to break the uncomfortable silence. "I believe God is raising the standard and wanting to take Damascus Road to a new level. Amen? And if you will,"—he looked around slyly—"that can be evidenced by the fact that God has blessed us with our first female minister, Minister Phillips. He's breaking us out of tradition, church. I've been pastoring this church for fourteen years and there are some things we are still doing that were done when the church started thirty years ago."

The dignitaries on the front row sat as rigidly as the two older reverends in the study were now.

"I'm sorry, Reverend Hubbard, but I don't see how that's out of order. If you think it's necessary, we could talk about it further in our next ministers' meeting. When is that? Second Saturdays? Next Saturday? Let's talk about it then."

Reverend Hubbard crossed his legs, rolled his eyes, and shifted his body in the direction of the door. "Since we don't have an assignment this morning, do you even want us to sit in the pulpit?"

Charity felt her eyes stretch open. She knew the older reverends could get an attitude, but he was being insubordinate. "The seating arrangements have not changed," Pastor King replied.

As if they had been resurrected from the dead, the ministers in the back began to encourage Charity in an attempt to convince her that she was more than capable of preparing the congregation to worship.

"All right, everyone has their assignments, let's pray and dismiss."

Everyone met in the center of the room and held hands. Charity stood between Reverend Miller and Minister Adams, and across the room from the older men.

"Minister Phillips, see me after service, please. Everyone bow your heads," Pastor King admonished. "Dear precious and wise heavenly Father, we thank You this morning for our life, health, and strength. I thank You, Lord, for these men and woman of God you have entrusted to me, and the sheep out in the fold, bless each of them, Father. Prepare this church for Your coming, may You find us to be a church without spot or wrinkle. Bless the furtherance of the worship services, and may our hearts and minds be stayed on You. In Jesus' name, we pray. Amen." Lifting his head, he said, "Go in peace."

The first two rows of pews on both sides of the church were reserved for its dignitaries. The deacons, charter members, and church mothers occupied the seats. Charity tried not to look at them as she focused on the praise and worship team. Charity looked out in the pews to find her best friend, April. She found her three pews back watching every move Minister Adams made. Charity smiled, shook her head at April, and closed her eyes so that she could visualize the words the praise team sang regarding welcoming the King into the sanctuary.

Charity focused on the words of exultation and found strength to do what she would have to after they finished this last song.

Before the soloist gave her final note, Charity was already at the podium with the microphone in her hand.

"Is He welcome this morning, saints? Is He welcome in this place? Then stand to your feet and welcome the King, invite Him in. When is the last time He sat down on you? Let us not sit down on Him."

The praise and worship team continued to sing softly, and Charity began to pray. And the more she prayed, the more the atmosphere changed at Damascus Road Baptist Church. Most people from the third row of pews to the back of the church and even those in the balcony stood. Some lifted their hands, some swayed from side to side, some had tears streaming down their faces, but they all looked relieved that something was happening.

"Oh Lord, You are welcome in this place," she prayed. "Have Your way, Father God. Lord, we know You to be a healer, heal right now in the name of Jesus. Someone needs a deliverer, deliver right now in the name of Jesus. Someone needs a provider, provide Lord in Your Son's matchless name. God, we know You to be a restorer, a waymaker, a mind-regulator, a heart mender . . ."

Charity could not believe how fast the words came to her mind to say. She felt uncomfortably hot, like she had a fever all over her body. Even her ears felt like they were on fire.

The praise and worship team ended their selection as she ended her prayer. The congregation's worship was so loud, Charity could not be heard. "God bless you, saints. We will remain standing and join in with our choir as they lead us in our opening song."

"I'mma stop calling you Lil' Bit," Pastor King said as Charity walked into his study after church. "You're a little ole thing but you pack a lot of power. I didn't know you had it in you."

Charity just blushed and sat in the chair facing his desk when he motioned for her to sit.

"Thank you, Pastor. I didn't know it was in me either. It was truly the anointing of God."

"You ain't telling me nothing I don't know. We could see it all over you. You know, our worship services will never be the same."

"Praise God for that. But you didn't call me in here to talk about me. Is there something I can do for you?"

"In fact it is; I wanted to apologize to you for the Reverends' behavior this morning. It's going to take a while for the walls of traditionalism to be broken down in this church, but I feel a change a coming. Be strong, Minister, you were called here for a time like this. I believe that you are going to be very instrumental in this transitional stage."

"Praise God."

Pastor King reached down to pick up his briefcase. "Have you seen *Today's Gospel* magazine yet?"

"The January issue?"

He looked at the cover of the glossy magazine. "No, the February one with Yolanda Adams on it. The one with your article in it."

"No. I didn't know they came out this early."

He handed her the magazine. "Page seventy-four."

Charity turned the magazine over and flipped through its pages until she found her article. Seeing her name and photo in the national magazine made her want to cry. "God is so awesome for making this possible."

"You know what I realized about your article? I was thinking about how you'll be ministering to people you don't even know, that you may never see, and in places you've never been."

"I didn't even look at it that way."

"Thomasina thinks the same thing and she called me last night. She would like for you to write an encouraging article about single mothers and Mother's Day. She said the word count and pay would be the same as it was for your 'I Have No Man' article. The deadline is Wednesday. Can you do the assignment?"

Without hesitating Charity answered, "Yes!"

He looked proud of himself as he slid a piece of paper to her. "Here's everything you need, including her phone number. Make me proud."

"Thanks for thinking of me, Pastor," she said, standing to leave.

"Remember the day I picked you up from school?" he asked. She nodded.

"You were what? Seventeen or eighteen? Now you're a grown woman. That goes to show how old I'm getting to be."

"I wasn't going to say anything but I've been noticing those gray hairs."

"Those come from keeping up with seven associate ministers," he joked.

Charity did remember the day he picked her up from school. He'd just been installed as pastor of the church and had implemented a "lunch with pastor" program wherein he'd draw a student's name monthly and have lunch with them. On the day he was supposed to have lunch with Charity, he arrived too late. So he asked if he could sit with her in her last two classes and drive her home. Charity felt awkward having her pastor follow her around school, but she also felt special. She was trying not to act too differently while he was there and risk having her classmates "call her out."

After school they talked all the way to Charity's house. Their conversation continued in the driveway for three hours as she slowly revealed that her biological mother was an alcoholic who had lost custody of Charity after her stepfather molested her. Charity was four years old when the Department of Social Services (DSS) took her from the hospital after recovery from a severe case of gonorrhea and placed her with her paternal grandmother, Louise. Pastor King learned that Louise initiated an open adoption and allowed Charity's mother to visit her. Charity was seven when Louise died, and her mother fought for and won her parental rights. Charity also told him about further occurrences of sexual assaults and continued physical abuse and neglect she had suffered while in her mother's care.

Charity didn't know why she was telling Pastor King all that she had gone through. All she knew was that when she talked to him, it felt like she was talking to God. It felt good to release all of her hurts and still find acceptance and unconditional love. That day was the beginning of her healing, and Pastor King gladly accepted the role as her spiritual father. She knew that there was a change in her attitude when she walked into the house that day introducing Pastor King to Mama Lorraine. She'd already explained to him how Mama Lorraine was Louise's daughter, who as soon as she was old enough made arrangements through the county to adopt Charity. Mama Lorraine made sure that her adoption case was closed and that Charity's mother's parental rights were permanently terminated.

It took Charity twenty minutes to get to her car. She had been stopped by at least fifteen people who wanted to thank her for blessing them during her call to worship. "Pastor should let you do it all of the time, rather than them dry old reverends," one person had even said.

"Minister Phillips," a male voice called out from behind her.

She had finally made it to her car and thought to pretend like she did not hear her name being called. She fumbled in her purse for her keys.

"Minister Phillips," the person sounded closer.

She turned around to find Minister Adams. "You're still here? You know you usually bolt out before Pastor can give the benediction good." She continued fumbling for her keys, hoping he didn't come to start a conversation. April would never forgive her if she let the cat out of the bag, and second, she made it a point to never talk to any male alone, no matter who he was. If it was one thing she was serious about, it was staying away from the appearance of evil.

He grinned. "I was sticking around to tell you how well you did on the call to worship this morning. You were awesome."

Click, click, she unlocked her sport utility vehicle by remote.

"Thank you. I'm sure you would have done just as good, if not better had he called upon you."

"I don't know. Especially after that royal treatment from the Reverends."

"I know, right?"

Minister Adams continued even though Charity looked like she was ready to jump into her Explorer any minute. "We make a good team, you and I," he said. Charity must have looked confused because he kept talking to explain. "While you were giving the call to worship I was backing you up on the piano."

She laughed. "Oh, I didn't notice. Thanks. And, thank you for the compliment." She looked around and saw people looking in their direction. "I need to go. I have to work on something for Pastor. You have a blessed week, okay?"

"Okay . . ." he looked like he wanted to say more. "You, too. Have a blessed week, too."

Charity was stressing over the magazine article. Backspacing every line she typed, nothing was good enough for a lead. She had only three hours to work on it. Emmitt would be dropping off Xavier at 5:00 and they were to be at Mama Lorraine's for dinner at 6:00. Maybe if she relaxed a little she could have the eight-hundred-word piece done by then.

"I can do all things through Christ, Who strengthens me. I can do all things through Christ, Who strengthens me," she repeated.

She read the "I Have No Man" article that Pastor King photo-copied from *Today's Gospel* magazine. She couldn't believe that she wrote such a powerful article on life after divorce. When she read the five tips on how to live as joyful single Christians, she realized that she didn't write the article by herself. *God, just as You helped me write that piece, I know You'll help me write this one. What do You want to say to single mothers about Mother's Day?*

She started typing by faith. Before she knew it, she had completed a modern version of the Bible story of Hagar and Abraham's separation called, "A Rose for Ishmael's Momma." Just as she was writing her byline at the end of the story, she heard a knock on the door.

"Who is it?" she asked just to be asking. She saw Emmitt's Nissan Pathfinder through the blinds.

"It's Xavier and Daddy, Mommy."

She opened the door and kneeled as Xavier ran into her outstretched arms.

"I missed you," she said, kissing him as much as he was kissing her. She watched Emmitt walk into the house without invitation and close the door behind him.

Charity was trying not to notice how handsome he looked in his fitted gray turtleneck sweater and black jeans, and gray and black snakeskin boots. He was standing in the foyer scanning the house. She was still holding Xavier, and closed her eyes, inhaling Emmitt's Cool Water cologne. She felt herself shiver from remembrance of how she would wrap herself up in his arms just so she could smell him. What she wouldn't give for an opportunity to do it now.

"Hello, Emmitt." She stood to greet him.

"Hey. Sorry we're late." He stepped back. "Traffic was a little bad getting here."

"That's okay, I needed the extra time. Would you like something to drink, or a sandwich to take with you on the road?"

"No, thanks, I'll be okay. I didn't come alone."

"Oh, did you bring James? Why didn't he come in?" she asked, opening the door to invite James in. He was still her friend too. But when she stepped out onto the porch, she saw the image of a female in the passenger seat. It was hard to make out who she was through the semi-tinted windows. She refocused her eyes to see if it was his mother before she jumped to conclusions. Realizing it was a woman she had never seen or heard about, she closed the door slowly trying to think of what to say next.

"She's just a friend," he started to explain.

"Xavier," Charity called. "Why don't you take your things to your room and get ready to go to Mah Mah's." When she was sure he was out of the living room, she continued. "You don't owe me an explanation about who she is. But I would've liked to have known that my son was spending time with someone I don't know."

"I thought about that. But since she ain't all that important to me, I just didn't know if I should tell you about her."

"She's not all that important? You mean, you would introduce our son to someone who's not *all that important?* How many other unimportant women does he know?"

"If she was all that, I would've brought her in here to introduce her to you."

"Whatever Emmitt, you've got someone waiting. Get on out of here."

"Lil' Man," he called to Xavier. By the volume of his television, they could hear that he was playing his PlayStation 2 video game system.

Xavier ran into the living room. He stopped short in front of his father. "Yes, sir?"

"Daddy's leaving. I just wanted to say thank you for such a good weekend. I'll see you in two weeks."

"Okay, Daddy. Tell Ms. Shawanda I said thanks for the Crash Bandicoot game, I'm playing it now."

Charity saw Emmitt mask his scowl by hugging Xavier. Charity walked over to the door and opened it for him.

"Good-bye, Emmitt."

"Charity, please don't—"

"Good-bye, Emmitt," she repeated, slamming the door behind him.

She was glad Xavier had run back to his room. She did not want him to see or hear her heaving over the toilet.

Chapter 5

CHARITY LOVED GOING TO HER MOTHER'S HOUSE, especially for Sunday dinners. It was the one place she felt absolutely free. There were no unrealistic expectations of her—not even from herself. No one cared that she was a minister or therapist. She could dress any kind of way, say what she wanted and how she wanted to say it, and do whatever she felt like when she was there. The more she thought about how good it felt to not be under the microscope, the faster she drove to get to Mama Lorraine's.

"Did you hear me, Mommy?" Xavier asked from the backseat.

"Mommy's sorry, baby, what did you say?"

"I have a little sister at my daddy's house."

"Umph, sorry," she apologized for driving up on the curb. "A little sister?" she asked, trying to keep her voice even and interested, and to keep the car on the road at the same time.

"Yeah. Her name is Destiny. Ms. Shawanda is her mommy."

"Is that so?"

"She can't talk all that good but she can sing 'Twinkle, Twinkle, Little Star' over and over."

"That's cute. How old is she, baby?" she asked, not believing that Emmitt would have another child and not tell her. Let alone

take care of another child, when he was not financially supporting his firstborn.

"She one, but she says she two."

"Did your daddy tell you that you're a big brother, or are you
saying that you are?"

"No, Daddy didn't tell me. I just know it."

"Oh." She felt relieved. *If Destiny was his daughter he would've
told Xavier that he was her big brother. Then again, I would've thought
he would have told me about this other woman.* "Baby? We're almost
at Mah Mah's house, let's play the quiet game until we get there,
okay?"

"I'm good at this game, Mommy. I bet I can beat you."

"We'll see. 1-2-3 go!"

Xavier was a talker. Charity had to admit that he got it honestly. She loved to talk. She'd always thought that she was either
going to become a talk-show host or a therapist. The latter came
easier. Emmitt was also a talker. So, the only way she could get
some peace and quiet was to play the quiet game. She had no idea
what she was going to do when Xavier got too old to play.

"Give your grandma a kiss, baby," Mama Lorraine said to
Xavier as he and Charity walked into the house.

"Hey, Mah Mah, I missed you," he said, kissing her on the
cheek. "Where's Sha-Lai and Raquan?"

"You're so used to them being here that you think they live
here. They're with they momma. They'll be here in a minute. Go
put your coat up and tell Mah Mah all about your time with that
pappy of yours."

"Hey, Ma," Charity said, hugging her mother, more so to keep
her quiet. Charity was against speaking bad about Emmitt in
front of Xavier.

"Hey, Cherry," she returned the hug. "You okay, baby?"

"Yes, ma'am. I'm good," she said, hoping she was convincing.
"Have you heard from Iesha?"

"Yeah, she's on her way. Go on and get your coat off. Your daddy's in there."

Charity's father was lying across the bed watching a movie on his wide-screen floor model television. He moved over to make room for Xavier and Charity to lie beside him.

"What'chu watching, Pah Pah?" Xavier jumped in the bed beside his grandfather.

"One of the old *Rocky* flicks," he answered.

Charity lay down on the bed. "Zavey, when your Auntie and I were little, Pah Pah used to show us all of the *Rocky* movies. Didn't you, Daddy?"

Xavier looked up at his grandfather and said, "Gosh, this movie is old."

"You better watch it, boy, your grandfather doesn't like anyone talking about his age."

"You're old too, Mommy."

"Xavier, you'd better stop while you're ahead," Mr. Brown said. "You doing all right, baby girl?"

She thought she must be transparent, considering she had not yet been in the house for five minutes and had already been asked twice if she was okay. "I'm fine, Daddy. I'm just a little tired. That's all."

"Pah Pah, I got a new sister at my daddy's house," Xavier said proudly.

Charity's father's eyes narrowed as he looked at her for an explanation.

"Yes, Daddy," she began choosing her words carefully. "Emmitt's friend, Ms. Shawanda, has a little girl named Destiny."

"Is she his?"

Charity shrugged her shoulders. "And she can sing 'Twinkle, Twinkle' can't she, Zavey?" she said, hoping her father would not ask more questions.

"Does your momma know?"

"No, but—"

"Mah Mah." Xavier ran out of the room to tell her the good news. "I got a new sister."

Charity stayed with her father, knowing she would be called for clarification.

"Charity Lachelle, come here."

Her father followed her into the kitchen. "Zavey, go play with the toys in the back. Raquan and Sha-Lai are going to be here in a minute. Go get things ready, okay?"

"Okay, Pah Pah."

"What is that boy talking about?" her mother asked before Xavier could turn the corner.

"Emmitt's girlfriend—"

"Girlfriend? You mean he found somebody who'd want his sorry behind?"

"Lorraine, let her finish."

"You shut up. Go 'head, baby. I'm sorry."

"All I know is that his girlfriend, Shawanda, has a one-year-old daughter named Destiny. That's all I know. I don't know if it's Emmitt's baby or what. I found out the same way you did, through Zavey."

Her parents stood there in silence. Either they did not know what to say, or what they wanted to say would be too ungodly to say in front of Charity.

"And—"

"There's more?" her mother interrupted. "You see there, Charles? The boy is still trying to ruin her life. I knew we should not have let Cherry—"

"Lorraine, please." Her father waved his hand to shush her. He motioned for Charity to go on.

"He brought her with him to drop Zavey off today."

Mama Lorraine held her hand over her mouth. She was glad to be distracted by clumsy knocking on the door.

"Y'all just in time," she said, letting Raquan and Sha-Lai in. "How you doing? Give your grandma a kiss."

"Hey, Mah Mah, hey, Pah Pah, hey, Aunt Cherry," they sang as they hugged every one they named. "Where's Xavier?"

"Back there in the back waiting on you," their grandfather answered.

"What's uuuuuup?" Iesha asked, walking in the door like a rapper with a limp.

"Girl, do you have to be so loud? Come on in here and close that door," Mama Lorraine said.

"I love you too, Momma," she said, hugging and kissing all over her face.

"Go put your coat up so we can eat."

"Sis, you chilling?"

"Hello, Iesha, I'm all right. How about you?" They hugged.

"Hey, Esha," her father spoke as he got the plates out of the cabinet. She walked over and kissed him on the cheek.

"Y'all been talking about me?" Iesha asked. "'Cause y'all mighty quiet. It ain't been this quiet in here since Cherry broke free from Mr. Jail." She laughed until she realized she was laughing alone. "My bad, what I miss?"

"It's okay, Iesha. I was just telling Mom and Dad that Xavier thinks he's a big brother because Emmitt's girlfriend has a daughter."

"Well, is he?"

"I don't know yet. I just found out on the way over here."

"From Zavey?"

Charity realized that if Iesha thought the situation was bad, then it was really bad. "May we please eat. I'm starving," she said, attempting to break the tension in the room.

"We ain't gone be watching a movie today," Mama Lorraine said as she sliced herself some butter and passed it to her husband.

Iesha kept her eyes on her plate.

"We're not?" Charity asked.

"Nope, today we're gonna talk."

"About what?"

Mama Lorraine looked at Iesha and then at Charity.

"I think we have a small problem in the Brown camp that needs to be discussed. Ain't that right, Esha?"

"I wouldn't say it's a problem—"

"Well, it sounded like a problem on Friday."

"You don't like working at Horizons do you, Iesha?" Charity asked.

"It's not that, Cherry. Momma seems to think I have a problem because I'm not like you."

"What?"

"Momma's always comparing us and when she do I get upset because I always get the short end of the stick. I always end up looking like the bad seed."

"Cherry, I don't compare y'all, do I?" asked Mama Lorraine.

Charity could see the hurt in Iesha's eyes. "Momma, I've worked hard to make y'all proud of me, to show you that I appreciate everything you've done for me. But there have been times I felt like you hold me on a higher pedestal above Iesha."

"Thank you," Iesha said, waving her fork at Charity.

"Charles, tell these girls how much I done struggled to treat them equally and how hard I worked to not show favoritism."

"That's true, girls. Your mom and I have talked on several occasions about what to do and what not to do for one because of the way it might appear to the other."

"I agree with what you're saying," Charity said. "You guys didn't give one of us something without giving the same thing to the other one. But I think what Iesha is saying is different. Esha, give us an example of what you're talking about."

Mama Lorraine rolled her eyes at the ceiling. "I done told you about treating us like we one of your clients. Leave that therapy mess in your office. We black and that mess don't work for us."

"I'll give you an example," Iesha offered. "When Cherry called us from that women's shelter and told us she had left Emmitt, Momma, you was so distraught you wanted to kill Emmitt yourself. But had that been me, you would've just overlooked it and fussed at me for messing with the wrong type of man." No one responded to her, everyone looked like they were more interested in what was on their plates.

"Okay, I got a better example," she continued. "I got my house before Cherry did. No one threw a housewarming party for me. But when Cherry bought her house, you would have thought Oprah was coming to town, the party was so big."

"Now, I'll give you that one," Mama Lorraine said. "You did *get* a house before Cherry. And we did come to your house for a housewarming dinner and we bought gifts for you. We threw a different celebration for Cherry because she *bought* her house."

"So, I don't deserve a housewarming party because I live in a Section 8 house?"

Mr. Brown interjected, "Honey, all Lorraine is saying is that a Section 8 house is rental property. Did we give you a house-warming party when you were renting apartments?"

"No."

"Okay then."

"Well, here's another example. I just started working my first job, and no one has said anything to me. I didn't get a congratu-lations or nothing."

"Esha, since when did you become so needy?" Mama Lorraine asked. "I never felt the need to praise you for every little thang. I thought you were the strong one. Cherry was the one who always needed to be praised and validated. She was the one with the bruised ego. Girl, working a job is like cleaning your room. That's something you supposed to do. Don't get me wrong, I'm glad you working. It's about time you see you worth more than a welfare check in the mail every month."

"And I'm glad to have you working with me," Charity added.

"Are you sure about that? I mean, I don't wanna embarrass you 'cause I don't talk like you, and I don't dress like you," she said sarcastically.

"Iesha Nicole, that's enough," Mama Lorraine intervened. "We getting ready to squash this. Don't nobody owe you nothing, and ain't nobody mistreating you. You need to get up off your high horse and realize that."

"I just want everybody to know that me and Cherry are two different people and that's okay. You wouldn't want two Ieshas, so you shouldn't want two Cherrys."

"Like I said," Mama Lorraine said, faking a smile so hard she was bearing down on her teeth, "we ain't the ones with the problem."

"Well, why did you want Cherry to give me a job?"

"'Cause you needed one."

"That's what I'm talking about. Y'all always talking about what I need. Since when did everybody become an expert on Iesha? According to y'all a job ain't all I need." She held out her hand to count on her fingers all the things she had been told she needed. "I need to quit clubbing, I need to quit depending on welfare, I need to go to church, I need Jesus . . . I need for y'all to let me be myself. I ain't hell-bound, but if I do go, it ain't like we on no family plan. I'll be going by myself."

Mama Lorraine shook her head at Iesha. "Everybody hold hands. We need to pray."

She paused so everyone could follow her lead. They bowed their heads, closed their eyes, and joined hands.

"Lord," she raised her voice. "Oooooh, Lord," she sang like a preacher in the climax of a sermon. "Let it be known, hah, by You and all Your heavenly angels, hah, that my daughter Iesha Nicole Brown, hah, bless her heart, hah . . ."

"Bless her Lord," Charity chimed in, realizing that her mother was having fun.

"She ain't hell-bound, hah, but if she do go, Lord, hah . . ."

"Have mercy, Lord, have mercy," Charity mocked.

"We just wanna thank You, hah . . ."

"Thank You, Jesus."

"That we ain't on her family plan. Hallelujah!"

"Hallelujah!"

"Let the church say, amen." Mama Lorraine could not keep

her composure any longer. She laughed like she was watching her *Madea's Family Reunion* video.

"Amen," everyone, including Mr. Brown, agreed as they laughed along with her.

Even Iesha laughed. That's one good thing about the Brown family, it was hard for them to stay mad at one another. Their sense of humor sustained them through some very tough trials. "Y'all the ones going to hell," Iesha said. "Making fun of the church. Y'all better check y'all policies, it might be better to get on that family plan."

CHAPTER 6

JOSEPH KNEW IT WAS CHEAP LABOR, but it was keeping him from being idle. "Idle hands are the devil's work tools," he remembers his mother telling him. He was a quality control manager for a furniture production company that outsourced its work to the prison. He supervised up to fifty workers and inspected the office and dormitory furniture they made. Most of the men had never worked before, or they had very few skills, which contributed to the many inefficiencies he would find in their finished products. His job was stressful. Oftentimes he walked the fine line between being a buddy and a boss to the workers. He liked to keep them encouraged because of the oppressive situation they were in, but they often mistook his kindness for a reason to be slack. The workers made furnishings by hand, therefore, their products were more expensive. He had to make sure their work was perfect and timely, because of the high demand for their furniture.

"Good morning, Brother Lee. You gone make someone a proud executive with the muscle you putting into that desk."

"Thank you, sir. It's turning out good, ain't it?"

"Oh yeah. You've become the furniture maestro around here. Keep up the good work."

"I will. Making furniture takes my mind off things," he said, sanding the wood. "I won't complain, though. Most of my needs are met here. I got a place to stay, a job, no debt, plenty to eat, and medical attention when I need it. But being here by myself is lonely. Making furniture fills that void for me. Every piece I make is important."

Joseph patted him on the back. "And it shows. You should meet some of the brothers in the fellowship. We have intercessory prayer every night at seven thirty in the Clayford building and we do Bible study on Wednesday nights at that time. You should come to Bible study tonight in the chapel. The meetings are guaranteed to chase away the lonelies."

"Maybe I will."

He went back to his desk after checking on the other workers. He knew exactly what Brother Lee was talking about. He condemned himself for prescribing the fellowship as a cure-all for loneliness. He had been leading the fellowship for two years and still had to deal with the aching in his heart to be loved. *Yes,* he scoffed, *Jesus is all I need. But it sure wouldn't hurt to know love on this side of heaven.* He opened the quality assurance paperwork on his desk, and, like Brother Lee, began to pore over his work.

Later that evening, Joseph went to the chapel for Bible study. He liked the evangelist who was coming in to teach tonight. Evangelist Wilhimena Graves was an older woman he could tell knew what she was talking about. He sat at the piano as usual to open up with one or two hymns. He played "Leaning on the Everlasting Arms of Jesus," as the group of twenty men sang along. Instead of playing another hymn, he began playing the chords to a song he felt that God helped him to compose. He closed his eyes when he saw the looks of confusion upon the men's faces. There used to be a time when he would've been too shy or scared to sing in front of a group of people. In fact, he knew that he couldn't sing, but he kept practicing, training his voice, and asking God for the gift of singing. He opened his mouth to see how well he had fared.

I know in Whom I've believed
I know Whose grace I've received
Oh, oh Lord, thank You for blessing me.
I know Whose words I've confessed
And I know that I shall be blessed
Oh, oh Lord, thank You for loving me.
Now-ow, Lord. Hon-or Your Word.
Keep me in Your will
I promise to stand still.
Oh, oh Lord, thank You for blessing me.

When he opened his eyes, he saw the men standing with their arms outstretched toward heaven. Tears were streaming down their faces. Again, he realized that God had answered another prayer. Evangelist Graves walked over to him and took the microphone.

"Brother, stand up," she admonished him. She turned to the crowd. "Y'all stretch your hands toward this brother. He is anointed." The men did as she said. She turned back to him and said, "Brother, God says He has heard every one of your requests. And just like He answered you tonight, He is going to answer you concerning your release from this place." The young man lifted his hands to receive her utterances. "Mark my word," she continued. "Your days here are numbered."

After the services, Joseph went back to his room encouraged.

Chapter 7

"GOOD MONDAY MORNING, IESHA," Charity greeted. "How long have you been here?"

"Hey. I got here around eight thirty. I just came on in after I dropped the kids off at school."

"Is everything all right at home? Because the sister I grew up with doesn't show up anywhere early."

"Well, this is the new me. Since our talk at Momma's yesterday, I decided that I don't have to prove nothing to anyone anymore—except to myself. So, I'm turning over a new leaf."

Charity hugged her. "Praise God. Does this mean you'll be going to church on Sundays?"

"Slow down, evangelist Holyfield, don't sling me into the ring just yet. I'mma do one thing at a time. And today, I just wanna learn how to do my job and be good at it."

Charity looked away. "Well, that's a good start."

"Don't look so sad. I'mma get back to church real soon. I'll probably come to yours because y'all got more men in your church than they do at daddy's church."

Iesha was the only one laughing. "Cherry, you all right?"

"Yes, I'm fine." She forced a smile. "Just thinking of the best way to start the day here. Let me go and put my things down and—"

"Hm-uhm. You lying. Did you talk to Emmitt and find out who that girl was he was with? Or if that's his baby?"

"No, I'm not even thinking about Emmitt, Iesha. I said I'm fine."

"That's what your mouth say . . . You ain't fooling me . . . I grew up with you . . . Know you like the back of my hand. Don't make me call Emmitt and cuss him out . . . 'cause I'll do it . . . Gone have the nerve to bring a chick to your house, hmph, you want me to call him?"

Charity laughed. Iesha was so much like Mama Lorraine that it was not funny. It didn't take much to get her riled up, and once she was going it was hard to get her to stop.

"Thank you, sis. For the third time, I'm fine. Let me go and put my things down and you and I can go over that little guide I made for you and see if you have any questions. Since you want to learn how to do a good job here." Charity walked off before Iesha could protest.

She opened the door to her office and walked over to her desk to put her belongings down. She wished she had a devotional book, something quick to help her get her focus. Tears blurred her vision. She rolled her eyes to the ceiling, to keep the tears away from her makeup. *Lord, I don't understand. I have faithfully prayed and believed that You would work on Emmitt and restore our marriage. And here we are, almost three years later, and he has a child by another woman. Father, I don't know how much more of this I can take. I love him . . . we have a child together, we had a life together. Why can't we be together?*

Charity knew that God was listening, but she didn't feel that He was responding. It felt like her mind was roaming at top speed. She knew she could shut it down by speaking aloud. "If a client of mine came to me in the same situation—they were divorced, their ex had a child by another person, and didn't give them the time of day, I would tell them . . . to move on. But what if that client was a Christian and knew that God didn't like divorce and believed that God was more than able to restore the marriage?" It took her longer to formulate a response to her own question. "I don't know . . . I don't know what I'd tell them." Unsatisfied with her answer, she tried again. "Okay . . . I'd tell them one of two things . . . One, I'd say that God is more than able to restore the marriage but that if He isn't restoring it, it's probably a blessing in disguise. Or I'd tell them that maybe it wasn't God's timing to restore it yet and they'd need to hold on. But the Bible says that God doesn't withhold any good thing from us and it also says that he who finds a wife finds a good thing." She sighed. Talking it out was giving her a headache. But the responses kept coming to her. "And then I'd tell them to quit punishing themselves because they were divorced. God hates divorce, but He loves the divorced."

Charity took a deep breath. She knew that she needed to let go of the outcome. "Thank You, Father." She dabbed her eye with a tissue and prepared herself to go back out to Iesha's desk.

"You ready?" she asked, smiling, standing like a black Vanna White ready to turn letters.

"Yeah. Girl, what'chu do back there? I need some of that."

"There isn't anything a little prayer won't take care of. Now, let's get to work. Do you have any questions about anything you read in the manual?"

"Oh, Lord. Sheeee's baaaaack."

"See, you're praying already."

"Whatever you say. I pretty much understood everything in the book."

"Good, I tried to put everything in there I could think of that you'd need to do your job. I'm sure some things will come up as we go along. Are you as nervous as I am?"

"Nervous? You don't look *nervous*."

"I don't know why I am. I guess because I'm new at this too. I've always worked for someone else. Everything has always been laid out for me. But now, I'm having to lay out my own way, and it's a little scary. I put everything I own and have at stake for this business and if something happened to it I don't know what I'd do."

"Well, so far, so good. You did a bang-up job with the open house, you got two people working for you, and both you and Harmony got people booked up till the end of the week. I don't know much about business, but for a first week, seems like you got it going on."

"See, that's why I'm glad you're here. You know you've always been able to do that?"

"Do what?"

"To make me feel better. Even though Mom doesn't see it, you've always been my biggest cheerleader. You knew just as well as everyone else that I had no business marrying Emmitt, but you were so supportive. You acted like you were just as happy as I was on my wedding day. Even as far back as when I was in school and girls would try to fight me, you were always there to take up for me."

"Well, I didn't want you to get your behind beat," Iesha laughed. "And as far as Emmitt goes, I just wanted you to be happy. But y'all been apart for two years and he still making you miserable. Ain't there something in the Bible that can help you with that?"

"That's just what God and I settled—"

The shrill ring of the telephone startled them both. Charity excused herself while Iesha answered the phone.

"Horizons Counseling Center, this is Iesha." Charity gave her a thumbs-up from where she poured a cup of Iesha's freshly brewed coffee.

"Yes, sir . . . uhm hum . . . yes, hold on one moment and let me get that information for you." It took her a few seconds to find the hold button.

"I can handle it," she said to Charity, who was looking at her questioningly. She flipped through the pages of her homemade manual.

"Thank you for holding, our DWI screening appointments are seventy-five dollars. When you wanna come in?"

Charity felt her eyes stretch wide, hearing Iesha speak improper English. She relaxed when she saw Iesha hunch her shoulders apologetically.

"Okay, I can get you in today at four o'clock . . . Will that work? . . . Okay, I got you down with Harmony Scott. Do you need directions? Okay, I'll see you at four."

"Not bad for a first phone call."

"I know, I have to concentrate really hard to talk like I got—I mean have—some sense."

"Speaking of Harmony, what time are we expecting her?"

"Her schedule says ten. Her first appointment is at eleven o'clock. You have an appointment at ten."

"Yes. With a Jeffrey Wright?"

"Yes, and then you're free until your one o'clock."

"What are you doing for lunch?"

"Traci and Mercedes are coming to eat lunch with me in the courtyard."

"Oh. I guess I'll call April and see if she can meet me for lunch. Since you seem to have everything under control out here, I'm going to let you work."

"All right then, you gone on back there and keep yourself together or I'mma call Emmitt and give him a piece of my mind."

"You are getting more like Momma everyday. Do you know that?"

Iesha smiled. "What? Being protective over you?"

"Yes." Charity smiled back. "But, it feels good to be loved."

Charity sat down at her mahogany wood executive desk and unsnapped her black leather-bound pocket Bible. She knew that if she were going to continue to walk in peace, she needed some Word to meditate on. She sat quietly flipping through the Bible waiting for peace about its passages. She slowed down in the Book of Isaiah and read chapter 54. It seemed like verses five and six just leaped off the pages and into her spirit. Rereading the verses helped her to understand them. *For thy maker is thine husband; the Lord of Hosts is His name . . . For the Lord has called thee as a woman forsaken and grieved in spirit, and a wife of youth, when thou was refused, saith thy God.*

"Thank you, Jesus. You are my husband and today that is more than enough. You know how to love me. You provide for me. You meet my every need. Thank You, Lord."

She encouraged herself by reading several Psalms until the unexpected sound of the phone's intercom made her jump.

"Charity, your ten o'clock is here."

"Thank you, Iesha. Let him know I'll be right out."

"Take your time, he's filling out his paperwork."

She went to the restroom to refresh her makeup and to make sure she was showing no signs of distress. *God forbid a therapist has problems of her own*, she kidded. She continued to praise God for lifting her spirit through His Word and presence. As she walked to the waiting area she reminded herself that she could do all things through Christ, Who strengthens her.

She extended her right hand to initiate a handshake to a well-dressed brown-skinned gentleman who was flipping through the pages of a *Black Enterprise* magazine from the coffee table. "Mr. Wright? Good morning. I'm Charity Phillips."

He stood to meet her. "Good morning." He looked at her left hand for a wedding ring. "*Ms.* Phillips. It's a pleasure to meet you."

She half smiled and pointed in the direction she led. "Follow me. My office is this way." She felt uncomfortable walking in front of him. Her whole backside burned, like someone with x-ray vision was watching her. "Did you have any trouble finding us?" she said, making small talk to diminish the discomfort she felt.

"No problem at all," he said, sounding like he was smiling and talking about a totally different subject.

"Come on in," she said, stopping at her office door to allow

Mr. Wright to walk in before her. She motioned to a chair in front of her desk. She didn't like conducting sessions from beind her desk, but at this moment she knew that was where she felt more comfortable.

She laid her daily planner on top of her Bible.

He leaned back in the chair and clasped his hands behind his head. "A Bible reader," he acknowledged. "My sign that I'm in the right place."

Charity smiled to be polite. She flipped through the chart that Iesha compiled with the paperwork he completed, and the case summary and recommendations from the court. "Mr. Wright, what brings you here today?" she asked without looking up at him.

"Ms. Phillips, I'd prefer you talk to me as opposed to that file."

"Forgive me, sir. I usually get a chance to review charts before I see clients. I apologize for not being able to do that today. Give me a few minutes, will you?" She read the five pages of information in less than three minutes and looked up at him. "Thank you."

"That's better," he shifted his weight to the front of the chair. "Now, I'll admit that I've had some problems in the past, but I'm not as bad as those papers make me out to be. And as far as those run-ins with the law," he crossed his legs. "I was at the wrong place at the wrong time, and with the wrong people. But I'm going to follow the court's recommendations, which is why I'm here. They sent me for a psychiatric evaluation. Waste of my time. I could've told him that he wasn't going to find anything. But he recommended outpatient counseling and the judge ordered it. Et cetera upon et cetera."

The one thing practicing therapy helped her do was not to let her feelings show and to emotionally detach from situations. *If I'd applied that principle to Emmitt two years ago, I'd be over him by now.* She remembered her graduate school adviser telling her that if she lets a client get under her skin, "that's a warning that you have some unresolved issues with someone they are reminding you of.

They may be reminding you of yourself or someone else. People are just a reflection of yourself." As she recalled that statement, she realized that this man was Emmitt with a different face. Just as charming and manipulative as he wanted to be. The psychiatrist may not have diagnosed him with anything, but she could think of a diagnosis. Sociopath.

She fixed a smile on her face. "Compliance. That's my sign that you're in the right place. What would you like to gain from therapy, Mr. Wright?"

His smile was incongruent with his body language. "You tell me. You're the therapist."

That was Emmitt up and down and she knew how to handle his type.

She made direct eye contact with him. "In order for us to make significant gain here, Mr. Wright, the goals we set will have to be mutual. Why don't you tell me what you would like to accomplish and I will help you identify how we can meet those goals."

He fidgeted in the chair and straightened his tie. "Uhm mum," he cleared his throat. "I would like to . . ." he started, regaining his composure. "Find out why sistahs have problems with brothers such as myself. Why they can't handle a fine, professional, and successful brotha like me. Every black woman I know—my mother, my sisters, and my wife—got their opinion about how I need to be living, what I need to be doing, and how I need to be doing it."

"Do you think that my race and gender will hinder us from working together?"

"Your sex—" He smiled, or smirked. "Excuse me, your gender and race is why the courts recommended you to me. They think I should work with a black female."

That sounded like a Judge Fulton recommendation. She made a mental note to call her. "Okay, that's one goal—to explore the resistance in your relationship with women who play a significant role in your life. I'd like for us to identify at least two more."

"You make it sound like that resistance is on my part. I told you, there is *nothing* wrong with me."

"You're right, Mr. Wright, there is nothing *wrong* with you. But I think exploring your role with the women you've mentioned might help you understand why you keep making wrong decisions and finding yourself in the wrong type of situations. And by the looks of the court's case summary," she said, flipping through his chart, "a female was involved in each charge."

"Where did you go to school?"

Charity looked pointedly at him. "We have about twenty more minutes in our session and it would benefit us best to use the time talking about you. Are you ready to proceed with your second goal?"

"I was just wondering if you know what you know because you learned it from the books or from your own personal experience. You look to be about my age. I don't know how you would be able to help me if you haven't been through the same thing."

"Nineteen minutes and counting."

"Just what I thought, book sense." He stood up and walked over to the window. "For a second goal, I would finally like to talk about a family secret. Something that happened between me and my sister Janice that my family doesn't talk about." He kept his back to her.

Charity waited in silence.

"Uhm mum," he cleared his throat. "I'm not prepared to talk about that today but I would like to get there."

"Very good. Two down and one more to go."

He walked back toward Charity and seated himself. "And finally," he said in the softest voice he'd used since he'd been there. "Since I see that you are a Bible reader, I would like to talk about how I can get back to where I used to be with the Lord. Are these three goals attainable?"

She retrieved a piece of paper from the desk's file cabinet drawer.

"This is a treatment plan," she slid it across the desk to him.

"We'll list the three goals that you have identified and I'll work on the objectives, the ways in which we can meet these goals. We'll meet twice a week for the first month, then once a week the next month, and eventually once a month until we terminate therapy. Does that sound workable for you?"

He nodded.

"Okay, when you return on Thursday, if you agree to the objectives, I'll have you sign the plan and we'll begin to work on them."

"I would like to meet three times a week." He smiled.

She kept on talking like she didn't hear him. As she flipped through to the end of his chart, she found something. "Mr. Wright, did the psychiatrist you met with talk to you about the findings of his evaluation?"

"Not really."

"Did he prescribe any medications?"

"Yes, he prescribed two, Resperidol and another one I can't recall the name of. He called it a mood stabilizer."

"Lithium?"

"Yes. That's it, lithium."

"Did he tell you why he was prescribing the medications?"

"Yes." He shifted in his seat. "He mentioned something about me being a schizophrenic."

"Do you know what that means, Mr. Wright?"

"Yes," he quipped. "I'm a well-educated man. I know what that is."

Charity softened. "Okay. Do you agree with his findings?"

"No. But because I have a maternal aunt who is a true schizo-phrenic, I do take the medications."

"Does that mean that your aunt had psychotic episodes, periods of time where she was not in touch with reality?"

"Shoot, yeah! I was scared of her when I was little. She was crazy. That's why I know I'm not schizophrenic."

"So, you've never had any episodes?" She didn't press when he refused to answer and took the expression on his face to mean that he hadn't. "Well," she admonished, "in order for us to work together, I need you to stay on the medications. And at some point I would like to meet with you and your wife. Okay?"

"Fine with me. Except that the medications are affecting our sex life and we've discussed me getting off of them."

"Don't make any decisions about that yet. Let's see how much progress we make in at least six weeks before you do. This is what I would like for you to do for homework." Before walking him to Iesha's desk to check out, Charity encouraged him to identify at least three black women he could relate to in a positive way. She asked him to find them through the music he listened to, the books he read, or through the television shows he watched if he could not come up with ones he knew.

"That'll do it for today," she said when they reached Iesha. "I'll see you Thursday. If anything comes up before then," she said handing him her business card, "call me, Mr. Wright, okay?"

He glanced at the card and smiled. "Call *you* Mr. Wright? How about Mrs. Wright?"

The progress she thought they made went right out of the window. "I meant, Mr. Wright, you can call me if something comes up."

"I know. I know. I just like the way you say my name—Mister Right. And that I am."

If he hadn't winked, she wouldn't have known he punned his name.

Wallace was nowhere to be found in the courtyard. Iesha had looked the place over twice. Even though there were countless people crowded in the two-leveled dining area, and the lines of the ten restaurants were extremely long, she knew he was not there. When it came to finding a man she was interested in, she had the senses of a lioness on the prowl for food.

"No you didn't!" Iesha heard Mercedes but did not see her or Traci. "These are Burberry's. Bur-ber-ry's. You betta watch way you stepping before I—"

"Sorry about that, ma'am," Iesha interrupted. She pulled Mercedes by the arm and Traci followed.

"Nah, E," Mercedes clumsily walked with Iesha pulling her arm. She looked in the direction of the woman who accidentally stepped on her foot. "That tramp stepped on my new shoes. And then looked like she wanted to bow up at me. I'll pull that corporate America weave out of her head."

"That woman did look like she was gonna hit her," Traci added.

"Both of y'all shut up." Iesha frowned. "I'dda looked like I wanted to hit you too. Y'all up in here acting like fools. Do y'all know where y'all at? Y'all cows embarrassing."

Traci and Mercedes looked at each other in disbelief.

Traci laughed. "What?" she asked Iesha. "Sadie, who did we have to pull out of the drive-thru window last week after she reached in to slap the cashier?"

"Esha."

"And who was the reason we had to leave the club early on Friday night because she heard someone talking about her in the bathroom?" she asked in one breath.

"Esha."

"That's what I thought. Now we embarrassing her."

Iesha laughed with them. "All right y'all got me. But this is different. I work here. How y'all gone start a fight where I work?"

"And the girl at Burger King wasn't working when you hauled off and slapped her?" Traci asked.

"Is y'all gone eat or drill me all day? I only got an hour for lunch."

"Uhm hum," said Traci. "Quit trying to perpetrate and keep it real."

"West sii—ede," Mercedes chanted.

Iesha held her head down and took three brisk steps ahead, pretending she was not with them.

"How 'bout some Burger King?" Mercedes laughed. "Maybe

that cashier can have it your way, E. Slap slap," she said, pretending to slap herself on both cheeks.

Iesha walked on before them to the Showmars counter and ordered her food. Mercedes and Traci stood in line behind her.

"Will you add an old-fashioned pita burger combo to that, with no onions?" a familiar male voice asked.

She turned around to find Wallace easing up beside her. He took out his wallet to pay.

"Hey, Wallace." Iesha blushed.

"A woman after my own heart. You remember my name."

"Do you remember mine?"

"Hmm, let me see," he said, pretending not to remember. "Keisha. Felicia . . ."

"Um, mum," Traci cleared her throat behind them.

"Oh, Wallace, these are my friends, Mercedes and Traci."

"Hello, ladies," he said, shaking both of their hands. "Any friend of Iesha's is a friend of mine."

"Hey-ey," they sang.

"Have you ladies ordered?"

"No, but if you paying we know what we want," Mercedes offered.

Iesha threw one of her straighten-up-or-I'll-kill-you motherly looks at them.

"What?" Mercedes asked.

"Ma'am, will you add their orders to ours?" he asked the cashier.

Wallace carried both trays to a table while the women fixed their beverages.

"Girl, he fine," Mercedes said, filling her cup with ice.

Traci put a lid on her cup. "He sure is and he got money. I didn't see nothing but twenties in his wallet. He's a good catch."

Iesha blushed. "Y'all please act like you got some sense. I don't wanna mess up anything if there is anything to be messed up." She led the way to the table where Wallace was standing.

"Are you going to eat with us?" Iesha asked him.

"No, I'm eating in the office today. I have some numbers to crunch for a two o'clock meeting."

"Oh," Iesha said simply. "Well, thanks for lunch. I would've liked to enjoy it with you."

"Uuuuhhh," the girls instigated.

"Then again, it's probably a good thing that you're not joining us," she said, looking crossly at her friends. "When will I see you again?"

"Don't worry about that, it'll be real soon." He winked, and walked away from them.

The girls sat in silence.

"Meow," Traci said, breaking the ice and dipping a french fry in ketchup. "Looks like we'll be going out alone this weekend, Sadie."

"Looks like it, huh?"

"Chi, please," Iesha said. "That man ain't said nothing about the weekend. Besides, that ain't nowhere near soon in my book," she laughed.

Traci bit into her pita burger. "Long as you don't let Sha-Lai know about him. You know what happened the last time?"

Iesha's smile turned into a frown. "I'll beat her behind if she do that again." She cringed after the words escaped her mouth, remembering what happened between her and Sha-Lai last night.

"What she do?"

"You remember, she answered the phone and called Mark by Greg's name."

"Oh yeah," Mercedes said, looking for pieces of grilled chicken in her salad. "She did, didn't she?"

"That was your fault." Traci plunged more fries into ketchup. "She wouldn't have had that information if you hadn't given it to her."

"That's why my chaps don't know my business," Mercedes continued. "If he ain't got a ring on my finger, my chaps don't know him. Shequanna's chaps done had three or four daddies. Every man she bring home they call daddy."

"Well, I know now," Iesha said. "Sha-Lai just getting to be too grown." She took another bite of her fish sandwich. "She runs her mouth too much and I messed around and hit her last night."

The girls looked at each other. "Messed around?" Traci asked. "You're infamous for whooping at least one of your chaps nightly. Every time I call, at least one of them done got one of the three B's before bedtime."

Traci high-fived Mercedes. "A bath, a beat down, or some Benadryl, and not necessarily in that order."

They all laughed. "Long as you ain't leave no bruises on her," Traci said. "You know they check them chaps at school these days."

"You right about that," Mercedes interjected. "That's how what's-her-name got her chaps taken away last year."

Traci snapped her fingers, trying to recall who Mercedes was talking about. "Um, um, Natalie."

"That's it, Natalie. Them white folks snatched all her chaps. That little boy went to school and told them Natalie whooped him. And that's all she wrote."

"Whatever," Iesha said, trying not to sound nervous. "They can lock me up for beating my child, but they'll never have to worry about locking my chaps up when they turn teenagers. That's what's wrong with chaps these days anyway. They mommas scared to whoop them. Ain't nobody gone tell me how to raise my chaps unless they helping me pay the bills."

"Preach, sister, preach," Mercedes mimicked.

"I ain't saying don't whoop her," Traci said. "I'm just saying don't whoop her on a school night. And whatever you do, don't whoop her in Wal-Mart, or in they parking lot."

They all laughed.

"I know that's right," Iesha said. "Had that woman on national TV after that camera taped her in the parking lot beating that little girl. That's a shame. You can't whip your chaps nowhere these days."

Traci seemed to get serious again. "Girl, you talk a good game, but you know if something happened to any one of them kids, you wouldn't know what to do."

"I couldn't even imagine. I don't even want to."

CHAPTER 8

EMMITT COULD NOT TELL IF THE THUMPING was coming from inside his chest or from the bass line of the song he was playing from his *Nellyville* CD.

But his suspicion was confirmed when he turned off the Nissan Pathfinder's ignition. Emmitt took the letter out of his manila folder to make sure he was at the right building. Davis, Watson, and Blalock, Attorneys at Law, Present Day Office Park, 433 Charlotte Executive Park Drive, Suite 203.

"This is it," he said, psyching himself up to get out of the vehicle and walk into the building's entryway. He talked to himself to slow his racing heart. *Calm down, Emmitt. Charity can't be everywhere. Charlotte is big enough to keep you from running into each other. This is what you want, right? The laws say the case has to be initiated in the city where the child resides. So just run in to see this attorney and go on back to Greensboro. A journey of a thousand miles begins with a single step. Go on in. Everything will be fine.*

"Good morning. I'm Emmitt Phillips," he said to the young woman sitting behind the desk in the enclosed area. "I have an eleven forty-five appointment with Mr. Blalock."

"Good morning, Mr. Phillips. Here's your paperwork," the receptionist said, handing him a clipboard with forms on it and an attached pen. "Please complete these and bring them to me when you're done. Mr. Blalock will see you then."

Emmitt was surprised at how calm he felt sitting there. He believed he was doing the right thing. He began to fill in the form for new clients. As the reason for the visit, he wrote, *I want my son.* Emmitt completed his paperwork and attached his pre-paid legal card to the clipboard as instructed. He returned the clipboard and completed form to the receptionist. It was only when he sat down that his heart resumed its racing.

He flipped through one magazine after another, not really interested in reading their contents or even attending to their photos. He just needed something to do with his hands, or to pass the time away, or something to quell his fears.

"Mr. Phillips," an older black gentleman called.

Emmitt walked over to him and shook his outstretched hand.

"I'm Attorney David Blalock, come on in," he smiled.

Emmitt followed him around the posh office suite. With all of the framed newspaper articles hanging on the walls regarding Mr. Blalock and his partners, Emmitt figured that they must be pretty good attorneys. He was glad that he chose him.

"Have a seat, Mr. Phillips," the attorney said, motioning for him to sit in one of the three chairs around a small table in the middle of his office. "I understand that you would like to counter-sue your ex-spouse for child custody?"

Emmitt twisted his eyebrows. "Counter-sue?"

"Yes, you want to reopen the child custody case that was awarded to your ex-wife and have it turned over in your favor. Right?"

"I guess. Can—"

"Before we go any further, I need you to be sure about what you want to do. This may not be an easy case to win."

"I just came here to find out if it is possible for me to get custody of my son."

"Anything's possible in the court of law, Mr. Phillips. Especially when you are sure about what you want."

"I am sure that I want my son."

"Why are you just now pursuing custody after three years?"

"Two years," he corrected.

The attorney looked at the dates on the paper. "You do realize that tomorrow is the first day of February?"

Emmitt looked like he was figuring out a math problem in his head. "It'll be three years next week. Is that good or bad?"

"Neither really. Let's talk about your ex-wife."

Emmitt looked away but nodded.

"Is she on drugs or an alcoholic?"

"No."

"Does she have a mental illness?"

"I think so," Emmitt couldn't help but laugh.

"What do you mean?"

"Oh nothing. Charity is a therapist. She counsels people with mental problems. I just think she's crazy."

"Do you have anything we might be able to use in court?"

"No," he frowned slightly. "Charity's not a bad person. I just want my son."

"Well, that kind of attitude is not going to get him back. Are you in favor of her keeping him?"

"No, but I don't have a good reason why she shouldn't, except that I want him."

"Why did you two separate?"

Emmitt looked down. "She claimed I was abusive."

"Were you?"

"I don't think so, but she won the case based on those grounds."

"Did you hit her?"

Emmitt hesitated. "I pushed her once. And the week before she left, she said I choked her."

"She *said* you choked her?"

"Yeah. I really don't remember. Things had gotten so bad between us, I could have just snapped."

"And how will we convince the courts that you won't 'just

snap' on your son? What is he, six years old?" the attorney asked, shuffling through the papers again.

Emmitt felt hot all over. "I would never hurt my son. I love him."

"And you didn't love your ex-wife?"

Emmitt shifted his weight in his seat. He contemplated walking out. He came looking for defense, not prosecution.

"Look, Mr. Phillips. You are not on trial here. But if you want your son back, you will be. And you can't give up or give away easily. Now, it seems like your ex-wife is squeaky clean—no drugs, no alcohol, no founded mental illness. She's a therapist—"

"A minister, has her own business, yada yada yada," Emmitt chimed sarcastically. "So, I should just give up?"

"I didn't say that. Times have changed. The courts are becoming more favorable toward fathers these days. If a father has, or in your shoes can get, a good case, we'll have a good chance to overturn the original case. Do you share custody currently?"

"No, she was awarded full custody, and my mother was awarded visitation."

"Run that by me again?"

"When the judge offered us joint custody, I refused. I wanted full custody or no custody. My mother was there and she asked the judge for at least visitation."

The attorney laughed out loud. "Lord, where was your attorney?"

"I didn't have one. I represented myself."

He laughed even louder. "You mean to tell me, you went to court on your own behalf on a child custody case? How old were you when all of this happened?"

He counted on his fingers. "Thirty."

"You know what they say, don't you?"

Emmitt was already angry, so he did not answer the attorney.

"They say the fool who represents himself has a fool for an attorney." He laughed harder, then apologized. "I just had to say that. I'm sorry. One thing is evident," he said, trying to pull himself together. "And that is that you love your son. Anyone who shows up without an attorney but still determined to fight for his cause is to be commended. We'll talk about that later. Tell me what you have to offer that your ex-wife cannot."

"Being a good father. A son needs his father—"

"But he also needs a mother, how will you withstand that?"

"I live with my mother—"

"Problem number one, I can tell you now, if you want to fight for your son, you are going to have to get your own residence. Does your ex-wife have her own place?"

"Yes."

"You are going to have to show how much you have changed over the past three years. You're going to have to show something for the lapsed time. And it wouldn't hurt to have something against your ex-wife to weaken her credibility."

Emmitt considered walking out again. Fighting against Charity was undesirable but doable. Fighting with his mother about moving out of her place was another thing.

"Can you do it?" the attorney asked.

"Do you mind if I call you by the end of the week?"

"Mr. Phillips, you've already waited two—tomorrow three—years too long. What is the hesitation?"

"I'm not sure if I'm ready for all of this."

"So, you're not sure you're ready to be a full-time father?"

Emmitt looked up at the ceiling. He exhaled as heavily and quickly as he inhaled. "All I know," he said, sitting upright in the chair, "is that my father was never there for me. He was only a check in the mail. I want more than that for my son. I want to be a father, a daddy. I don't want my son to be where I am. I'm thirty-two years old and I feel obligated to stay with my mom. I don't want my son to have to fulfill my role in my absence, like I'm doing for my dad with my mom. Yes, I'll do what's necessary to get my boy."

"Well, you've got yourself an attorney," Attorney Blalock held out his right hand for Emmitt to shake. He explained the proceedings. It was too much information for Emmitt to understand or retain. All he could think about was how he would break the news to his mother. He felt sick to his stomach.

"I know you didn't call me to eat lunch with you and that's all you're going to eat?" April asked, watching her best friend pick over a plate of rice pilaf, macaroni and cheese, and a roll. "What, you on a carbohydrate diet or something?"

Charity tried to perk up. Meeting with Jeffrey Wright drained her energy. "I really haven't had much of an appetite since yesterday, but I know I need to eat something. This is all I could find that I might want to eat."

April waved her hand over her food as if she were performing a magic trick and smacked her lips every time she paused. "Well, I'mma enjoy my buffalo wings . . . my baked potato smothered in melted cheddar cheese, bacon bits, and sour cream . . . and my tossed salad with creamy blue cheese dressing."

"You just be careful driving back to work. I'd hate for you to fall asleep on the road. You know how you do after you eat."

"I know that's right," April agreed. "So, what happened yesterday that you can't eat?"

Charity chewed longer than needed, pretending like her mouth was full. She had been doing well until she met with Mr. Wright and then she had to meet April for lunch. She hadn't had another opportunity to pray or meditate on Scripture. "I was actually doing pretty good until I met with my last client. He reminded me so much of Emmitt that it sent me into a tailspin. I haven't had time to process it all yet."

"Well, I'mma do you like you do your clients. Give me the version that we can resolve in an hour."

Charity looked at her watch and forced a smile. "Now I know how my clients must feel." Her smile faded just as quickly as it appeared. "I realized this morning that I'm going to have to let my hopes of reconciling with Emmitt go."

"I know you know what that is?"

Charity rolled her eyes. Usually she and April agreed on everything, especially spiritual matters. But she knew what she experienced earlier. "I know it's called spiritual warfare."

"You got it! That ain't nothing but an attack of the enemy—"

"I know that, but right now I just want to talk about what's going on in the natural. Sometimes you have to deal with reality."

"But your situations always work out, don't they?"

"Yes, until the next thing comes along."

"The Bible says you will always have—"

Charity held up her hand. "April, please. I don't want to talk Bible right now. I just want to be straight up." April threw her hands up and sat back in the chair. "For instance," Charity continued. "Let's look at my relationship with Emmitt. We have been divorced for two years. And for those two years, I have prayed and believed God and done everything in between believing that my marriage would be restored. And Emmitt is still the same. Every time he pulls one of his little stunts, I stick my head in the heavenlies and say that the enemy is trying to steal my marriage again, he's trying to get me to give up. So, I pray harder. I'm just not sure I want to keep doing that."

"Sounds like an attack to me. But since you're talking about the *natural*, what did Emmitt do?"

Charity pushed her rice around the plate with her fork as she spoke. "When he dropped off Xavier yesterday, he didn't come alone." She looked up at her best friend. "He had a girl waiting in the car for him."

"That don't mean nothing," said April.

Charity could only imagine what kind of expression was on her face.

April continued, "The enemy ain't gonna just *give* you your husband back. You're gonna have to take him. The Bible says the kingdom of God suffereth violence and the violent taketh by force."

Charity made direct eye contact with April. "So when I take him by force, do I take his one-year-old daughter, Destiny, too?"

April's mouth dropped wide open. She grabbed Charity's hands. "Oh, I'm so sorry."

"Me too."

The two sat in silence and just held hands. Finally, April prayed and asked God to strengthen Charity and give her wisdom. She prayed protection over her emotional well-being and upon her spirit. Then she prayed for herself, asking God to give her the right words to say and to be a source of encouragement.

"Amen," they verbalized their agreement to the prayer in unison.

Charity used a napkin to wipe the tears that rested on her cheek. "Thank you for that prayer."

"Please. That's the least I can do."

"It means more than you know. So," Charity changed the subject. "Has Minister Adams made any moves yet?"

"No, nada, nothing. All he does is speak and keep going."

"Have you thought about saying anything to him?"

"A woman is to be found, not to find."

"I know, but the least you can do is unearth yourself," Charity giggled. "Would you like for me to hook you up?"

"No, I'm still recovering from the trauma of your last hookup. Matchmaking is not your forte."

"Well, let me just introduce you two. I want to start letting people know how blessed I am to have you as a friend."

"No, it's the other way around. After church yesterday, I was proud to say that I was your best friend. You had the whole church up worshipping God. The good reverend doctors have never been able to do that."

"And, they are not happy campers right now."

"So?"

"Like I need to ruffle feathers in the church. The glass ceiling for women is thicker in the church than it is in the workplace."

"The way Pastor was talking in that church meeting,

some things are getting ready to change. You better get prayed up because I believe you are going to play a major role in it."

"That's what I'm afraid of."

Iesha was still beaming and replaying everything in her mind that Wallace said and did at lunch. She flitted around the office suite straightening up the magazines in the waiting area, cleaning up the coffee area, and neatly arranging the papers on her desk. She was sure that today was one of the best days of her life. She had met a man who was different from the men she usually attracted. To her that was a sign that she was really changing.

Sha-Lai's and Raquan's fathers both were what she called "roughnecks." They were a challenge to get, hard to keep, and almost impossible to get rid of. Just last week, a man in a pair of jeans with a sag low enough to display the contour of his muscled behind would've had her slobbering at the mouth. But that was until she met Wallace. She didn't know a man could look so sexy in a suit. As far as she was concerned a roughneck could never pronounce her name in the same way a brother in a suit could. Wallace pronounced her name as I-e-sha. It sounded like music compared to the one syllable she was used to hearing. Iesha.

The ring of the telephone reminded her that she was at work.

"Horizons Counseling Center, this is Iesha . . . Yes, I'm Sha-Lai Brown's mother. How can I help you? . . . Sick? Is she all right? . . . Oh, good," she said in relief. She looked up to acknowledge Charity coming in from lunch.

"Another appointment?" Charity mouthed with a look of excitement on her face.

Iesha shook her head and scribbled a note that it was the school's guidance counselor. "Uhm mum . . . Yes ma'am, physical discipline? . . . Yes, I do physically discipline my children but . . ."

Iesha saw Charity's expression. She'd gotten on Iesha many times for putting her hands on Sha-Lai and Raquan. Iesha now wished she had listened.

Iesha looked at her watch. "Yes, ma'am. I can be there at

three . . . I would like for y'all to know that I don't abuse my children. I just made a mistake. Me and my daughter talked about it right after it happened. So, I would appreciate it if you—"

"Hello, ma'am?" Charity took the phone from Iesha, who was crying and raising her voice. "My name is Charity Phillips. I'm Ms. Brown's sister. She is really upset right now, is there any way I can help? . . . Yes, ma'am . . . Okay, I'll have her there at three."

Charity hung up the phone. "Do you want me to get Harmony to take my one o'clock?"

"No," Iesha said blowing her nose. "Harmony's not back from lunch and this is your one o'clock coming in now. I'll be all right. I'mma call and talk to Momma."

"You sure you want to call Momma right now? I can get out of my session if you want to talk."

"You're right, calling Momma's the last thing I need to do. I'mma just go to the bathroom and get myself together."

Charity grabbed her sister's hands, hoping Iesha would receive the same strength Charity had just received from April. "Okay, but don't go anywhere. I'll be free to talk after my session. Do you think talking to Harmony might help?"

Iesha forced a smile. "Girl, don't make me cuss."

Iesha handed the client a clipboard, and Charity went to her office to pray that God would use the situation to draw Iesha closer to Him and not drive her farther away.

CHAPTER 9

CHARITY AND IESHA WERE ON THEIR WAY OUT THE DOOR when Iesha asked if she should let Harmony know they were leaving.

"Is she in session right now?" Charity asked.

"No. I think her next appointment isn't until three o'clock."

"I'm going to warm up the car. Will you run back there and tell her to lock up when she is done? Let her know that you're riding with me and that your car is still out front."

Iesha knocked on Harmony's door. When she did not hear a response, she knocked again. She opened the door to get a piece of paper to leave a note on her chair.

Harmony was sitting Indian-style on a mat on the floor, with her eyes closed. Iesha couldn't decide if she should disturb her. She knew that Charity didn't like to be disturbed while she was praying. Then again, Charity doesn't pray like this.

"Harmony?" When Harmony didn't move, Iesha called her again, but louder. "Harmony?" Iesha walked slowly over to her and put her hand on her shoulder and yelled, "Harmony!"

Harmony jumped and Iesha screamed. "Why you didn't answer me?"

"I didn't hear you. I was meditating."

"I called you three times. Seemed like you were in a freaking trance or something. You scared me."

"I'm sorry," Harmony said, pushing herself up off the mat. "I'm preparing for the workshop I'm giving this evening, 'Change Your Mind, Change Your Life.'"

Iesha shook her head. "Whatever. I'm just glad I didn't walk up on a dead body. Charity sent me in here to tell you that she's leaving with me, so you'll have to lock up. My car's out front, I'll pick it up later."

"Okay. Tell Charity to say a prayer for me for the workshop tonight. I want to help my participants be all they can be."

"What army are you enlisting them into?"

"The Lord's army, of course. We all could use a little help finding joy and happiness in our everyday lives, grasping a hold of our higher selves, and tapping into our potential within."

Iesha shook her head and closed the door. *That woman ain't playing with a full deck of cards.*

Charity and Iesha arrived at the school almost thirty minutes early. The drive had been completely silent except for small talk about the terrible way people in Charlotte drive. As much as Charity loved to talk and as much as she usually had to say as a minister and a therapist, she was at a loss for words. She had never seen Iesha look so somber.

"Do you want to talk?" Charity asked as she parked the car.

Iesha looked in the direction of the school. "I don't know what to say. I just hope they don't take my kids away."

"I bind that up in the name of Jesus. My niece and nephew aren't going anywhere. What exactly did they say to you?"

"Charity, look. On the way home from Momma's I got to thinking about all that was said and done and I just . . ." She paused, trying to think of how she could explain what she meant. "I was just frustrated. Sha-Lai was whining about her head hurting. And I just hauled off and slapped her. The mark the school sees on her face is the print from these two rings." She held up her hand for Charity to see. "Cherry, I don't want to lose my kids."

"Well, let's pray about it."

Iesha started crying again. "I can't pray. I don't feel right going to God just because I need something. I know He's tired of my promising to do better if He'll just get me outta this and get me outta that."

"Iesha, that's a lie from the pit of hell," Charity said, retrieving some tissue out of her glove compartment for Iesha. "You have to trust God in this situation. He loves you and wants you to commit your life to Him. Give your life to Him, Iesha, He's the only one who can help you out of this."

"But if I come, I wanna come correct. I don't want to break any more promises."

"And you don't have to. Remember earlier this morning? You said you were turning over a new leaf. Well, God heard your confession and He wants to help you do it. Without Him you can't." She took Iesha's hands to pray. "If you could've done it by yourself, you would've done it already. Do you mind if I pray with you?"

"Yes, please pray for me. And while we're at it, pray for me to be saved."

Warm tears streamed down Charity's cheeks. She let go of Iesha's hands long enough to raise her hands to God in thanksgiving. She took her pocket Bible out of her purse and turned to Romans 10:9. "Iesha, salvation is a gift from God to us. It's not something we have to earn or pay for. Jesus Christ paid the price for us on the cross more than two thousand years ago. Our salvation is based on Romans 10:9, read what it says here."

Iesha leaned over and read the verse: "That if thou shalt confess with thy mouth the Lord Jesus, and shalt believe in thine heart that God hath raised Him from the dead, thou shalt be saved." She read it again silently. "That's it?"

Charity nodded. "That's it. We confess what we believe and we walk it out. If we believe that Jesus is Lord, we walk like we are under His reign. We live according to the way He does things, we have what He says we can have, we do what He says we can do, and we believe that we are who He says we are. And, we find all these things in His Word." She held up the pocket Bible. "Are you ready to accept Christ as your Lord and personal Savior?"

Iesha took a deep breath. "Yes."

"Good. I want you to repeat after me." As soon as Iesha nodded, Charity saw tears roll down her cheeks. "Lord, I come to you in the name of Jesus . . . Your Word says in Acts 2:21 . . . that whosoever shall call on the name of the Lord . . . shall be saved . . . I'm calling on You . . . I pray and ask Jesus to come into my heart . . . and be Lord over my life according to Romans 10:9 . . . I confess that Jesus is Lord . . . and I believe in my heart that God raised Him from the dead . . . I am now reborn! . . . I am a Christian . . . I am saved."

Charity and Iesha locked themselves in an embrace and comforted each other.

"We better go in," Charity said, patting Iesha on the back. "Are you ready?"

Iesha looked at the clock. "As ready as I can be." She pulled down the mirror on the passenger's visor. "I look rough."

"No, you look like a concerned mother."

They walked toward the elementary school building. Not even the winter chill could speed them up. They followed the signs to the office.

"Good afternoon, ma'am," Charity approached the heavyset white woman at the desk. "I'm Charity Phillips, here with my sister Iesha Brown. We're here for a three o'clock appointment concerning Sha-Lai Brown."

The woman smiled slightly, or slightly frowned. Her expression was difficult to read. "Oh yes. The conference room is right this way," she pushed herself up off the chair to lead them around the corner. She led them into a room where six people were already seated. A short, brown-skinned gentleman with a balding head and a wide smile stood with his hand extended to Charity, as she was the first to walk into the room.

"I'm Mr. Robinson, the principal here at Thomasboro."

Charity accepted his gesture. "I'm Charity Phillips. I'm here with my sister Iesha Brown." She looked over her shoulder at Iesha.

Iesha stepped forward to acknowledge Mr. Robinson but refused his handshake. "Where're my kids?"

"They're next door working on their homework. They—"

Iesha turned toward the door. The people who were seated stood simultaneously like the mob squad. Mr. Robinson held his hand out to stop her. "They are expecting you after this meeting is over."

Iesha dusted his hand off of her. "Well, let's hurry up and get this over with then."

The others sat down. Mr. Robinson pulled out two chairs for them to join the others at the table. "Please have a seat."

Iesha locked her knees. "I don't want to sit down."

Charity whispered in her ear. "You sit. I'll talk."

Iesha looked intently at each person in the room. She sat down with her arms folded across her chest.

"Mr. Robinson," Charity said, breaking the silence. "Will you please explain to us what is going on?"

He cleared his throat. "Yes, but before we get started, I'll go around the table so these folks can introduce themselves?" he said, directing his attention to the five people who were with him.

A middle-aged white woman with a blond Halle Berry haircut spoke up. "I'm Mrs. Sauvain, the school's nurse."

Charity liked the iridescent fuchsia shirt the woman wore who spoke next. "I'm Ms. Tuttle. We spoke earlier." She blinked her eyes a few times and then took her glasses off. She pulled at her eyelashes, like one was stuck in her eye. "I'm the guidance counselor," she said, still messing with her eye.

"Hello, Ms. Brown." Charity smiled. It was good to see a black woman at the table, she knew she'd be on their side. "I'm Sha-Lai's teacher, Mrs. Davis."

"I'm Mr. Mance . . . Raquan's teacher," offered a white man with a few gray strands moussed over to one side of his balding head.

Charity and Iesha looked at each other with the same question on their faces. Charity's facial expression told Iesha that she did not know why he was there either.

"Ms. Brown," the woman in the last seat called. "I'm Dawn Styre. I'm a social worker from the Mecklenburg County Department of Social Services."

"Lord, have mercy," Charity whispered, and shook her head.

Iesha frowned and leaned forward in the chair. "DSS? How y'all gone call DSS on me?" she asked as she slammed her fist against the table. "I have not abused my children."

"Iesha, please." Charity turned to whisper to her sister. "Don't give them what they're looking for. Calm down." She turned to the principal, "Mr. Robinson, we can understand a conference being called to address the situation, but why has DSS been involved?"

"In the state of North Carolina, the law obligates any citizen to report to DSS any case in which they suspect a child is being abused. Mrs. Davis noticed a mark on Sha-Lai's face this morning, and when she asked her about it, Sha-Lai told her that she had been fighting with her younger brother. In less than an hour, Sha-Lai complained that her head was hurting and was sent to see Mrs. Sauvain, the nurse. Mrs. Sauvain inquired about the mark as well. Sha-Lai told her that you 'messed around and slapped her on accident.' When the nurse talked with Sha-Lai's teacher, they realized they'd gotten two different stories. That's when Ms. Tuttle, the guidance counselor, was called. And then DSS was called."

"Okay but—" Iesha started.

"That's understandable," Charity said, cutting off Iesha. She thought it would be best if Iesha remained quiet. "But why is Raquan's teacher here?"

Iesha nodded to let Charity know that she was going to ask the same question.

The social worker answered. "Once a report is made, we begin an investigation. That just means we gather as much information as we can. We start with the school and then the parents. In cases where there is more than one child in the home, our investigation includes them as well."

The guidance counselor added, "To aid the investigation, the school provides information that in many cases helps the parents. We submit attendance records, the child's grades, parent-teacher conference reports, anything we can find with hopes that it will paint a favorable picture for the family."

Charity could tell that Iesha did not trust the guidance counselor. "So, have you already started getting information or is that what we're here for?"

"Yes, to both of those questions," the guidance counselor answered.

Iesha snapped, "Well, did what you turn over to DSS paint a *favorable picture?*"

The social worker intervened. "Ms. Brown, I can understand your frustration right now. Let me assure you that the Department of Social Services is not interested in taking away your children. Our goal is to thoroughly investigate reported cases of abuse to make sure that the children are safe. In a very large percentage of cases reported to us, abuse is not substantiated and the cases are closed just as quickly as they were opened. But I need you to cooperate with me if you want your case to be one of them."

Iesha relaxed her shoulders a little bit.

The social worker continued. "Your case is mildly difficult. According to the school's report, this is what we have in your favor—Sha-Lai is a straight-A student, her progress reports are all good, except that she is an excessive talker," the social worker smiled.

Iesha returned her smile and relaxed a little more. Charity reached for and squeezed her hand.

"She has perfect attendance since kindergarten, and you don't have a prior record with DSS. Your son's grades are just as good in spite of poor attendance. And it is noted that he has severe asthma and requires significant medical attention. But," she said firmly to prepare Iesha for what she would say next. "We have a child here with a bruise above the shoulder. Ms. Brown, in North Carolina, the law considers bruises on the lower part of the body, below the waist," she demonstrated, "as less significant, depending on the type of bruises. If the bruises are higher, say for instance the chest area, these are more significant. And bruises above the shoulder are considered most significant and could result in immediate removal of the child or children."

Iesha squeezed Charity's hand. Charity was already praying.

Calmer than she was fifteen minutes ago, Iesha felt more comfortable talking for herself. "So, do you still need information from me?"

"Yes. Tell us what happened between you and your daughter. As you're talking, I will be taking notes. This will enable me to draw up a report for the courts." Iesha stiffened. "Ms. Brown, it's not the type of court you're thinking. In five days you will have a case review hearing. It's a small, informal, and quick process. Meanwhile, you must look over this safety plan," she said, digging in her burgundy leather briefcase to retrieve a piece of paper. "Hopefully, you will agree to sign it. It's an agreement that you will not physically discipline your children."

"Yes, I will sign it," Iesha said eagerly.

"Read it carefully, Ms. Brown, because if you are found in violation of any of its stipulations, your children will be placed in the county's care. Let's just have you tell us what happened first and then we'll go over the form, okay?"

Iesha inhaled to compose herself. She let go of Charity's hands so that she could use hers to talk.

"We were driving home from my mother's after dinner last night," she spoke only to the social worker. "It was already past the kids' bedtime. Sha-Lai was complaining of a headache, but I thought she was just sleepy and whiny. She always complains that something hurts when she's sleepy, just so she won't have to go to bed. So, I told her to lay down until I could give her some medicine when we got home. My son was asleep in the back and I told her to be quiet so she wouldn't wake him up. But she kept leaning up toward the front of the van, whining. I did yell at her and told her that if she didn't lay back and put her seat belt back on, I was going to whoop her." She wiped her face with both of her hands like she was washing her face without a facecloth. "And she did for a little while," she continued. "My family and I had a heated discussion over dinner and I was playing it over and over in my mind, and Sha-Lai kept calling my name and whining. Before I knew it, I reached in the backseat and hit the only part of her body I could reach with my right hand, while my left hand was on the steering wheel. I slapped her on the face." She shrugged her shoulders when she could not think of anything else to say.

The nurse broke the silence by tapping her fingernails against the table to get Iesha's attention. "And then what did you do?" The others shifted in their seats restlessly as if they'd heard enough. "Sha-Lai told me," the nurse added warmly. "And I think the others should know."

Charity looked at Iesha for explanation.

Iesha continued to wipe the tears as they fell from her eyes. Then she spoke. "As soon as I realized what I'd done, I pulled over to the side of the road. I got out of the car and crawled into the backseat with them. Raquan was still sleeping. I pulled Sha-Lai in my arms and I apologized to her. I explained what I was going through and told her that I didn't mean to do what I did. I told her that I'll never slap her in her face again. I held my child for as long as it took for her to know I meant what I said. We were there so long that she fell asleep. I cried all the way home. I honestly did not mean to slap her, and definitely not hard enough for my rings to leave a print on her face."

"Thank you, Ms. Brown," the social worker said. "I think I have everything I need for my report. Did you get a chance to read that safety plan?"

Iesha took a few minutes to read the triplicate copy plan that indicated that her signature was her consent to a home inspection, no physical discipline policy, and an appearance in youth and family court. Iesha asked Charity for a pen to sign the form.

"Do you have any questions, Ms. Brown?" the social worker asked.

"I understand the form. But will I be able to walk out of here with my kids?"

"If you sign the form, yes. If you refuse, no."

Charity handed Iesha the pen and she signed the document.

"Your hearing will be on February 10, in Family Court, courtroom 103. If you have any questions, or problems, call me at this number." She circled her phone number on a business card. "This copy is for you." She handed Iesha a yellow copy of the safety plan. "Is Thursday a good day to do the home inspection?"

Iesha looked at Charity for approval for the time off. Charity nodded.

"Yes, ma'am. Thursday will be fine. Any particular time?"

"I will call you on Wednesday. I have your work and home number." The social worker stood up. She extended her hand for Iesha to shake. "Thank you for your cooperation. I'll see you on Thursday."

Iesha accepted her handshake. The social worker shook Charity's hand.

The principal and the others rose from their seats. "Ms. Brown," the principal called, "if you follow me I'll take you to your children."

Charity and Iesha said good-bye to the others. Iesha thanked the nurse before she was escorted out of the room. Sha-Lai was helping Raquan with his homework when the principal opened the door to the after-school room where they were.

"Momma," Sha-Lai and Raquan sang, running over to Iesha. Being mindless of the people who were watching, she knelt down, held them both, and cried. "Thank You, Jesus," she whispered with her head buried in their embrace.

CHAPTER 10

CHARITY PLOPPED DOWN on the Italian leather love seat in her family room. She had already put Xavier to bed. She flipped through the television channels with the remote control in one hand and a bowl of mint chocolate chip ice cream in the other. "This has been the longest day of my life," she mumbled. "Definitely been a manic Monday." She let the television rest on TBN and watched the remainder of Joyce Meyer's *Life in the Word* broadcast. As she listened to the message on getting control of your emotions, she sorted through her mail. She pulled a small wastebasket to the couch. "Don't need you," she said, discarding a credit card offer. She threw another packet in the trash. "Don't need a home equity line of credit, and my last name is no longer Brown." She opened and read the next few pieces of mail. "Oh shoot." She ripped open the last envelope. "I forgot about the banquet." She read the information on the complimentary pair of tickets. "This weekend? I totally forgot."

She looked at the clock on her VCR and hoped it was not too late for her to call Pastor King at home. She needed an escort for the banquet and knew he would have a recommendation on whom she should ask.

"Hello, Sister King. This is Charity, how are you?"

"Fine, Minister Phillips. How are you?"

"I'm good. I hope it's not too late to be calling, but I wanted to ask Pastor for some fatherly advice. I need his recommendation for an escort to a banquet."

Mrs. King laughed. "And you gone trust Pastor?"

Charity joked. "I know, right?"

"That's sweet of you. I'm sure he'll be honored. Hold on a minute."

Charity listened closely to see what Mrs. King would tell her husband about the caller waiting for him on the line.

"Hello, you've reached the Love Connector," Pastor King joked.

"Lord, I got a feeling I'll never be able to live this one down."

He chuckled. "I hear you need a date for a banquet?"

"No, I need an escort," she clarified. "I sit on the board of directors for Grace House, and their annual black-tie formal is Friday. Who would you recommend that I ask to escort me?"

"Do you want a wolf in sheep's clothing, or a sheep in a wolf's outfit?"

"Pastor." She cast a look she'd never give him in person.

"Okay, okay. I have three people I'd recommend, knowing I won't have to worry about you while you're with them. I'll go a step further and say that I recommend them in this order. So if the first one can't go, then call the second one."

"Okay."

"My first choice is Minister Adams." Charity rolled her eyes to the ceiling; she should've known he was going to recommend him. She'd be glad when April would make it known that she liked the man. "If he can't make it, call Brother Stratford. And my last choice is Brother Ingram. Now, if he can't make it, I suggest you don't go," he laughed.

"Thank you, Pastor. That helps a lot."

"Do you know how to reach them?"

"Yes, Love Connector. I know how to reach Minister Adams. He may know how to reach the other two."

"All right. I'm just trying to help you out. If you want any beauty secrets, I'll have to put my wife back on the phone for that."

"That's okay. You know Sister April will help me with that."

"She sure will. You know what I call her, don't you?"

"Oh Lord, what Pastor?"

"I call her a first lady. She carries herself like she's the President's wife."

"She does, doesn't she? Thanks, Pastor. Tell Sister King I'll talk to her later."

"You're welcome. Let me know who's going with you so I can call and make sure they're in line."

"Pastor, I think it's past your bedtime."

"Good night, Minister Phillips."

Charity would not trade her pastor for the world. She looked in her minister's handbook to get Minister Adams's phone number. He was not home, so she left a message for him. "Hi, Minister Adams. This is Charity. I'm calling because I need a favor," she said in a childlike voice. "I called Pastor for his help and he recommended that I call you. I have a black-tie affair to go to on this Friday night—way short notice, I know. But I need an escort. Will you check your schedule and see if you'll be able to go with me? I already have the tickets. Don't worry about a tux, a nice suit will do. Oh, the banquet starts at seven, and it's at the uptown Adam's Mark Hotel. Call me when you get this message. Thanks."

Her stomach turned flips as soon as she hung up the phone. She hoped Minister Adams wouldn't get the wrong idea. *I did tell him that Pastor King recommended him, right?* Then nervousness set in. What in the world were they going to talk about? Then she decided that she'd had enough of this. She dialed April's phone number.

"Hey, Toot, what are you doing?"

"Ironing my clothes for tomorrow. What about you?"

"Eating ice cream and watching your woman of God."

"You know I'm on it. She's talking directly to me."

"I called to let you know that I called your pastor to ask him who I should ask to escort me to Grace House's banquet on Friday. He gave me three names. Guess who they are?"

"If they go to Damascus, you ain't got but three choices," she joked.

"Guess."

"Who?"

"Your husband, Brother Stratford, and Brother Ingram."

"Who are you going to ask?"

"Well, he suggested I ask them in that order."

"Oooooh, I hope you go with Michael so you can put in a good word for me."

"Oh, now you want my help?"

"Might as well."

"Since when did you start calling him Michael? Ya'll on first-name basis now?"

"No, but we will be after you talk to him on Friday night."

"You're silly. I was actually hoping you would talk to him before then. Like at Bible study."

"Yeah, right."

"Girl, this has gone on for long enough. He'd be married by the time you got up the nerve to tell him. Don't you think it's time you said something to the boy? It has been a year and some change."

"That's why you've got to do it for me. I'm scared. What if he doesn't like me?"

"This is not the April I know. But who else could bring out the weakness in a woman, but a man. Go on and finish ironing your clothes. I'll talk to you later."

Iesha adjusted her shower spout to receive a massage from the downpour of steamy water. She closed her eyes and turned backward. She tilted her head back into the water and allowed herself to be cleansed from head to toe. She shampooed her hair and lathered her body with Caress soap. As she rinsed herself with the hotter-than-tepid water, visions of the day's activities flooded her mind. She felt herself shake inside. When she could no longer contain her emotions, she gave herself permission to cry, and her whole body quaked. She fell to her knees and thanked God for giving her a second chance to raise her children right.

After she dressed in her pajamas, she found in a junk drawer the only Bible she had in the house. It was one of those pocket New Testament Bibles that included the books of Psalms and Proverbs. She opened it to the Psalm she halfway remembered from her childhood Sunday school classes—Psalm 23. She felt stupid when she did not understand the first verse. She called Charity for clarification.

"Hey, Sis, you sleep?"

"Almost. Is everything all right?"

"Yeah, I just have a question."

"Yes?"

"I'm reading Psalm 23 and I'm trying to figure out why it's saying that the Lord is my shepherd and I shall not want Him."

Charity could not help but snicker. "I'm not laughing at you, I'm laughing with you. When I first started reading the Bible, I thought the same thing."

"So, it doesn't mean that?"

"No, it's saying that because the Lord is our Shepherd, our Guide, and our Provider, we will not want or need anything."

"Oh, I get it."

"Do you mind if I get my Bible and we go over it together?"

"No, I would like that."

Iesha was so proud of herself when she got off the phone with Charity. She felt good about her new life. She knew she needed to call her mother but decided that she did not want anything or anyone to ruin what she was feeling. She said the Lord's Prayer before retiring to bed, then slept like a baby.

CHAPTER 11

JUST WHEN HE WAS ABOUT TO BE OVERWHELMED with loneliness, Joseph received a blessing. While the godsend was not a wife, he felt it put him one step closer to her. There was no other way to explain it. His magazine subscription lapsed more than two months ago. When he didn't receive an issue last month, he was not expecting the one that came today. Out of all the issues that could have come, he received the February one, whose cover touted the headline for an article on Valentine's Day for singles. Just what he needed—some encouragement. He read *Today's Gospel* magazine expectantly. Midway through the publication, the title "I Have No Man," caught his eye. As he read the testimony of a single woman from Charlotte, North Carolina, his heart beat so fast he thought it would leap out at her on the page.

He was so stirred by the story that he ran to his best friend's room to tell him about it.

"Man, you've gotta read this," he said, shoving the magazine in Allen's hands.

"Okay, Brother Word. What message from God have you found this week?"

He overlooked Allen's suspiciousness. "No, man, this is different." He pointed to the photograph on the page. "I think I just found my wife."

Allen shook his head. "Okay. I know you are a man of faith and I know that you *do* hear from God. But, come on, don't you think this is a little extreme?"

"I know this sounds crazy. But I know what I felt when I read her article."

"And what do we know about feelings?"

Like a child being chastised Joseph parakeeted, "That they come a dime a dozen."

"That's right, we are not moved by our feelings; by what something feels like. We move by a knowing, which God gives us through His Holy Spirit."

"I know that you're right, but—"

"Joseph, you soak up everything. You're a sponge for the things of God. When you hear a preacher preach something, you hold on to it fervently. Whereas the rest of us hear something and we forget about it after a couple of days. But you continue to watch the words you speak, you make your confessions daily, you sow seeds all the time . . . and you're the one who gets results. You're the one who signs and wonders follow. But *you* have to find balance because you're walking a fine line between sanity and insanity. And thinking that you've found your wife between the pages of a magazine would be—"

"Insane." He took the magazine from Allen and held it up as if he were going to read it to him. "I know, man, but just hear me out. This minister from Charlotte wrote this article called, 'I Have No Man.' It's like her testimony of being single and struggling to be content. In it she likens herself to the paralyzed man in John 5 who'd been lying at the pool of Bethesda, the one Jesus asked if he wanted to get well."

Allen shifted his weight impatiently. "And? She'd be your wife because?"

"I'm getting to that. The paralytic didn't answer Jesus, but he told Him that he couldn't get well because he had *no man* to help him into the pool when the angels would stir it. And that's how she got her title, 'I Have No Man.' Isn't that clever?"

Joseph saw the look on Allen's face that seemed to ask, *And?* So he continued talking. "She was saying that she gets lonely and sick of being single sometimes when she dwells on the fact that she doesn't have a man to come home to, or to spend time with, or to help her care for her son. But—"

"Wait a minute, your *wife* has a child? You're willing to marry a woman who has a child that ain't yours?"

"Just as Joseph did for Mary, and raised Jesus."

"Whatever. Just tell me what *thus sayeth the Lord*," Allen mocked.

"God hasn't said anything. I just feel—believe, that she's the manifestation of my prayers. She's everything I prayed for in a wife. I asked God specifically for someone who has been through something; she's divorced. I asked God for Juanita Bynum, but seeing that she's married now, I'll settle for a woman in the ministry. Now, tell me this ain't God."

"I know better than to challenge you when you're bent on a revelation."

"I'm just attracted to the anointing on her. The way she writes, how she interpreted the Scripture, and she didn't mind exposing herself and telling her testimony. And to top it off, the woman is beautiful. My heart thumped the whole time I read her message."

"So, you think she's your wife because your heart thumped?"

"Never mind, man. You don't understand."

"You're right, I don't understand what you're saying. But I do understand what it feels like to be out here with no family and no one to love. I do understand the desperation to do anything to get rid of loneliness and the aching for someone to call, to write, or to have them visit. I understand that. I just don't want you to believe something stupid and make it worse on yourself. That's all."

"I am going to write to her. I just want her to know that her missive blessed me."

"Write her?" Allen took the magazine. "What kind of magazine is that where you can write to people?"

"It's *Today's Gospel*. And her address isn't in here." He snatched the magazine back. "It says here that she's a minister at Damascus Road Baptist Church in Charlotte. I'm going to send a card for her there." He continued as if he could read the perplexed expression on Allen's face. "What makes it all more ironic is that my baby sister lives in Charlotte. I'mma ask her to look the address up for me."

"I should've known you already had a plan."

"Can't you see God's hand in all this?"

"You're a better man than I am, that's all I can say. So while you're doing all of this are you going to tell her that you're at least six hours away? I mean if she as lonely as it sounds, don't you think she'll be disappointed to know where you are?"

Joseph dropped his head. "Okay, how about I do this? How about I bring the situation to intercessory prayer team tonight and see if something comes from there before I proceed?"

"I think that's the smartest thing you've said since you've been here."

Joseph turned to leave the room.

"Wait," Allen stopped him. "I still wanna read that article. I want to witness this anointing for myself."

Joseph tossed the magazine to his friend. "See ya in about thirty minutes."

At 7:30 p.m., Joseph answered the knock on his door and let the nine members of the intercessory prayer team into his room. The men were always on time, starting and ending promptly. For those of them who had wives or girlfriends back home, 8:00 p.m. was the best time to call and if they were going to get a good place in the phone line they needed to be there at 8:00 on the dot. The lines for the phones could be ridiculously crowded.

Brother Hankins delegated devotional tasks to two of the

intercessors. As the men joined hands, Hankins asked for prayer requests and concerns.

"I have a prayer need," Joseph said. "I would like to ask God for wisdom about how to handle a situation. Please pray for God's wisdom and His will concerning me and a minister friend of mine named Charity Phillips from Charlotte, North Carolina." He closed his eyes and waited to hear the next prayer request.

Joseph listened as a few others submitted concerns and needs. Brother Hankins asked if there was anything else to consider for prayer. No one said anything. Joseph opened his eyes to observe the group. Every head was bowed and every eye closed. Most of the brothers were still holding hands. Some were swaying from side to side, some were waiting, and some were already praying quietly. One of Joseph's friends, Brother Hunting, was praying in the Spirit.

"Brother Hunting," Brother Hankins called to him. "Will you pray for us tonight?"

Brother Hunting could still be heard praying in tongues, but he acknowledged the request by nodding. "Thank you, Jesus," he said, beginning his prayer. "Heavenly Father, we thank and praise You for being so awesome and wise. Thank You for Your righteousness, provision, and loving kindness. Thank You for allowing us to come to You tonight by Your grace and mercy. We have requests to lift up to You tonight, Father. We promise to trust You with the outcome of them, Lord. You are faithful and just and Your ways are perfect. I come to You on behalf of my brother, Lord. Thank You for preserving a wife for him in Charlotte, North Carolina . . ."

Joseph's eyes popped open. *Did he say what I think he just said?* He looked over at Allen to see if he had heard him too. Allen was looking at him with the same expression. Joseph took it as confirmation, smiled, and bowed his head to focus on the rest of the prayer.

Chapter 12

It was Tuesday morning and the Word of God wasn't the only thing that quickened Charity's spirit. A 5:30 telephone call from Emmitt had been just as jolting. She was studying her daily devotional Scriptures when the ringing phone startled her.

"Hello?" she answered expecting an emergency.

"Good morning, Charity. It's me, Emmitt."

"Is everything all right?"

"Yeah, I just wanted to catch you before you started your day."

"For?" She was annoyed when his voice did not sound as urgent as a phone call at this time of morning should.

He paused. "I was calling to ask you for your work address . . . I would like to send you something."

"Did Xavier leave something?"

"No, this is something for you."

"For me?" Her response was between blushing and disbelief.

"Uhm hum. Where do I send it to?"

Before she could answer she had a flashback of anger about Shawanda and their daughter Destiny. "Look Emmitt, I don't have time for any games. I'm not interested in receiving a wedding invitation. Nor am I interested in a family photo of you and your new family."

He chuckled. "Girl, you're crazy. Didn't I tell you I wasn't ever getting married again?"

"Oh, don't act like I ruined it for you."

The tone of his voice changed. "Sweetie, I didn't call you to fight. I called to see if I could get your work address. Are you going to give it to me?"

There were certain things about him she couldn't resist, little things that made her want him. Like the tone of voice he was using; it was a decibel above a bedroom whisper. She squeezed her legs together so that she would think only with her head. A big part of her still loved him and would do anything to have her marriage restored. What she wouldn't give to have her son's father in the home with him. She softened, "Emmitt, I'm afraid to trust you. Every time I do, I get hurt. Which means my trust is in the wrong place anyway. So, I'm going to trust God on this one."

"That's the way it should be anyway."

At least they agreed on that one thing. And to Charity that was evidence that God was performing His Word concerning their reconciliation.

"What is it that you're sending?"

"It wouldn't be a surprise if I told you. Now would it?"

She praised God silently. "Is it good or bad?" she asked with a chuckle.

"I'll let you be the judge of that."

"I can't wait to see this. Are you ready for the address?"

"Uhm hum."

"It's a long address, so I'll give it to you slow. On the first line put Charlotte Executive Park . . . Present Day Office Building." It sounded like he gasped for air. "Emmitt, are you there?"

"Yeah, uhm. I just got the hiccups." He made another noise but it was different from the one she heard at first.

"Oh. Did you get the first part?"

"Yeah, go ahead."

"On the second line put Horizons, Suite 505 . . . care of Charity Phillips . . . and lastly the zip code is 28269."

"When should I expect the surprise?"

"What's today? . . . Tuesday? . . . You should have it by Monday."

"I'll tell Iesha to look out for it."

"Iesha?"

"Yes, she's my admin—my secretary," she said, remembering that Emmitt used to accuse her of relaying bigger words to intimidate him.

"All right then. I know you gotta get ready to get Lil' Man up and get ready for work, so I'm going to let you go."

The throbbing between her legs started again. "Emmitt, when are we going to talk?"

"Soon. You go on and do what you have to do. Don't be late on my account. Wrap up; the Weather Channel says that Charlotte's morning low is twenty-eight degrees out there. Don't forget to lock up and drive carefully."

She crossed her legs and pressed them together, hard. It felt good to know he still cared. "Thank you."

He sounded like he was smiling. "No, thank you."

She wanted to end the conversation with a confession of her love for him, but Emmitt hung up before she could. It seemed abrupt but the way he thanked her did sound like he was saying good-bye.

She looked at the clock and noticed she was running behind, but this was worth it. She knelt and thanked God for answering her prayers concerning her husband. "And whatever You send through him, Lord," she confessed. "Be it flowers, a check, or a ring. I receive it in Jesus' name."

By the way Iesha set up the conference room, it looked like a second open house was about to take place. She wanted their first staff meeting to be memorable. On a purple linen cloth that she had centered on the executive meeting table, she placed three goblets she had brought from home, a pillar candle, cheddar cheese, crackers, a fresh fruit tray, and a bottle of sparkling white grape juice. She lit the candle and turned on the flash for the disposable camera.

"Charity's going to be so surprised," she announced, clapping her hands.

"It's not good to be seen talking to yourself, young lady."

It was one thing that Harmony's voice annoyed her, and another that it took her forever to say whatever she had to say. Iesha pivoted on one foot to face her. "You've got some nerve to be talking, Ms.-tap-into-the-potential-within."

Harmony walked past her to put her belongings on the table. "Oh, darling. The power of quiet time can be profoundly healing. It's like showing up for an appointment with God."

Iesha looked her up and down. Harmony was dressed in a lavender tie-dyed frock with black tights and brown moccasin-looking shoes. "I'm sorry I gave you the impression that I have time to talk to you. But this conversation will take more time than I have to give. So, if you'll excuse me, I'll go get the rest of what we'll need for this meeting."

By the time Iesha reached her desk to retrieve the agendas she had typed, she found herself praying. "I'm sorry, God. You're going to have to help me with that woman. I just can't do her. But . . . that doesn't give me a right to be nasty. Forgive me." She untaped the paper from her computer that held a list of scriptural verses, which Charity had made for her. She read from the paper. "I am a new creature in Christ. Old things have passed away. I am redeemed from the law of sin and death. In all these things I am more than a conqueror. Amen."

Harmony was reading the newspaper when Iesha returned. Iesha sat across from her. "Hey, Harmony." Harmony lowered the paper. "I just wanted to say I'm sorry for the attitude I just gave you."

"That's okay, young lady." Iesha cringed at the sound of her voice. "I know it's hard when you have a lot on you."

Iesha raised her eyebrow. "What makes you think I have a lot on me?"

"I'm a therapist, remember?"

"Oh." Iesha felt relieved for a sensible answer.

"I guess it's a gift. Charity has it too. Seems like she can see right through me."

"Is that so?"

Iesha figured she didn't have anything to lose and decided to open up to Harmony. "Yeah. I'll never forget the time we went to this Chinese shack on the west side for lunch. These two dudes walked in and stood behind us while we were looking at the menu boards. I turned around to tell them they could order their food because we couldn't make up our minds. Charity turned around to let them know she agreed. Before they could even move forward, she nudged me and told me we needed to get out of there. I thought she was just paranoid because we were on my side of town. But as soon as we got into the car, we heard yelling, screaming, and a couple of gunshots. I drove like crazy while she called the police on her cell phone. Ever since then, she's only got to tell me something once, and it's done . . . She calls it listening to the Holy Spirit."

"Now that's what I'm talking about, tapping into the power within. All of us possess that ability."

Iesha shrugged her shoulders. "I guess."

"You guess? There's a piece of God within us all. I've been reading this great book, *A Course in Miracles*. I'm going to have to let you borrow it because it'll help you along your spiritual journey. I've learned that man is God and God is man, and that we have so much potential within ourselves. The only thing that stands between us and God is ignorance of who we really are."

Iesha shook her head as if she were trying to shake water out of her ears. "Let's change the subject, because you're making my head swim."

Harmony's face disappeared behind the newspaper again. "What's your zodiac sign?"

Now this was a subject Iesha could relate to and have a decent conversation about with Harmony. "I'm a Leo to my heart."

"Leo," Harmony read from the paper. "What you neglected forty-eight hours ago commands immediate attention. Family, employment spotlighted. Love walks in today."

Iesha cocked her head back. "What? That's why I don't go by those things anymore. They don't make any sense. Let the horo-scopes tell it, I meet a new love every day."

Harmony bent the paper back enough to see Iesha. "What it's saying is that whatever you did forty-eight hours ago is con-suming you, it has all of your attention. And it has to do with your family or your job, or both. And that you will meet someone today."

"Okay, I'll give you the first part. That's true. But if I meet someone I could fall in love with today, you and I are gonna be buddies for the rest of our lives."

Iesha watched Harmony's mouth turn up into a grinch-like smile.

"You shouldn't smile like that, makes you look like evil. See what Charity's horoscope says, she's a Capricorn."

"Capricorn. Long-awaited news can relate to one who played an important role in the past. Spiritual values surface; you adopt a philosophical attitude where family, loved ones are concerned. Don't let past interfere with future success."

"Can you translate that, please?"

"Charity is waiting for something from someone who used to be important to her. Because it's been a long time coming, she questions what, or whom, she believes. She's still living her life in the past and people are concerned about her." Harmony lowered the paper.

"I don't know about that one, Harmony. I don't know anyone who is as strong in their faith as Charity. If any of us are con-cerned, it'd be about her being too strong in her faith, but not because she ain't strong enough. So I don't know about that one."

"It didn't say specifically what you'd be concerned about. It just said that you would be."

Iesha looked at the clock. It was only 9:50. *Ten o'clock, please come on*. Harmony must've seen her look at the clock, because she said, "Besides, it's too early to say it's not true. It's just nine fifty. The universe is still in motion, orchestrating and aligning things to push us toward being our higher selves. Only some of us won't go. Too afraid. Too busy holding on to hurts and pasts we can't change. If only we knew how great we were. How divine we are. If we'd only quit holding on to this sin-sick-soul mentality."

"Earth to Harmony. Girl, do you ever have plain conversations? Hel-lo, we were talking about horoscopes."

Harmony picked up the newspaper again. "I'm a Gemini, the twins. It says that I am no longer plagued by indecision. I know what I want and what I have to do to get it. Proceed with my plans. Don't hesitate to pull strings."

"Yours is pretty cut and dry."

Harmony reached into her pocket. "I know, but I got my lucky rabbit's foot just in case."

"Iii-uh." Iesha cringed. "What in the world is that?"

"A rabbit's foot. The kind they sell in the stores are not real, this one is an orig—"

"Well, well, well." Charity strolled in. "What did I ever do to deserve such a wonderful staff?" Iesha was glad that Charity's eyes were focused on the food on the table, because if she had caught Harmony slipping that dingy rabbit's foot back into her pocket, she would've had a fit. "Look at this spread," she heard Charity say.

"I wanted our first staff meeting to be special."

"Thank you, Iesha." Charity walked over to hug her sister. "This is special."

Harmony agreed. "It is special. May I make a toast?"

"That would be nice, Harmony," Charity said. "But I would like to lead us in prayer."

Iesha winked at Harmony. She told her Charity was strong in her faith. Harmony bowed her head, but as her head went down it looked to Iesha like she rolled her eyes.

Charity began the prayer softly and asked God's blessing upon

Horizons and its staff. Harmony coughed. As Charity's prayer became more fervent, Harmony's cough worsened. Charity prayed louder so that she could be heard over the coughing. Charity prayed that demons who would try to hinder God's work from being done would be bound up in Jesus' name. Harmony's cough had become so wrenching that she started gagging and excused herself.

It was obvious Iesha was talking to a man on the phone. Her smile was as wide as a Cheshire cat's. Like a teenager in love, she giggled while she talked and twisted her hair around her fingers.

"Wallace, you're so silly . . . I was wondering when I'd hear from you again . . . Friday night? Uhm . . . Yeah, I do have to check my schedule . . . I'm just kidding. Friday night sounds good . . . Yeah, I can hold . . ."

She doodled hearts on her desk calendar as she waited for Wallace to return to the conversation. She sat up straight when a deliveryman walked into the suite.

"May I help you?" She surprised herself, noticing that she wasn't using her seductive tone of voice. Either she was changing for real or the man she really wanted was on the other line. *He ain't my color anyway.* She watched him walk over to her. He was cute, but too dark for her. *Not enough milk in the coffee.*

He smiled. "Yes, ma'am. I'm Terrence Davis from Delivery Direct and I have a delivery for . . ." He looked at the electronic clipboard. "For Ms. Charity Phillips."

She held up her finger to let him know she would be right with him. Wallace came back to the phone. Her smile grew wide again. "I have to go," she whispered. "I think my sister's horoscope is coming true. Harmony, the weird lady I was telling you about, read me our horoscopes this morning. My sister's said she was waiting on something and a deliveryman is here." She looked up at him to see if he could hear her. He had taken a few steps back to give her privacy. It looked like his eyes were closed. "This might be what she was waiting on," she continued. "Call me later for directions to the house. I'll see you Friday night."

Iesha hung up the phone loud enough so that the deliveryman could hear. She didn't know how else to wake him up. He opened his eyes. "Mr. Davis, I hate to call your boss and tell him you're sleeping on the job," she joked.

"So, if I give you the number, would you promise to call?"

She cocked her head to the side. That was different. A pickup line without crass. She looked at him peculiarly. With other men, Wallace included, she could read them and know what they wanted. But there was nothing familiar about this man. His long eyelashes made his drowsy eyes look sexy. His stare was intense but inviting. His smile nervous but sincere. His name was created just for him. *Terrence. Dark, tall, and bald.*

"Sir, Charity is still at lunch." She looked at the clock on her computer. "She should be back in a few minutes. Would you like to wait for her?"

"I guess that's a no on that phone call," he grinned.

She blushed.

"I'll tell you what." he continued. "I'll go get Ms. Phillips's delivery out of my truck. That'll give you a chance to think about taking my phone number and maybe she'll be back by the time I return."

He turned to walk away. "Umph umph umph," she moaned, shaking her head. "There is a God."

"Uhhhh, those are some beautiful flowers," Charity said to the delivery person as they were getting out of the elevator together.

He smiled and held the arrangement of blue moon roses and pink tulips, enclosed with greenery and cascading white lily of the valley flowers, up to his nose. "And they smell good too." He held them out for her to get a whiff. She stopped and closed her eyes while she inhaled the floral fragrance.

"Mmmmm," she moaned. "God is awesome all of the time."

"And all of the time He is awesome," he smiled. "Praise God,

it's good to know that I have a sister on the same side of the bat-
tlefield."

"Amen, you know it!" Charity stopped in front of the office
suite, expecting that he would pass by. "Have a good day in the
Lord!"

He looked up at the suite number above the door. "You
wouldn't happen to be Ms. Charity Phillips, would you?"

"Yes, I am."

He handed the bouquet of flowers to her. "These are for you."
While she pecked through the flowers for a card, she heard him
ask, "Who is she?"

Charity looked up. "That's Iesha. My sister." She looked at his
left hand and smiled when she didn't see a ring. "And she's single.
And saved."

He grinned. "And beautiful."

Iesha joined them. "Ya'll talking about me?"

"And she's perceptive," Terrence said. "I like that."

Charity took a few steps back so that Iesha and Terrence were
standing alone. "Well, you two get to know each other." Charity
pushed them a little closer together, thinking that it was good to
have Iesha that close to a man of God at last. "I've got to go and
find out who these flowers are from."

Charity couldn't get to her office fast enough. She wasn't
expecting anything from Emmitt until Monday. She'd just talked
to him this morning. She read the card that was tucked between
the flowers. "Yes, I'll go. Michael Adams." She was disappointed.
I don't want flowers from you, April does.

If it wasn't for Harmony coming through the door, Iesha
could've stayed there talking to Terrence all day.

"I've got to go," she told him.

"Me too. I've got a few other deliveries to make."

Harmony walked up to Iesha and whispered in her ear. "I see
that love did walk in for a Leo today. That means we're buddies

for life." Before Iesha could think of a response, Harmony was already gone.

Iesha took a step away from Terrence.

"Is everything okay?"

Iesha thought for a moment and tried to laugh away what she felt. "Yeah. Just a silly joke we made earlier. She was reading horoscopes and it said—"

Terrence shook his head. "I'd hate to ruin your first impression of me, but I have to say this . . . We Christians have no business reading, let alone believing, in horoscopes. Unbelievers dabble in that mess because they don't have a God to guide them, they use horoscopes to do that. But our steps are ordered by the Lord."

"I should've known better, and I sat there and told her that if that horoscope came true she and I would be buddies for life."

"Is she saved?"

"Oh yeah, my sister doesn't play that. But the more I hear her talk the more I can see differences in what she believes and what my sister believes."

"What about what you believe?"

"I just gave my life to Christ yesterday."

"Praise the Lord." He hugged her. "Welcome to the Body of Christ. No wonder the devil's trying to introduce you to horoscopes. He's trying to keep a foothold in you."

"This is going to sound stupid, but if horoscopes are not of God, how do they come true?"

"They don't come true. They're illusions; they have the appearance of truth for people who believe in them. The devil knows what you're looking for and how to present it to you."

Iesha was confused but didn't feel comfortable asking what she really wanted to know. Did that mean that he was an illusion too? Maybe that was his purpose, to come and say just what he said.

"What are you thinking?"

"This is going to sound stupid too—"

"Quit beating yourself up. You're a one-day-old baby, you're not supposed to know everything. If Christians asked more questions, we wouldn't have so much witchcraft in the church."

"Well, if horoscopes don't come true and they're illusions, then that would mean that you wouldn't be the *love* that was supposed to walk in today."

"How about we leave that up to God and not the horoscopes?" Terrence took her right hand in his. "I'd love to stay, but I'm working." His voice was deep and soft. "I'd hate for my boss to get a call saying that I'm sleeping on the job." He grinned and kissed her hand before letting it go. He handed her one of his business cards. "When you call, you don't have to worry about telling my boss I was asleep. He won't believe that. But if you tell him I was praying, he'll know that you're telling the truth."

Iesha turned the card over without reading it and wrote her phone number on the back. "I prefer to be called."

"That's even better." He took the card and turned to walk away. He looked back when he got to the door and waved.

Iesha waved back. No man had ever left her speechless.

Chapter 13

EITHER CHARITY WAS STUPID or he still had it like that. Emmitt didn't know which was most true. How could she possibly believe that he would be sending her a surprise, when he had not given her the time of day in almost six years? *She'll be surprised all right.* A smile came across his face. "I know what it is. She's still hooked on Big Daddy," he said, referring to the part of himself that used to belong exclusively to her. He knew that if he brushed up against her the right way, or got close enough for her to smell his cologne, or if he kissed her lips, it would be all over.

He didn't know if it was his security guard uniform or realizing that he had been in the same vicinity as Charity and did not run into her that made him feel bravado. Out of all the attorneys in the city of Charlotte, how could he have possibly picked one that was so close to her, in the same building? He shook his head and muttered, "It's a small world." He remembered he was at work when he faintly heard his name on the CB radio he carried. He listened to see if it would be called again.

"Officer Phillips, please call the main office. Officer Emmitt Phillips, call the main office."

His hands felt thick and clumsy as he fished for the two-way radio attached to his belt clip.

"This is Emmitt Phillips, over," he answered.

"Phillips, report to the station. You have an urgent message, over."

"Did they say who it's concerning? Over."

"Your mother, over."

"I'll be right there, 10-4."

Emmitt made his way to the station as fast as he could to obtain the message to call his mother's physician as she had been hospitalized. He could not figure out what to do first, whether to call the hospital or to drive over there. "Please, Lord, let everything be all right," he prayed. He dialed the number written on the pink memo paper and waited for someone to answer.

"Yes, this is Emmitt Phillips, I'm returning a call to a Dr. Metcalf," he tried to sound as calm as possible. "Hello, Dr. Metcalf, this is Emmitt Phillips, Elaine Phillips's son . . . Yes, sir, is she okay? . . . You ran some tests? . . . Chest pains? Yes, sir, she has them when she's under a lot of stress . . . No, sir, I don't think she's under stress now, not that I'm aware of . . . Yes, I can bring her medications . . . Room 772 . . . I'll be there in less than an hour . . . Thank you, Doctor . . ."

Driving like a madman raised his blood pressure faster than it got him home. He would swear that people were driving slowly just to spite him. "Get out the way," he yelled, and with his hand shooed an elderly woman in a Cadillac. He was more focused on the conversation he had with the physician than he was on the road. The car may as well have been on automatic pilot as visions of what his mother could be going through distracted him. *She's probably hooked up to life support. Not breathing on her own. Got tubes everywhere.* This was more than he could bear. He needed to hurry and get there. He pulled into his driveway like he had crossed the finish line at the Indy 500. He was in such a hurry he didn't realize he was turning off the ignition without shifting into park.

He let himself into the house and went straight to his mother's room. Her room was kept as usual. Aside from the opened mail scattered across her bed, there was no evidence that anyone had been in the room. He wondered what had happened. All of his mother's medications were neatly lined up on her dresser. He counted twenty-six bottles, picked them up individually, and read the labels to see if he recognized any of them. Her sleeping pills were there, as were her migraine medications. There were also some bottles he didn't recognize, and he didn't know what they were used for. The more he read, the more overwhelmed he became. This was wasting time. He looked around for something to put the medications in. He decided to take all of them. He lifted the half-full bag of trash out of her wastebasket and got an empty bag from underneath it. He swept all of the prescription bottles into the bag.

He was on his way out of her room when one of the pieces of mail caught his eye. He could see the bold, black writing from where he was: NO PLACE LIKE HOME: HIGHLAND BRIDGE APARTMENTS. He put his hand over his chest as if the piece of mail scared him, or at least to keep his heart inside his chest. *That can't be what I think it is.* He snatched the papers off the bed and uncovered other pieces of mail addressed to him. He uttered a few choice words. He did not expect that he would receive any of the apartment applications so soon. He had just requested them yesterday. This is not the way he wanted his mother to find out. He threw the applications back on the bed and resumed his race to the hospital.

He hated hospitals. He became nauseous just thinking about the fact that he was getting ready to set foot in one. It reminded him of the two months he spent in the hospital recovering from injuries sustained after his car skidded off the icy roads into an embankment during a snowstorm. He was on his way home from East Tennessee State University for winter break when he lost control of the car. To this day that is all he remembers, besides the fact that he was forced to withdraw from the university—an emotional scar that hurt worse than the scars that could be seen.

He recalled how supportive Charity had been when she

learned about the accident. He was told that she immediately drove to the hospital to be by his side. She was right there when he regained consciousness and she drove back and forth from school as he recovered. He was surprised that his mother allowed Charity to visit him at their home upon his discharge. Just remembering Charity's kindness at that time reminded him of why he asked her to marry him in the first place. She'd rejoiced with him when he learned to walk again, when he confessed Christ as his Savior, and a year later when he returned to ETSU. He returned to school a new man and felt that he wanted to live a better, more settled life. In order to repay Charity for her kindness, he asked her to marry him. The first year of their marriage was good, but the weight of having a new baby, and being torn between his mother and his wife, was more than he could withstand. He was beginning to hate everything and everyone, including himself and God. He admitted to himself that he had done some mean and hateful things to Charity. But he would swear on the Bible that he did not choke her.

Emmitt sighed. Remembering all that he'd gone through with Charity only slowed him down. He rehearsed one of the things he used to hear her say all of the time, *My past is not my present*. With that thought, he speeded himself up and walked into the hospital. He saw a GET WELL SOON balloon in the window of the gift shop and decided that he wanted to get something to cheer up his mother. He raced into the gift shop and asked for one of the Mylar balloons. He stood at the counter looking around the store while a petite woman with a silver bouffant blew up the balloon with helium. He spotted a light brown, stuffed teddy bear with GET WELL SOON engraved on its sweater. He walked over, picked it up, and brought it to the counter.

"Will this be all for you?"

"Yes, ma'am."

"Your total is $24.05. Who do you know that's sick?"

"My mother."

"I'm sorry to hear that. I'll say a prayer for her."

Emmitt took out his wallet to pay her. "Thank you, ma'am. Have a good day."

On the way to his mother's room, he beat himself up about the excessive time and money he spent in the shop. Then he soothed himself thinking, *I'd rather spend money on her while she's alive than after she is dead.*

It was obvious that he was nervous by the countless times he repositioned the bear and balloon from arm to arm. As if it might have changed since the last time he looked, he kept checking the room number he'd scribbled on the scrap of paper. Reaching her room, he stood at the door to brace himself. He leaned in closer to see if he could hear anything from inside. He heard someone talking and was disappointed. He wanted to be left alone with his sick mother. He was getting ready to tap on the door when he heard laughter on the other side. *Who could that be laughing as his mother was laying up in the hospital sick?* He gave a quick warning tap and thrust open the door.

He could've sworn he saw his mother laughing when he peeped into the room, but the closer he got to her bed, the worse she appeared. Maybe it was his aunt Elisa or his granny that he'd heard laughing.

"Hey, Emmitt," Elisa greeted. "Thank you for the bear," she joked.

He walked past her to get closer to his mother's bedside. "Hey, Momma." He leaned over to kiss her. "How you feeling?" he asked.

She clutched her chest. "I . . . think . . . I . . . ," she said brokenly.

He put the teddy bear next to her in bed and pulled the covers that were gathered at her waist up over her shoulders. "Just relax, Momma. I'm here to take care of you."

He acknowledged Granny. When he turned to tie the balloon to the bedside tray, he saw his aunt shake her head at his mother.

"I know, Aunt Elisa," he said. "I hate it when she's sick too."

• • •

"Hey, Mr. Wright," Iesha greeted over the telephone. "How're you doing?"

"I'm fine, Iesha. Is there a problem with my appointment for Thursday?"

"Oh no, sir. I'm calling to find out if you know anyone who does any good car detailing?"

"Why, yes. It's funny that you ask. That's what I do for a living—"

She interrupted him. "I know. That's why I'm calling you. I would like to surprise Charity by having her car detailed. Can you bring your things here and do it?"

"Oh yes. When are you talking?"

"I'm going to take her out for lunch Friday, if you can detail the car while we're gone."

"No problem, just leave her keys with me. And I'll have it done in less than an hour."

"Good." She clapped her hands excitedly. She wanted to do something nice for her sister since she had a hand in introducing her to Terrence. If Charity had not received the flowers, she would've never met him. "Thank you so much, Mr. Wright. I'll talk to you more when you get here on Thurday."

After Iesha hung up, she made a list of all the cleaning supplies she thought she would need to get ready for the DSS inspection. *Mop, broom, smell good, sponges, Ajax, and some new dishrags.* Housekeeping was not one of her strengths. She did what she had to do to keep the living room presentable, but beyond that, the house was what Mama Lorraine called "nasty." If anyone could help get her house in order, it would be Mama Lorraine. Iesha just hated that she would have to tell her that she messed up—again.

"Hey, Ma," she spoke into the phone. "What'chu doing? . . . I'm at work . . . Yeah, she's got a client . . . I need a favor . . . Will you help me clean my house? . . . Yes . . ." Iesha sucked in her breath and exhaled as she spilled the news in one breath. She shifted in her seat, doodled on her calendar, and held the phone away occasionally as Mama Lorraine cussed her a little bit, and consoled her a little bit. "Thank you, Ma, you're a lifesaver. Speaking of saving lives, I gave my life to Christ yesterday . . . Charity did . . . I'm for real this time too, Momma . . . Thank you, Mah . . . I'll be home by five-thirty tomorrow . . . Okay, thanks . . . I love you too. Bye."

That wasn't too bad. Either that or I've messed up so many times I'm getting used to her I-told-you-so speech. She tore up her shopping list. Mama Lorraine had told her she would bring "the good stuff" with her.

Charity hurriedly completed her documentation on her last session. She needed to leave work early today. April would be meeting her at the mall at four o'clock so that they could find a dress for the banquet. She looked at her watch. It was 3:30. She knew she didn't have enough time but she wanted to stop by the church and pick up a letter that had come for her. Mrs. Johnson, the church's administrative assistant, called to tell her that she would hold the letter for her in the office. When Charity asked, Johnson said it looked like a card. *Why would someone send me a card to the church?* She could not wait to find out.

She'd ignored the first two rings of the telephone, but when it rang a third time, she yelled at it. "How many times can a phone ring? I'm trying to get outta here!" She picked it up on the fourth ring.

"Hello? . . . Hello, Emmitt . . ." She shuffled her feet like she was shouting. *Thank You, Jesus.* "Your mom's in the hospital? I'm sorry to hear that." She rolled her eyes. *Wonder what it is this time? When is this man going to wake up and see how manipulative his mother is?* Charity knew Elaine all too well. Every time she felt like her relationship with her son was being jeopardized she would become conveniently ill, and Emmitt would be right there with her, patting her like a baby. Charity thought back to all of the hospitalizations she had witnessed.

There was the time when she and Emmitt took her out to

dinner to tell her that they'd become engaged. Within an hour she was rushed to the hospital for food poisoning. Then a few days before their wedding, she was hospitalized for high blood pressure. When she learned that Charity was pregnant, she developed a thyroid problem. Charity would bet anything that the hospital's medical records department had a shelf reserved solely to house all of Elaine's charts.

"Is she going to be okay? . . . A heart attack? . . . How long did the doctor say she would be there?" *Just what I thought, he hadn't even talked to the doctor yet.* Charity knew what his mother's diagnosis was, she probably just had a bad case of gas, as much as she eats. Charity thought about it for a minute. She realized that his mother had not been hospitalized since their separation and divorce. She has stayed out of the hospital for almost three years. Something had to be getting ready to happen for her to be there now. *I wonder if he talked to his mom about reconciling with me.* That thought brought a smile to her face.

"Does your mom need anything? Do you need anything? . . . I just want you to know that Zavey and I are here for you . . . Okay . . . Well, keep us posted . . . We'll talk to you later . . . I love you, bye."

She could have slapped herself. That was not supposed to come out of her mouth. He must have been just as surprised as she was. All he said was, "Okay."

CHAPTER 14

CHARITY WAS RUNNING BEHIND but still anxious to pick up her mail from the church. She pulled into the parking lot as if there were a gleaming HOT DOUGHNUTS NOW sign at Krispy Kreme. She sprinted into the church.

"Hi, Mrs. Johnson," she greeted.

"Hey, Minister Phillips. How's it going?"

"All is well. How about yourself?"

"I'm good." Mrs. Johnson turned around in her chair to access the file cabinet behind her desk. "I have your mail right here." She pulled out a pink envelope. "Who do you know in the Bluegrass State?"

Charity raised her eyebrows. "Kentucky?" She looked at the return address on the card. "I don't know anyone in Kentucky. Minister Joseph Nelson?" She wanted to read it, but when she looked at her watch she decided that she needed to go. "Thanks, Mrs. Johnson. I've got to go. I'm meeting Sister April at the mall." She turned to leave. "Tell Pastor I said hello." She sped out of the parking lot and while waiting at every red light, she read the card and two-page letter.

She was back to sprinting after she parked her car at the mall. There was no doubt in her mind that April would be on time, tapping her foot and looking at her watch. She walked aerobically to Group USA Warehouse, the retail store that she and April shared as a favorite. The sight of April tapping her foot and lowering her arm after looking to see what time it was on her watch made Charity smile. *I know my girl.*

"I was determined to be on time," Charity greeted.

"Girl, when are you ever on time?"

"I know," she laughed. "But at least I'm less than ten minutes late."

They walked into the store.

"Uhhhh!" April went running. "This is you, Charity." She tugged on a long, shimmering gold, spaghetti-strapped dress.

Charity turned her nose up at it. "You know I'm too black for that dress."

"You're always talking about you too black for something. If that's the case, you need to wear something that'll lighten you up."

"Lighten me up, yes. But to brighten me up to the point where I can't be turned down, no."

"The Bible says that you're the light of the world."

Charity shook her head. "Come on, Sister Word." She pulled her by the arm and led her to another rack of dresses. "What do you think about this?" She pulled a dress off the rack and held it up for her friend's approval.

April looked sideways at the graceful, black, ankle-length sleeveless dress. It had a sequin design around the neck and a front split. "It's nice. Definitely sexy, you gone have to use your anointing oil on your left leg with a split like that."

Charity held the dress up to her body and looked in a nearby mirror. "Do you think it's too sexy? I don't want to send the wrong message."

April laughed. "And neither do I. You're going out with my man."

Charity laughed too. "Let's go to Belk's and Dillard's. If they don't have anything, I'll come back and get this one."

"Girl, get that dress with your Size 2 behind. You look good in everything. I ain't never seen nobody who could make a pair of jeans with a T-shirt look classy. Get that dress."

"No, let's keep looking. We'll come back."

After an hour of going from store to store, Charity was growing frustrated. "If I try on another dress, I'm going to scream." She put a black dress with a silk apricot draped neck back on the rack. "I need a break." She looked at her watch. "Let's go get some ice cream. I have another hour before I pick up Xavier. I think I want that first one we saw in Group USA."

"Fine with me. Some cherry pistachio ice cream sounds good right about now. I'll follow your lead."

Charity knew Concord Mills Mall like the back of her hand. She led her friend through two concourses before they reached the food court. Charity stopped April before they headed toward Baskin-Robbins. "You know how we do with ice cream, right?"

April nodded and looked Charity in the eye. "You have something you want to talk to me about?"

"Yes, it just happened and it's going to sound really strange, but—"

April's eyes widened. She placed her hand over her chest. "Oh my God. You gotta breakthrough in your marriage, didn't you?"

Charity snapped her fingers. She'd forgotten to tell April about Emmitt's phone call and the surprise that he was sending to her. "Oh yes. I believe I've received restoration of my marriage, but—"

April threw both of her hands up and did a two-step shuffle. "Thank You, Jesus. Hallelujah. The prayers of the righteous availeth much."

Charity looked around to see if anyone was looking. She could not believe that this girl was really shouting in the middle of the mall. Charity locked her arm in April's and led her to a nearby table with chairs. "Girl, you are a wet wick, the smallest spark can light your fire." April was rocking back and forth trying to contain herself. "I know you've been praying for Emmitt and me and God is truly answering your prayers. But what I want to talk to you about is this." She retrieved the pink envelope from her purse and gave it to her. "Find us a table closer to Baskin-Robbins and read it while I order our ice cream."

Charity prayed as she walked to the counter. She needed divine instruction and she hoped God would use April as a mouthpiece. She was intrigued by the contents of Minister Nelson's letter and wanted to respond, but didn't know if she should. She didn't know if she was nervous and just wanted to get back to April or if the cashier deserved the attitude she was giving her. She knew the teen-aged employees saw her standing at the counter, but they kept talking as if their conversation were more important than doing their jobs.

"Hel-lo?" she called to get their attention. One of her biggest pet peeves was unprofessional people.

The young girl glanced back at her male coworker as she sashayed toward Charity. "May I help you?"

You can stop chewing that gum like a cow for one thing. "I'd like two scoops of mint chocolate chip and two scoops of cherry pista-chio." Charity dug in her purse for her wallet, annoyed with the cashier who just stood there like she was waiting on something else. Charity forced a smile, "How much do I owe you?"

The cashier sucked a bubble from the gum she was chewing back into her mouth. "Ma'am, you have to tell me how you want your ice cream. Do you want it in a cup or a cone?"

What difference does it make? Charity pursed her lips together to hold her tongue, then spoke like she was talking to someone whose second language was English. "I'd like the mint chocolate chip in one cup, and the cherry pistachio in another."

"That's all you had to say the first time."

Charity cocked her head to the side and pointed at the cashier. "Look, little girl . . ." She stopped mid-sentence, remembering who she was and to whom she belonged. She took a deep breath. "Please go get my order before I say and do something that we'll both regret." Charity looked at the cash register to find the cost.

Even though the old Charity was dead and buried, it only took a second to resurrect her.

April was still reading the letter when Charity returned with the ice cream. She sat the tray on the table. To try and feel April out she said, "Girl, I about went off on that little girl at the cash register." When April didn't look up, Charity continued. "So should he be one of my clients?"

April did not lift her eyes from the letter. "No, he seems to be where he needs to be. But if you're thinking about writing him back, you might consider making an appointment somewhere."

Charity sat down and started eating. "It's courteous to at least acknowledge that I received his letter."

April refolded the letter and slid her ice cream closer. "That's how women get killed these days—being courteous. Charity, the man's in jail, he's not looking for courtesy, he's looking for a pen pal."

"He just wrote to say that he was blessed by my article in *Today's Gospel*."

"And he also wrote you a two-page story about his life."

"He was just explaining how he got to where he is."

April sighed. "You're talking like this is normal. Like it's okay to receive correspondence from a criminal. I'm sure your article was nice, but do you think this is the first time he was so inspired that he wrote to an author?"

Charity didn't respond. She asked God for divine instruction, and she had to accept what she was given.

April continued. "Don't get me wrong. Aside from being locked up, he sounds like a nice person. He writes well. Sounds like he has a relationship with Christ. And that's commendable considering most men in jail turn to the Nation of Islam. Seems like he sincerely wants you to know that he's a good person who made a mistake. But the fact remains that he's in jail."

"I'm surprised. I thought you would've been all in the Bible on this one. Giving me Scripture after Scripture about how I need to write back because the Scriptures say, 'judge not that you be not judged' or at least when Jesus said . . . better yet, let me show it to you . . ." Charity took the pocket Bible out of her purse and flipped through its pages. "Here it is, Matthew 25:36, 'I was in prison, and You came unto me.'"

"No, you didn't. You know good and well Jesus ain't never been to prison. He was teaching a parable about judgment."

Feeling foolish, Charity kept up her argument. "Okay, you got me on that one. Paul and John the Baptist, two of the greatest men of the Bible, were imprisoned, and considering all of the mess we did back in college, we might've served some time too."

"Now I'll give you that one. We should've served some time for the mess we did."

"I'm not looking for a husband. I just want to write back and thank him for his kind words and let him know I'll be praying for him."

April opened the letter again. "Dear Minister Phillips," she read. "Your 'I Have No Man' missive in the February issue of *Today's Gospel* blessed me so much that I wanted to tell you thanks and to encourage you to keep letting our Lord and Savior use you. I tried hard not to write you, telling myself that it was a foolish idea, but you and I know God uses foolish things to confound the wise. I felt an unction in my spirit to contact you. In fact, the babe in my spirit man leaped as I read your testimony. I know the Spirit led me to find you." She put the letter down. "Charity, you need to be prayerful about what spirit he was led by."

Charity picked up the letter. "What? I thought that was sweet. I bet if he weren't in jail, you'd be telling me to go for him. Look at him, the boy is fine."

April looked at the picture that he had sent again. She had to admit Minister Nelson was handsome. "I sure would tell you to go for him," she said, spooning her now-melted ice cream.

"Like you said, he sounds like a nice person who made a mistake—"

"Yep, a felonious one. A police officer who got charged with aiding and abetting."

Charity shrugged her shoulders. "He said he didn't know his partner was crooked."

"How can a police officer with over ten years' experience not know his partner was accepting bribes from the people they stopped?"

"I don't know. He said his partner framed him when he got caught and said that Minister Nelson knew all along that his partner was accepting bribes."

"I guess the good thing is that they were never able to find any evidence against him. You know how we can find out don't you?"

"Find out what?"

"If he's telling the truth or not."

"How?"

"We can look it up on the Internet. They have those Web sites where you can look up inmates and see their crimes, their sentences, and everything."

"You need to stay off Court TV."

"I wouldn't write him back until I at least did that."

Charity considered April's suggestion. It sounded like a good idea. "Do you know how to look it up?"

"Yeah. I'll do it when I get home and call you." April sipped a spoonful of melted ice cream. "He only got a five-year sentence, so he is probably telling the truth. How long has he been there?"

"Two years."

"What is the world coming to? Police officers breaking the law they're supposed to uphold."

"I know. Emmitt is the one who should've been in jail . . . for domestic violence."

"Yeah, but he wouldn't have gone to a federal facility. I know you've already made up your mind and I honestly don't think responding is a bad idea. I just don't want you to give the wrong impression, or for him to get the wrong impression. You know? Your real dad's in jail, isn't he?"

Charity nodded.

"Why don't you ask him for advice?"

Charity sucked her teeth. "I know you've lost it now. You want me to write my father and tell him that someone from jail wrote to me and to give me advice on what to do?"

"No. Ask him how inmates find their pen pals. And if you're bold enough tell him about Minister Nelson."

Charity looked at her watch. "Let's go get this dress," she said, standing. "I refuse to write Brother Abdul for advice. I only told you because I was seeking godly counsel. I'm not interested in what his Allah has to say. That's evidence of one truth you spoke about Minister Nelson—he is to be commended for turning to God. I'm still praying the same for my father."

Emmitt parted his mother's graying hair and scratched her scalp with a rattail comb. He'd performed this service since he was eight or nine years old. His mother, grandmother, and Aunt Elisa affectionately called him the "head honcho." It never failed that the recipient would be asleep within ten minutes. His mother had fallen asleep minutes ago. He brushed her hair back with his fingers and massaged her scalp. He was glad she was resting.

When he was done he sat in the mint green recliner beside her bed and watched the television play silently. All the while his mind was on his mother. He knew that her heart attack was a result of the hard life that she'd lived. His alcoholic and abusive father walked out on them when he and Greg were toddlers. Consequently, the boys watched men come and go. There were plenty of times they fought to protect their mother or them-selves from the men she brought home or allowed to move in. Emmitt remembered when he was eleven years old. His mother was driving her van and her boyfriend was in the passenger's seat. The boyfriend was yelling at Elaine when Emmitt climbed boldly up to the front of the van to intervene and threatened the man. His mother begged him to return to his seat. As Emmitt turned back, the boyfriend grabbed him by the shirt and tried to pull him over his lap. He opened the van door to throw Emmitt out. Fortunately, Emmitt's lanky body was too long to be pulled over the round hump that divided the driver and passenger's seats. Emmitt did not remember how that ordeal ended or why the man didn't come back to hurt him later. But one thing was for certain, for his mother, he would do it all again. She married and divorced two times after that relationship.

Emmitt knew that he was her love child. What he lacked scholastically, he compensated for athletically. He was so agile and talented that by high school he'd become a decathlete. His mother worked two jobs and never came to any of his games, but he knew she was proud of him. She watched his interviews on the eleven o'clock news and read and clipped all of the newspaper articles about him. To this day, his many trophies and awards were displayed on three shelves in a cabinet in their living room.

There was a short, rapid knock on the door. He looked at his mother to make sure she had not been disturbed. The door opened before he could get up to open it.

A doctor tiptoed toward him and initiated a handshake.

"I'm Dr. Metcalf," he whispered. "Are you Sleeping Beauty's son?"

"Yes," he laughed nervously.

The doctor motioned for Emmitt to follow him outside to the hallway. "Did the tests from her heart attack turn out okay?"

Dr. Metcalf looked puzzled. He flipped the chart over to look at the room number and then turned back to look at the number on the door. "We ran some diagnostic tests. The results are normal. The tests showed no organic basis for a *heart* attack. We are certain that your mother had a panic attack."

"Panic attack? What's the difference between that and a heart attack? We have a family history of heart attacks."

"It's understandable that your mother thought she was having a heart attack. The physical symptoms of a panic attack are so identical to a heart attack that we have to run diagnostic tests like the EEG and EKG to make a definite diagnosis. Your mother's test results were normal."

Emmitt was not convinced. "So, even though she was having chest pains, could hardly breathe, and felt like she was going to die, it wasn't a heart attack?"

"Like a heart attack, a panic attack involves a sudden onset of extreme apprehension or fear and is usually associated with feelings of impending doom. Palpitations, chest pain, breathing difficulties, nausea, feelings of choking, chills, and hot flashes are some of the symptoms. But they can be so severe that the patient believes he is dying of a heart attack."

Emmitt tuned out Dr. Metcalf. "Mr. Phillips," the doctor attempted. "Has your mother been under a lot of stress lately?"

"She's always under a lot of stress," he quipped.

"Aside from the usual, has her comfort zone or routine daily life been threatened in any way?"

Emmitt looked sideways toward the ceiling. "Not that I can think of. We're in the process of adopting my son, but she is in favor of that."

"Will getting your son create any changes for her?"

Just then Emmitt remembered finding the apartment applications that she had opened and left on her bed. A twinge of guilt gripped him so hard his eyes watered. "In order to get my son," he started slowly, "I have to move out of my mother's home. I went looking for apartments yesterday and requested a few applications. When I went home to pick up her medications for you, I found two application packets that she had opened and left on her bed."

The doctor scratched his head. "Bingo, Mr. Phillips. Will this be your first time living apart from your mother?"

Sheepishly he responded. "No, sir. I went away to college and I used to be married."

"How was your mother's health when you moved out then?"

"Okay."

"Did she require any medical attention?"

Annoyed, he answered, "Yes. But I don't understand why you're asking me all of these questions."

"I'm wondering if your mother suffers from a panic disorder. I'm not a psychiatrist—"

"A psychiatrist? She doesn't need a psychiatrist—"

"Mr. Phillips, I'm just saying that people with panic disorders have just what your mother had today when she found those applications. And I would bet that if you thought about it long enough you might remember other occasions when she required medical attention during times of significant events."

Emmitt didn't know if he believed what the doctor was saying. He did know that he had heard this before, from Charity. Charity was always trying to convince him that his mother was "co-dependent" and that he needed to set some boundaries. She was always talking in that therapy language he didn't understand. He hated that she put him in the middle, between her and his mother. Charity would be on one end showing him where the Bible says for a man to leave his family and cleave to his wife. His mother would be on the other end telling him that nobody ever loves anybody like their own mother. "One day I'mma be dead and gone," she would say. "And you'll finally realize that I wasn't trying to control you. I was telling you right."

"Mr. Phillips?" the doctor called, as if he had been trying to get his attention for a while. "Have you ever heard of codependency?"

Emmitt lied and shook his head no.

"That's a type of relationship where there are no clear boundaries between two or more people. The people involved do not know where they begin or end, they are so enmeshed with the other person. If the other person ever left, the first person would feel empty, incomplete, and even abandoned."

Emmitt shifted his weight onto one foot.

The doctor continued. "We have social workers in the hospital who would be available to talk with you and your mother. Would you be interested in a consultation?"

If he did not know better, he would have sworn that Charity

had something to do with this. She was always trying to get him to see a therapist.

"No thanks." He looked at his watch, hoping the doctor got the message that his time was up.

"Well, if you change your mind let us know. A social worker may be able to help you talk to your mother about your moving out. I'd like for her to stay overnight and be discharged in the morning. So you have until then to think about it." He stuck his hand out for another handshake.

Emmitt hesitated, then weakly shook his hand. Anything to get him on his way.

He tiptoed back into the room. He was relieved that she was still sleeping.

CHAPTER 15

IESHA LOOKED THROUGH HER CD COLLECTION. After a long day at the office she needed some working music. Something energizing, because it was going to take an all-nighter to get the house in decent shape. She selected her Missy Elliott CD and put it on track number 2. She danced all the way to Raquan's and Sha-Lai's rooms to make sure they were cleaning underneath their beds. If she had gotten on them once, she had gotten on them a thousand times about stashing dirty clothes, books, and toys under there. The beds housed more clothes than the closets, and the closets were still cluttered. Clothes strewn on the top shelf, clothes halfway hung in the middle, and clothes fallen atop their shoes on the floor. "These chaps are trifling," she muttered. She shuddered, realizing how much she sounded like her mother.

"Momma, I found my Yu-Gi-Oh! trading cards," Raquan said, looking up at her and showing her his finds.

"It's amazing what you'll find when you look for things. What else is under there?"

"Clothes," he sang while going through the heap of items. "My other Power Ranger bedroom shoe, socks, my LeapFrog Pad—"

She didn't have the time to hear him sing each item he'd discovered. "Put those clothes in the hamper and those toys in your toy box, please." She stepped out of his room and moonwalked to Missy's beat down to Sha-Lai's room. Sha-Lai had finished cleaning underneath her bed and was straightening her closet.

"How're you doing in here?"

"Good. What do you want me to do after this?"

"You ain't nowhere near done with that closet. You'll need to get a chair so you can fold those sweaters on that top shelf. All of the clothes and shoes you can't wear, bag it up. We'll take it to The Salvation Army. After you've done that, you can clean out that toy chest."

"Okay," Sha-Lai replied, and returned to rehanging her clothes.

Iesha watched her daughter like she was someone else's child. *Who is this compliant child and what did she do with my sassy-mouthed daughter?* She left Sha-Lai in her room and walked back to the living room so that she could vacuum and dust. It dawned on her that the school meeting must have scared Sha-Lai, too. She hadn't been a problem since Monday when it all happened. Iesha sprinkled deodorizer on the carpet and began to vacuum.

She jumped when she saw the front door open. If the vacuum cleaner hadn't been so loud she would've heard Mama Lorraine come in.

"Girl, that thing makes more noise than it picks up dust," Mama Lorraine said. "Turn that toy off. I got the real deal out in the car. We gone steam this nasty rug."

Keeping her children depended on whether or not she passed this inspection, so her mother's comments were more comforting than offending. "Where's the steamer at? In the back or in the trunk?"

"In the trunk. Grab that box beside it while you're out there."

On her way out, she heard her mother call for Sha-Lai and Raquan. "Where my grandbabies at?"

· · ·

It took everything she had not to slam the door behind her mother. It was past eleven o'clock and Mama Lorraine would've still been cleaning if Iesha had let her. After Mama Lorraine failed to catch Iesha's third hint that it was time for her to leave, she called her father and told him to tell her to come home. That almost failed. As far as Iesha could tell, the house was clean hours ago. She worked alongside as Mama Lorraine led her into washing walls, scrubbing floorboards, cleaning the oven and refrigerator, and mopping every floor in the house, including the visible spaces between the washer and dryer. Iesha surveyed the place as she went from room to room to turn out lights. The house was so clean one could eat off the floors.

She was gathering her things and preparing for a shower when she heard a knock. She figured that Mama Lorraine must've left something. She swung the door open without asking who was knocking.

"Momma—"

The two men laughed. "You know Mama Lorraine is in bed," one of them offered.

If looks could kill, Kenny and Nookie would be on their way to Beasley's Funeral Home. Iesha looked them up and down and rolled her eyes. She could tell by their glossy red eyes that they were high.

"May I help you?"

"Oh, so it's like that now? You gotta take our orders for us to see our kids?"

She turned back to look at the wall clock. "In case you didn't know," she said, facing them again, "my kids are asleep by nine o'clock. And since I'm taking orders, I regret to inform you that the drive-thru is closed for tonight." She tried to slam the door, but Kenny held his foot in the way.

"You ain't got to be nasty. My child support is current. How about yours, man?"

Nookie took a step forward. "Mine too." And they walked past her into the house.

She followed them. "Your child support doesn't give you a season pass to use whenever you feel like it."

"Girl, chill out," Kenny warned, including a few choice words. "Since when do you have a problem with us stopping by?" They made themselves at home on the living room couch. Nookie reached for the remote control and turned the television to BET.

She cursed herself for being stupid. *As long as I'm a mother, this is the price I gotta pay for getting mixed up with these two fools.* Kenny and Iesha grew up together on Rush Avenue. He was three years older and was like a big brother to both her and Charity. Even Mama Lorraine called him the son she never had. He organized many street games for the neighborhood children to play. He taught Iesha and the others football, softball, volleyball, and kickball. Iesha knew Kenny liked her because she was such a tomboy and could play just as well as any neighborhood boy.

As things began to change, so did their relationship. Iesha's body was one of the first things to change. Mama Lorraine thought Kenny was just coaching Iesha in sports, but he began coaching her in other personal matters, like sex. Her behavior varied, and she and Mama Lorraine were always arguing about something. She remembered how Kenny had come to her saying that Mama Lorraine had asked him to talk to Iesha for her, because he was the only one who could put some sense into her head. Kenny then urged Iesha to tell her mother about the baby. She was five months' pregnant when she told her parents.

She was so into her thoughts, she didn't notice that Nookie had gone outside. He was returning with a twelve-pack of beer.

"Y'all have to go," she admonished. "I'm not down with our little get-togethers anymore."

Nookie handed Kenny a beer and offered the same to Iesha. She held up her hand. She knew he was probably used to her resisting the first drink and then giving in. But she was determined to uphold the commitment she made to God. "I don't drink anymore."

Nookie pursed his lips. "Since when?"

"None of your business," she frowned. "I have to work tomorrow, so I'd appreciate if y'all just left. You can see the kids tomorrow."

Nookie twisted off the bottle's metal cap. He sipped the beer. "Pass the Heineken and mind your business," he sang, mocking an old LL Cool J song.

She rolled her eyes and got out of her chair to turn the off television. Although Kenny had a lot of mouth, he was more tolerable than his cousin Nookie. Sha-Lai had not yet turned two when Kenny was arrested for drug trafficking. For the six months that he was away, he made arrangements through Nookie, his partner-in-crime, to financially support Iesha. On one of her many lonely nights without Kenny, she confided in Nookie and one thing led to another. The moment happened so fast that it was still a blur in her mind. Yet, in spite of all the drama, the three of them remained friends and had become closer than they were initially. When one of the guys would come to take his child out for a visit, he would take the other child as if it were his own. Kenny and Nookie financially supported both children.

"Did you give up this too?" Kenny asked, waving a thick marijuana blunt in the air.

"Yes," she answered weakly.

Kenny lit the blunt and took a long, deep drag. "This some . . . good stuff . . . here," he choked. She sighed out of frustration, inhaling the pungent aroma. She remembered the house inspection tomorrow.

"Nookie!" she yelled. "Get your drunk behind out of here." She jumped up to pick up the beer bottle he dropped on the floor. "Man, you got beer everywhere."

She walked to the door. "Ya'll got a choice. You can get your mess and go voluntarily or I can call the police and have you escorted out involuntarily. Take your pick." By the way they moved, she knew they could tell she wasn't playing.

• • •

Charity chuckled, thinking about Mama Lorraine and Iesha cleaning together. *Better her than me.* She waited for peace before ending her prayer. She prayed protection for Iesha and thanked God in advance for His favor with her home inspection. She thanked God for keeping her motives pure and guiding her fingers as she wrote a response to Minister Joseph Nelson.

She turned on the computer in her home office and read his letter again to see how she should respond. Although he requested photos of her, she decided she wouldn't send any. She picked up his picture. His smile was contagious. She could not help returning a smile. But her smile faded remembering where he was. *Lord, what is this feeling in my heart? Why am I thinking about this man? Wondering about him? He's in jail and will be for another three years. I ain't waiting on Emmitt that long, let alone a man in jail.*

She decided to pray for Minister Nelson and send a short note to let him know that she'd cover him in prayer. She typed a letter on her ministry letterhead, hoping to convey that she wasn't interested in a personal relationship. This was strictly business. She typed out five sentences, expressing her gratitude for his kind words about the article and signed off by letting him know that she would continue to pray for him. She read her letter several times to make sure it could not be misconstrued in any way.

It was Thursday, and Emmitt was anxious to take a break. His mother hadn't been home from the hospital twenty-four hours and yet she was working him overtime. Her latest request was a glass of Pepsi over ice.

"Anything else?" he asked, handing her the beverage.

She sat up in bed. "I-hiiiii," she sipped. "No, baby, this is it. Thank you."

"I'm getting ready to run some errands. Do you need anything while I'm out?"

"Where are you going?"

A scowl came across his face. "Momma, do you need anything?"

"I ain't trying to be in your business. I was just asking where you were going so I wouldn't have you going out of your way."

He gave her the same look he gave Dr. Metcalf, letting her know he was not convinced. "I'm taking Shawanda to Wal-Mart and then we're taking Destiny to that McDonald's with the indoor playground."

"Umph. I don't know what you see in that little bald-headed girl, and her little ugly baby—"

"Ma, do you want something from Wal-Mart or McDonald's?"

"Boy, get your draws out of your butt. You weren't that protective over your own wife, and you gone disrespect me for a floozie."

"I'm sorry, Ma—"

"Now, I appreciate you taking care of me but you are not going to treat me any kind of way in my own house. If you gone disrespect me, don't even call me Momma, just call me Elaine." She put her hand over her chest.

"Momma, are you okay?"

"Yes, I'm fine." He saw a tear slide down her cheek. "I just hate being a burden to you. You don't deserve a sickly mother. I just wish I would go on to glory so you wouldn't have to take care of me. I know you would move out on your own if I weren't so sick, wouldn't you?"

He didn't know how to respond and thought carefully before he spoke. "Momma, don't talk like that. You're not a burden to me. I'm your oldest son and all you have, why wouldn't I take care of you?" He wiped her tear and brought the bottle of medication she asked for. He watched her chase down the anti-anxiety pills with Pepsi. He stayed with her until he felt comfortable leaving. And that was not until an hour and a half later, when she'd fallen asleep.

He left the house angry, feeling the same way he had when he and Charity were together. He had chosen his mother over his relationship again. Shawanda was going to be pissed at him for not answering his cell phone, or returning her messages over the past two hours. He psyched himself up to face her. She would just have to understand that his mother is sick and needs him. *If she can't understand that, then she can do just what Charity did, leave me alone. Don't make me no never mind.*

Charity thought about her session with Mr. Wright and laughed. He completed the homework assignment she'd given him. The three black women he could positively relate to were Jada Pinkett Smith, Vivica A. Fox, and Queen Latifah. He said that he had always been impressed by their roles in the movie *Set It Off*. If she didn't know any better she would swear that he'd stopped taking his medications. He seemed to be tired today. He didn't have too much to say and he wasn't as grandiose as he had been on Monday. "That man is crazy," she mused. As well educated as he seemed, Charity thought that he would have identified at least one historical black female. Charity flipped to the front of his chart to see where he worked. He was the owner of Wright Away Auto Detailing. She pretended to shiver. *I wouldn't let that man touch my car with a ten-foot pole.*

Chapter 16

The mailroom employee was looking strangely at Joseph. He waved at her. He knew that she'd seen more of him in the past week than she had in the two years he'd been there.

"It's Friday, Nelson. I know you're expecting something from the courts," a petite black woman with fat goddess braids said from behind the counter.

"Oh yes," he quipped. "All the time. I'm expecting my immediate release any day now."

"I knew it had to be something because you've been here every day this week. You usually only come once or twice."

He considered her comment and made a mental note to change his routine. He hated to be predictable. When he got to his mailbox, he retrieved a small pile. He shuffled past a musical instruments catalog, a brochure from the correspondence Bible college he was enrolled in, and a few letters. When he read the return address on an ivory linen envelope, he thrust his right arm out and pulled it back in, "Yes!"

The mailroom clerk ran around to where he was. "You got it? You got your papers?"

He chuckled. Even though he mostly spoke by faith, he was

amazed that people trusted what he said. "No, ma'am." He held up the envelope. "This isn't from the courts, but it's just as good."

"You're a good man, Nelson. I ain't never seen you down. Even when you didn't get what you were expecting, you're satisfied with what you got."

"That's because I serve a mighty God."

Joseph was so into reading Minister Phillips's letter that he stood in the same spot until he was done. He waved good-bye to the mailroom clerk as he raced to the weight room to meet his friends.

"Allen! Hankins! I told you!" he yelled across the room. He was frantically waving the letter in the air. "She wrote back."

Allen dismounted the stationary bike and wiped his brow with the white washcloth he took from the waist of his gray sweat-pants. Hankins finished his last set of sit-ups before he got off the mat. Joseph's grin was so wide that his friends grinned with him. "I told you man," he declared. "God is awesome. It ain't nothing He won't do for those who seek Him."

Allen took the letter from him.

"Read it out loud," Hankins demanded.

Allen cleared his throat. "Dear Minister Nelson. I wanted to promptly acknowledge your letter and thank you for your kind words about 'I Have No Man.' It was definitely the Spirit of God who encouraged and blessed you through the article. Thank you so much for encouraging me. Keep reading *Today's Gospel*, per-haps we will meet again in its pages. Stay blessed as I will keep you in my prayers. Minister Charity Phillips."

Joseph folded his arms in suspense as he waited for his friends' response. Allen looked as if he couldn't believe what he'd just read.

"Man, I'm in awe," Allen said, shaking his head. "This has kicked my faith up another notch."

Hankins reached for the letter. "Forgive my doubt and unbe-lief. I gotta read this for myself."

Joseph stood there basking like he'd just performed in a major production. "I told y'all. Just because we're in here doesn't mean that God has forgotten about us. He cares about us and even our smallest desires. While this letter ain't but five sentences, she wrote back."

Allen was still shaking his head when he took Joseph's hand and laid it on his head. "Man, lay hands on me so that anointing can rub off on me."

"You ain't seen nothing yet."

Chapter 17

"Hey, Mr. Wright," Iesha called as he was coming into the suite. "You're right on time. Charity's still in session."

He looked at the office clock. "How much time do I have?"

"About an hour. We're just going down to the courtyard for lunch."

"All right. I need to go ahead and get started." He handed her a duplicate form. "Fill this top part out for me. This is the invoice."

Iesha looked at the form. "This is for Charity. Should I put her address on it or mine?"

"Put hers on there. I use the addresses to send my customers coupons and other special promotions."

Iesha considered writing a fake address but she could not think of one, and he needed to leave before Charity uncovered their secret. "Here you go. How much do I owe you?"

"Since it's a surprise and it's for my therapist, I'll do the car for forty dollars."

"You know she drives an Explorer?"

"It's still forty dollars. You got the keys?"

She had to lie to Charity to get her keys. Iesha told her she thought that she lost her earring in the Explorer on Monday when

Charity drove her to the school. She reached under the desk to get her purse. Mr. Wright gave her the top yellow copy of the form and he took the pink copy. She gave him Charity's keys, paid him the money, and shooed him off. She heard Charity coming down the hall, talking to her client.

Iesha threw her purse under the desk and pretended she was looking for something on the floor.

"Iesha?" Charity called.

She rolled her chair back and sat up. "I'm right here. I dropped my pen." She lifted her pen for Charity and her client to see.

"Will you check Ms. Rutledge out and book her again in two weeks?"

"I got it."

"Ms. Rutledge, you take care. I'll see you in two weeks."

Charity walked back to her office.

"Don't take too long back there," Iesha called after her. "I'm hungry."

They ordered from Schlotsky's and sat down to eat. Charity blessed the food.

"Charity, have I told you lately that I like working for you?"

Charity smiled. "No, but I'm glad you do. Have I told you lately that I like having you work with me?"

"No, but I'm glad you do."

They both giggled, ate, and talked about everything that came to mind. Charity remembered to tell Iesha to watch for Emmitt's package, which should arrive on Monday, and talked about going to the banquet with Minister Adams that night. Iesha talked about being nervous about her date with Wallace. Somehow the subject turned to Harmony.

"I see you and Harmony are getting along better."

Iesha raised her eyebrows and nodded her head. "Yeah, pretty much. She turned out to be cool."

"See. You have to get to know people. You can't judge a book by its cover."

"Oh, I still think the sister is a little out there, but at least she knows when to come back to earth. Literally."

Charity laughed. "You're silly. I like Harmony. Once you get past her earthiness, you'll find that she's really a wise woman."

"How in the world did y'all two hook up?"

"I met her at a counselors' conference about two years ago. We were in a session where we had to split up in groups, and she and I were assigned to the same group. I learned so much about myself in that one group we were in. During one of our assignments I shared my goal about opening a private practice and she encouraged me to do it. So I told her if I ever did I would look her up. *Voila!*"

"Girl, I done told you about that West-side French you speak." Iesha finished the first half of her club sandwich. "Y'all's meeting sound like a divine intervention."

"I'd say so."

"Do you think she's *really* saved, though?"

"Yes or she wouldn't be at Horizons. I don't care how good of a counselor I thought she was, if she was not saved she wouldn't be here. I will not be unequally yoked with anybody. That's why Emmitt and I are not together."

"I was just asking because Terrence said that reading horoscopes is wrong and she was reading them on Tuesday."

Charity could feel the wrinkles in her forehead. "Oh yeah, we don't play that. That's witchcraft." Charity thought back to Tuesday to see if she could remember anything significant. Then she remembered the staff meeting, her prayer, and Harmony's coughing. She decided to keep her thoughts to herself and deal with Harmony in her own way.

Charity motioned for Iesha to turn around to see who was standing behind her.

"Wallace!" she gasped. "I was just telling my sister about our date tonight."

He held out his hand for Charity to shake. "Nice to meet you, ma'am."

"Hi, I'm Charity," she greeted. She continued eating in attempts to ignore the two of them acting like kids with high school crushes on each other. When Wallace left, Charity encouraged her sister. "He seems nice and he's nice looking. Does he work in Present Day?"

"Yes, his office is upstairs. He's a financial analyst."

"Now I know where to find you when you ain't around." She looked at her watch. "Are you about ready?"

Iesha looked at her watch. "Oh no. We have a few more minutes. I have a surprise being done for you. It should be ready by the time we get back."

"Uhhh. What is it?"

"A surprise."

"Give me a clue."

"Okay, just one. You were complaining about how dirty it was the other day."

Charity looked confused. "Let's see. What do I have that's dirty? Momma's mouth?"

"You better not let your momma hear you say that. But that's not it."

"My house?"

"Nope."

"Dirty? I can't think of anything."

"That's 'cause you a neat freak."

"I give up."

"Okay."

"Huh!" Charity inhaled with her mouth wide open. "I know what it is. My nasty car!?!"

"You got it."

Charity looked even more confused. "What's being done to it?"

"I have one of those traveling auto detailers cleaning it in the parking lot."

"That's expensive. This man was going to charge me a hundred and fifty dollars. Did you get a good deal?"

"Get all outta my business."

"Thank you, thank you," she said as dramatically as a contestant being crowned Miss America.

"What company is doing it?"

"You're not going to believe it." Iesha leaned in closer. "I hired Wright Away Auto Detailing."

The name sounded familiar to Charity. She thought for a moment. "Oh my God. Iesha please tell me that's not Jeffrey Wright's company."

"What?"

Charity threw the used napkins and straw wrapper onto her tray and stood to take it to the trash can. "Oh my God. Girl, let's get out of here. Just tell me he doesn't have my keys."

Iesha's mind was racing so fast, she couldn't answer or speak. She just followed behind Charity who was visibly upset.

"I'm sorry, Cherry. I was just—"

"Is there any chance you gave him my address?"

The tears Iesha shed were all the answer Charity needed. She left Iesha standing there sobbing, and like a mother looking for her lost child she ran back to Horizons. Harmony was at the front desk when Charity entered. Harmony had a confused look on her face. Seconds later, Iesha came through the door.

"Charity, your patient Jeffrey Wright came by, but he was looking for Iesha." Harmony opened Iesha's top drawer on her desk and fetched Charity's keys. "Iesha, he told me to give you these keys and let you know that he's all done with your car. I know you didn't hire him to work on your car."

"I didn't know . . ."

Charity took the keys from Harmony before she turned to go to her office. She heard Harmony tell Iesha, "Honey, you never hire a client. I don't care what profession you're in. And you never give a serviceman your whole set of keys. Didn't you hear about that woman who went to have her car repaired and gave them her whole set of keys? They made a copy of her house key and broke into her house and raped and killed her."

Charity stormed off to her office. Since no crime had been committed she couldn't call the police, but she could, however, call a locksmith.

Minister Adams would arrive in thirty minutes to pick up Charity, but she still wasn't ready. She'd left work to wait at home for a locksmith who'd told her that he'd be there at 3:00. That was an hour and a half ago. The first two locksmiths she called were booked through Monday. She wished she had called Minister Adams earlier and canceled, but she didn't want to disappoint Angel and Guy, the directors of the Grace House. She justified that going to the banquet would probably do her some good and take her mind off things.

"Lord, Psalm 127 says that unless *You* build the house, the laborers work in vain and unless *You* keep the city the watchmen stay awake in vain. God, I have no choice but to trust You. Keep my boundaries intact, Father, as You have promised. I bind up the works of the enemy and rebuke fear in the name of Jesus. I call my house, my son, and myself safe. In Jesus' name I pray, Amen." In attempts to keep a positive attitude she kidded herself, "At least I don't have to drive tonight." She'd felt violated earlier driving home from work in her sports utility vehicle.

The doorbell interrupted her race against time to get dressed. She was grateful that Minister Adams was twenty minutes late. She limped to the door with one shoe on and the other in her hand. "Hello," she greeted. She stepped to the side and ushered him in with the shoe in her outstretched hand. "Come on in. Let me get my jacket and purse."

She turned to walk away. He gently grabbed her by the arm and pulled her into him for an apologetic one-armed hug. "I'm so sorry I'm late. I was held up at the shop."

She pushed herself away. "That's okay. I needed the extra time." She hoped she didn't offend him, but she really wasn't in the mood to be around anyone.

He pulled a corsage of white roses from behind his back. "I was held up at the florist shop buying this for you."

Her lips spread into a sincere smile. She sighed. "Ohhh. You're so sweet. Thank you. I needed this; today's been one of those days."

"You're welcome." He followed her instructions to sit while she went to another room to gather her belongings.

"Are you ready?" Charity returned to find him with his arms sprawled across the back of her sofa and his feet on her coffee table. He was acting like he lived there. His making direct eye contact with her as he stood caused Charity to drop her gaze.

"I was born ready for this moment." He held out his arm for her to take and they walked to his car arm in arm.

The ride began uncomfortably silent. "You look very nice," she said in an attempt to make conversation.

He sighed. "I'm sorry." He looked over at her and then back to the road. "In my thoughts I have told you over and over how beautiful you are, and how lovely you look tonight, but I failed to say it out loud. You look extraordinary."

"Thank you, Minister—"

"It's okay for you to call me Michael."

"Thank you, Michael." She looked out the window. She needed to erase today's event from her mind. She prayed Psalm 91:2 silently. *I will say of the Lord, He is my refuge and my fortress: My God; in Him will I trust.*

"A penny for your thoughts."

Attempting to regain her composure she replied, "I was just thinking of a good way to tell you about my friend."

He looked disappointed. "A male friend?"

"Oh no, Sister April Cloud."

"Oh yes, the light-skinned young lady you're usually with in church?"

"Yes, her."

"What about her?" He laughed like he was getting ready to hear a good joke.

"She would die if she knew I was breaking it to you like this. But, she likes you."

His smile changed into a frown. "Oh. So that's why you're always so short with me?"

She laughed heartily and relaxed a little more now that the attention was off of her. Ignoring his question she started talking about April. "April is beautiful inside and out. She has a wonderful spirit. I couldn't have asked for a better armor bearer. I've known her for five years, and she has never been anything other than a woman of prayer and faith. You'll really like her when you get to know her."

"What if I told you that I'm not interested in getting to know her?"

Charity sat silently for a moment. "You're entitled to that," she laughed. "But that doesn't mean I wouldn't keep trying to get you two together."

He looked like he was enjoying the conversation. "Do you know what she likes about me?"

"Yes, she thinks you're the best thing since sliced bread. She's always talking about how fine you are and how nice a smile you have. How articulate and refined you are. When you preach, she hangs on every word you say. And when you sing, the girl squirms in her seat. She adores you."

He blushed. "What do you think?"

"About what?"

"About me?"

"I think you guys would make a good couple."

"I'm not letting you off that easily. I meant what do you think about *me*?"

She went straight into her detached therapist's mode. "I think you are a very nice young man whom I would recommend for my best friend."

"Oh, that's cold."

"What?" She blushed.

"So, there is no way you would consider getting to know me for yourself?"

"Okay, I say this respectfully, so I pray that I don't offend you. I think you're a very nice man and Pastor King speaks highly of you, which is commendable. But my best friend likes you, so I would never consider you for anything except a boyfriend for her. Now, how about some music?" She moved to turn on his radio. "I like this song." She bobbed her head to The Cross Movement's "Cry No More."

He turned the music down. "I apologize if I offended you and I understand your position. So, let's start over . . . What do you do for a living?"

"I'm a therapist."

"And I bet you're a good one, too."

For the rest of the ride to the banquet, laughter and conversation came easily for the two of them. They talked about their childhoods, college experiences, dating, marriage, and ministry. They were both surprised to learn how much they had in common. Charity was more convinced than ever that he'd be perfect for April.

The evening had not come soon enough. Iesha needed a night out on the town after surviving the week she'd had. A run-in with DSS on Monday, the home inspection yesterday, and the hurt she'd caused her sister today made her court hearing victory bittersweet. Her case was closed and a night out would be the best way to celebrate. During the home inspection, Ms. Styre, the social worker, had worked her last nerve. Iesha refused to believe that checking the refrigerator for food, the stove to see if it was working properly, and the bathroom for toiletries, was really a part of the procedure. She was just being nosy. *Now I know why all of those social workers were killed a couple of years ago in Rowan County. Barging into people's houses.* Iesha knew the woman was just doing her job, but some things were ridiculous. Like the fact that she noticed the empty beer bottles in the recycling bin. She didn't have any business looking in there. Iesha knew she didn't believe her story about her relationship with the kids' fathers and how they just dropped by whenever they felt like it. She even explained to her that she had just gotten saved and no longer drinks. Ms. Styre listened patiently and appeared to understand but Iesha easily tired of all of her questioning.

She surveyed herself in the full-length mirror, turning this way and that, to get an all-around view of her red halter dress. She was smoothing it out at her hips with her hands when the phone rang. She figured that it was Wallace, and he'd probably be calling for better directions. Even though she grew up in Charlotte, she was terrible at giving directions.

"Hello?" she greeted in her sexiest voice.

"Hello, may I speak to Iesha?"

She paused before answering because she did not recognize the voice. She got suckered into paying a debt one time when a smooth-sounding brother from a creditor she owed called her. She couldn't bring herself to cuss him out like she had done his predecessors. "This is Iesha. Who's this?"

"Hey you. It's Terrence."

Pretending she did not remember she asked, "Terrence?"

He chuckled. "I'm sorry. That was pretty presumptuous of me to think you'd remember. We met on Tuesday when I delivered flowers to your sister at the office."

"Ohhhhh yeah," she made her voice go up a few octaves. "I remember now. What are you up to?"

"I know this is very last minute, but I'm over here starving and I wanted to know if I could take you to dinner with me."

Disappointed, she answered, "Oh man. I'm on my way out the door going to dinner."

"May I ask you a personal question?"

"Yes?"

"Are you dating anyone?"

"Not really."

"What does that mean?"

"This is the first time that I'll be going out with this person."

He sounded more upbeat. "Good. I won't feel so bad when you decide to leave him for me."

From her window she could see Wallace getting out of a black Lincoln Navigator.

"Well, I gotta go. He just pulled up."

"May I ask you another question?"

"Ter-rence," she whined.

"Is he saved?"

"I don't know but I'll find out."

"That should always be your first question."

"Okay, Daddy. Thanks for the tip."

"I'm not trying to preach. I just want you to know that you won't know what you've been missing until you get with a saved man. If you're not too busy, will you call me tomorrow?"

The doorbell rang. "Yes. I'll call you tomorrow. Good night."

She hung up before he could respond. "I'm coming," she called, loud enough to be heard through the door.

"Hey, gorgeous," Wallace greeted with a kiss on the cheek.

If it weren't for Terrence's comment about saved men, she probably would've enjoyed the greeting much more than she was able to now. "Hey. I'm ready. Should we be leaving?"

He looked at his watch. "Yeah. Our reservations are at seven and we might have to fight dinner traffic."

Wallace grabbed her coat and held it up for her to slide into.

Chapter 18

Tonight, Charity was so proud to be a board member for the Grace House. Guy and Angel, the program directors, had done a lot with a little to give this fund-raising banquet. Because of their charm, ability to work together, and good reputation in the community, many people came out to support their cause. Charity spotted the city's first black mayor, a black television news anchorwoman, and several other prominent black Charlotteans.

Charity and Minister Adams walked into the ballroom. It was tastefully decorated in black and silver. Everything was perfect. She was sure that other board members were just as pleased to see how much their hard work paid off. They solicited donations from several local businesses. The African House loaned the black wrought-iron centerpieces for each table. The Charleston House Restaurant catered the food for free. The Northwest School of the Arts would be performing between recognitions, awards, and speeches. Afterward, DJ EZ Ice would provide music for dancing.

"This is absolutely wonderful!" Charity beamed as an usher escorted her and Minister Adams to the table reserved for board members.

"It is," he replied. "How long have you served on the board?"

"Two years. I'm the secretary and grant writer."

"You must be proud." He pulled out the seat for her.

"I am. This is an excellent turnout for our first fund-raiser. The directors are tithing 10 percent and giving another 10 percent in a scholarship to a high school senior. That person should be here tonight."

"Praise God."

They both looked up when they heard a light commotion. Guy and Angel were walking toward them and bantering back and forth. When Charity and Angel made eye contact, they both squealed in delight.

Charity turned to Minister Adams. "These are the directors, Guy and Angel. They fight all of the time." They both stood up to greet them.

"Charity, you look fabulous dah-ling," Angel said dramatically before hugging Charity.

"Merci, mon ami." Charity stepped back to get a better look at Angel's purple and blue sparkling cocktail dress. *"Très jolie."*

Guy smiled and started singing, interrupting them with a popular tune.

"Hello, Guy." Charity hugged him to stop him from getting louder. He was getting into his song and starting to dance. "Angel and Guy, this is a dear friend of mine, Minister Michael Adams."

Angel hugged him and Guy shook his hand. "Charity's told me a lot about the Grace House. I'm honored to be here with her tonight to support you and your cause."

"Thank you," they replied in unison. Angel winked at Charity and slightly pulled her aside. "Girl, he's a keeper. You better hold on to him." Angel dismissed Charity's motherly look, turned to Guy, and said, "Come on, it's about time to do the welcome."

Charity and Michael returned to their seats. "She's a good woman," Michael smiled. "And she gives godly counsel."

"So, you heard what she said?"

"Yes, you better hold on to me." Then he leaned over closer to whisper in her ear. "It's okay with me if you introduce me as Michael, rather than Minister."

She fanned herself with the program she held in her hand. His being so close to her neck and ear sent a wave of heat through her body. Afraid of what she might say, she nodded and took a sip of ice water. *Jesus keep me near the cross.* She relaxed when other board members joined their table.

Charity and Minister Adams talked during the banquet as easily as they did during the ride. She didn't know he was so silly. He joked about everything from people's outfits to the tough pork loin and rubbery green beans. Charity laughed politely at his comments. But when a woman tripped on the stairs leading up to the stage and Minister Adams said, "And God is able to keep you from falling," her hand across her mouth could not contain the spray of iced tea she spat.

She wiped her mouth and dress with the linen napkin and tried to stifle her laughter long enough to apologize. "Stop it! And pay attention!" she demanded, and playfully hit Minister Adams on his knee. She could see that it was a struggle for him to be quiet. Every now and then he leaned over to her, caught himself, and leaned back in his chair. She commended him with a thumbs-up.

"La—dies and gentle—men," the DJ announced like a circus ringmaster. "It's time to get your dance on and I'm your DJ for tonight, DJ EZ Ice. We're going to be jamming to some old school beats. I'll be taking requests in a little bit. By the way, if you have not yet given your donation, it's not too late. There are several ushers with baskets circulating through the crowd. Give your contributions to them. Make sure they are real *ur-shers* please. The *ur-shers* are dressed in white shirts and black pants. Do not, I repeat, do not give your money to someone who is in a suit or formal gown. Those are not *ur-shers,* those are thieves." The audience laughed. "Here's a tune that'll get you to giving."

The O'Jay's' "For the Love of Money" echoed through the ballroom and transformed the quiet, composed audience into a hands-raised-in-the-air, body-swaying crowd that rushed the dance floor like church folks in an all-you-can-eat buffet line. The incandescent lighting was replaced by floating circles of red, green, and blue lights.

Charity was writing a check when Minister Adams turned to her. "I hope you dance."

"Here?"

He looked at her like she was speaking French again. "Yes. I'm a minister, but I think God knew that even before He gave me the gift of dancing."

"I know we can dance, but should we be dancing to that?"

"How old were you when that song came out?"

Charity thought about it for a few seconds. "I don't know, a toddler maybe."

"Okay, so when you hear it, does it bring up any negative thoughts or feelings?"

"No."

"Well, I hope you'll join me on the dance floor."

She remained glued to the chair.

He leaned in closer to her so she could hear him over the music. "Charity, we are in the world, but not of it. As people of God we must find a balance in all things. Scripture says that an unbalanced scale is an abomination. Yes, most secular music has sensual messages, beat, and tempos, but some do not. The most important thing you can do to determine whether or not you should listen or dance to a secular song is to see what effect it has on your spirit. Now if they play Jodeci, 2 Live Crew, or Snoop Dogg and the Dogg Pound, we need to leave. Because you don't want to see the old Michael." He laughed. "He was a play-ah from the Him-a-lay-ahs."

Charity laughed too. "Okay, but if I embarrass you out there, I don't want to hear it."

He took her hand and led her first to an usher to deliver their donations, and then to the dance floor. When he found an empty spot, he turned around to face her. He was doing a simple two-step move.

Charity followed his lead, except that she moved more stiffly than a candidate being led to a baptismal pool full of cold water. All kinds of questions went through her mind. *When did I get so stiff? Why am I so uncomfortable? Is this really okay?* She then thought back to her college days when she was the life of the party. Parties didn't get started until she arrived. She would easily move to the center of the dance floor and dirty dance with the best of them. Men would leave their partners and stand in line to dance with her. The whole crowd would clear out and watch her as she danced with each and every one of them. The more the crowd cheered, "Go Cherry, Go Cherry," the more she rolled, gyrated, or lowered herself to the ground.

"Are you okay?" Minister Adams yelled over the music.

She nodded. She thought of what Michael said earlier about dancing being a gift. She got angry at herself for not being able to move freely now when she used to dance like a fool. When Michael Jackson's "Don't Stop 'Til You Get Enough" came on, she loosened up a little. Minister Adams smiled in approval. By the third song, they were dancing like partners. Cheryl Lynn's "To Be Real," one of Charity's old favorite songs, began to play, and she chuckled when she remembered how she used to dance with her back turned toward her partner and her behind in his groin. *I cast that down in the name of Jesus.* That was her sign that she needed to sit down. She told Michael that after this song, she wanted to go back to the table. But the DJ slowed the music down and played The Moments' "Love on a Two-Way Street."

"You gotta dance with me on this one," he pleaded.

Charity liked the song, too, so agreed. They kept a safe distance. Minister Adams closed his eyes, and she wondered what he was thinking. She studied his facial features. He was cute, not necessarily handsome. He always kept his small Afro neatly combed and cut. She liked his sideburns. His caramel complexion was smooth, and his lips were full. She dropped her gaze when he opened his eyes.

He watched her intensely. At one point she held his gaze.

"Never look a man in the eye if you don't want him to know what you're thinking," he told her.

She led him off the dance floor without saying anything to him. When they got to the table, she sipped her water; they rested at the table until the program was over.

Iesha was not used to having doors opened for her. She had already gotten out of the car by the time Wallace got around to the passenger side.

"Oh no, let's try this again," he said. "Tonight, it's all about you."

She climbed back into the Navigator. He opened the door and took her hand to lead her out of the vehicle and into the restaurant. CAMPANIA. Iesha read the sign to herself. Wallace opened the door for her and took her jacket. The host welcomed them and greeted Wallace by name. Iesha sat in the chair that Wallace held out for her. She was smiling so hard her cheeks ached.

"I hope you like Italian," Wallace checked. "Campania is the best Italian restaurant in the city."

"If the food is half as good as the ambiance, I'll agree." She looked around and admired the golden walls, rich wood, and candlelight. The starched white table linen and extensive set of silverware made her nervous. She wished she could remember the etiquette she and Charity learned in charm school.

"The food is exquisite," Wallace continued. "Probably as authentic as you can get."

The server arrived and informed them of the chef's recommendations for the evening. Wallace listened intently and moaned after each suggestion. Iesha studied the menu, trying to find out what the server was talking about. That's when she noticed the prices. She gasped. She put her hand over her mouth, imitated the sound, and made her body jump. "Hiccups," she explained to both the server and Wallace. The cheapest thing on the menu was a six-dollar salad. She entertained herself by trying to pronounce the dishes, *Linguine Posillipo* and *Gamberi Mergellina*. She thanked God for the descriptions under each entrée.

"I'll give you a moment to decide. Which of our fine wines may I get for you?"

"A bottle of '94 Chardonnay," Wallace ordered.

Iesha's eyes were still on the menu. She was nowhere near ready to make a decision.

"I'm going to order the *Costoletta alla Pompeii*," he beamed. Iesha must've looked confused because he offered a translation. "It's a charbroiled veal chop that's smothered in an herb garlic butter. It's so good it'll make you wanna run home and slap your momma."

"Well, I'mma stay away from that, because my momma don't play. I'm looking for the chicken dishes."

He picked up his menu and directed her to the chicken section. "Look on the inside, on the right page, second column. See all the *pollo* listings? Those are the chicken entrées. I bet the *pollo cacciatore* is good. That *pollo balsamico* doesn't sound bad, either."

She read the descriptions of each. "I think I'll try the *pollo cacciatore*. It's chicken sautéed with bell peppers, onions, tomatoes, garlic, and mushrooms. That does sound good."

Iesha kept trying to relax. She didn't know if she was nervous because this was her first date with Wallace, or if it was because she thought Wallace might want to be compensated for the $200 he was going to kick out for dinner. The maître d' poured their wine.

"Relax," Wallace insisted. "You look so tense. I don't have any expectations of you." Only the corners of her mouth turned upward. "You don't have to worry about using the right utensil. You can even slurp out of your glass if you want to." He laughed at himself, making her laugh too. "You don't have to impress me, I'm already impressed, with'cho fine self."

Wallace continued talking while they waited for their food. Iesha listened and waited patiently, knowing he would invite her to talk about herself. During the one week that they'd been communicating, she hadn't talked much about herself. Mainly because he hadn't asked. He was always doing the talking, and it was always about himself. Tonight she learned the rest of his life story. How he'd grown up poor but was determined to have more as a man than he had as a boy. He went to North Carolina A&T State University and studied accounting and finance. That's where he learned to make and manage his money, and that's where he decided he wanted to help other people do the same. He was still talking when the server delivered the food. She was so bored that she found herself wishing she'd gone to dinner with Terrence. Every now and then she looked up from her dish to nod and say, "uh huh." He was so self-absorbed he didn't notice that she wasn't listening. Even though her meal was excellent and the chicken melted in her mouth, she couldn't eat. She wanted to go home.

"How's your meal?" he asked, carving his chop like he was sawing a piece of wood.

"It's good. I just don't feel so hot."

"Anything I can do?" he asked seductively.

She wanted to scream and tell him that his boasting was making her sick to her stomach. "No." She forced a smile. "I think I'm coming down with that twenty-four-hour bug my kids had last week."

"You have children? How many do you have?"

Finally, a question about her. But it hit her like a ton of bricks—he was only interested in one thing. They'd been talking all of this time and he didn't know she had children.

She pushed her plate away. "I have a nine-year-old daughter and a seven-year-old son, Sha-Lai and Raquan." She paused. She finally had the opportunity to talk about herself and she didn't know what to say.

Wallace looked thoughtful. Iesha thought he would guide her by asking more questions. "I don't have any children. I would like to have some though," he said, raising his eyebrows.

Her stomach churned. "I'm sorry, Wallace. I'm coming down with something. Would you mind if we ended our night early?"

He looked annoyed. "No, I don't mind. I understand."

He obliged too easily. Iesha thought he must have a trick up his sleeve. She followed his lead and arose from her chair after he did. He thanked the waiter and left.

"Wallace, did you pay?"

"Did I ask you to?" he snapped. "Of course I did."

Iesha looked at him like he was crazy. "Just take me home, now."

He softened. "I'm sorry. It's just that this evening is not going like I planned. I wanted to wine and dine, and get to know you."

"Oh yeah? How well did you get to know me over dinner?"

"Hardly. Our evening was not going to stop after dinner. I had other things planned."

She picked up her pace. "Obviously."

He unlocked and opened the door for her. As he walked around to let himself in, she smiled to herself. It was only 8:30. If she was lucky, Terrence would still be hungry.

"Iesha, I really am sorry. Will you let me make it up to you?"

"Wallace, you don't have to make anything up to me. I blame myself just as much as you're blaming you." She smiled, even wider when he started the car.

He drove to her house mostly in silence. When he pulled into her driveway, he was barely parked before she opened the door. "Wait! Can I at least say good night?"

She grabbed her stomach. "I'm sorry, the ride made me a little queasy. I'm trying to get to the bathroom as quick as I can."

He touched her forehead and then her neck to see if she was feverish. "Let me follow you in to make sure you're okay. I'd like to at least tuck you in."

She realized that she was going to have to turn this up a notch; he was not catching the drift, and time was of the essence. *I'mma have to get ghetto on him.* "Look, I'm not some poor little girl that's looking to be rescued. Or some ho looking to be paid for. 'Cause if that's what you think, you can back this thang up and get on up outta here."

She stormed to her front door. For effect, she wiped her eye.

Not even a minute after she slammed the door closed, he was ringing the doorbell. She pinched herself and thought of every bad thing she could to muster up tears. When a steady stream flowed down her cheek, she cracked the door open.

He looked worried when he saw that she was crying. "Oh, Iesha. I'm sorry. What can I do? I mean, what happened? I don't want to leave like this."

She couldn't believe that he was falling for her drama queen routine. She knew it worked on roughnecks, but was annoyed to see it work on educated brothers, too. "I just want to be alone. I'll call you tomorrow."

"Are you sure?"

"Yes." She slammed the door. She didn't move until she heard him drive away.

Terrence's number was the last entry on her caller ID, so she dialed him back. She pounded her fist on the bed when his voice mail picked up. "Hey, Terrence, it's Iesha. I was hoping you'd be at home and still hungry. If you get this message within the hour, call me. Maybe we can catch a movie. If not, give me a call tomorrow. Talk to you later, bye."

Chapter 19

It was either now or never. Emmitt decided that today was the day to tell his mother about his apartment. He and Shawanda paid his deposit and first month's rent yesterday and James was going to help him move in tomorrow. Since his mother was usually in a good mood on Sundays, he thought that today would be a good day to break the news.

"Ma?" He tapped on the bathroom door. "You don't have to cook this morning. I'm taking you out."

"You are?" she hollered from behind the door.

"Yes, you need to get out and get some fresh air. When can you be ready?"

"Uh . . . give me fifteen minutes."

The first part of his plan was compete; now on to the hard part. It was difficult to decide if he should tell her about the apartment before breakfast and take her to see it afterward, or wait until after breakfast and just take her to see the apartment. He decided on the latter. The last thing he needed was for her to show out at Shoney's.

He let her do most of the talking on the way to the restaurant. He didn't want to prematurely break the news. He did take her on the long scenic route, driving past the apartment complex, hoping she would say something about them. But she didn't.

"Has Charity gotten them papers yet?"

"No, ma'am. She should get them tomorrow."

"I should've known she ain't got them yet, 'cause we ain't heard from her. You talk to the baby?"

"No, I'mma call him tonight."

"You must have something important to talk to me about, since you taking me out."

He swallowed hard. "No. I just want to get you out of the house."

"Boy, please. I carried you for nine months and two weeks, went through fourteen hours of labor, and raised you for thirty-two years. I know you better than that. What is it?"

He pulled into someone's driveway, made a U-turn, and went the other way. "I want to show you something." He pulled a paper from his glove compartment and looked at it. He drove up to a gated apartment complex and entered the five digits recorded on the paper. The gates retracted.

Neither of them spoke. He drove past the clubhouse, the mailboxes, a playground, and two complexes before he parked the car. He hopped out and opened her car door for her. "This is what I want to show you."

He led the way to a lower-level apartment and with his key unlocked the door. He turned back to invite her in and to see her response. He was surprised that she was not yet distraught. "Momma, I didn't know how to tell you this, but the attorney told me that if I wanted to get Xavier I needed to get my own place. I don't want to move, but I have to for the baby." He didn't care that he called Xavier a baby, he was treading lightly with her.

"I know." She reached into her purse and pulled out an opened envelope. "This came on Thursday." She handed it to him.

It was a letter from his attorney outlining all of his recommendations and the proceedings they discussed. Emmitt contained his anger—she was making it easier for him to leave her.

He wondered if this was the first piece of mail she withheld from him. "Momma, why didn't you say something to me or at least give me my mail?"

"I was going to, but it was the day after I got out of the hospital. You'd gone to Wal-Mart."

Emmitt remembered what the doctor said about her faking a heart attack and about their codependent relationship. He decided to test her. "Momma, what else have you been keeping from me? What did the doctor say about your *heart* attack?"

She looked away. "He said it was mild and that if I eat right, limit my salt and pork intake, and take my medicine I should be fine."

"What kind of medicine did he give you?"

She stopped to think. "Wait a minute, I'm your momma. Why are you questioning me?"

"Momma, Dr. Metcalf told me about the tests he ran. I know you didn't have a heart attack—"

"You don't have no respect for me. I don't know why you're still calling me Momma. I told you to call me Elaine, with your disrespectful self. I never talked to my momma the way you do me. You treat them heifers in the street better than you do me. If I didn't have a heart attack, you sure is trying to give me one."

Emmitt surprised himself by not backing down. "He also told me I need to go to some Codependents Anonymous meetings. Something to help me learn how to be your son, and not your husband."

He knew his words cut like a knife. But he was determined to be free from her today. The sting from her slap across his face was duller than the guilt he felt.

Emmitt braced himself; he saw her clenched fists by her side. Then, it looked like she changed her tactic. Instead of hitting him, she clutched her chest and started gasping for air. He watched her let herself fall to the ground. "Em—Emmitt, call 9-1-1."

"Oh no you don't. Get up, Momma. I'm not falling for this mess no more. Get up!" *She's getting good at this game.* He stood there watching as she rolled her eyes up into her head. He wanted to be funny and hand her some lip balm; her lips were so dry they looked purplish. "Okay, you win, Momma." He yanked his cell phone from his belt clip and dialed the first two digits of the emergency number. "I'm dialing 9-1-1 for real, you can get up now."

He wasn't surprised when she didn't move. He knew she wanted him to call the paramedics. He let her lay motionless at his feet.

"May I get the paramedics to Highland Bridge Apartments? I'm in 5000-A. I think my mom is sick . . . I don't know, she says she's having trouble breathing . . . No, she's not talking now . . ." He was annoyed with all of the operator's questions. All of this nonsense for nothing. The operator asked him to check her for a pulse. Even though he was a security guard and trained in CPR, he thought his techniques were off because he didn't feel anything. "I don't know, can y'all just hurry up?" He shook his mother. She didn't respond. He was starting to get scared. "Momma? Momma? Get up! Come on, Momma, get up! I believe you." The operator told him that the paramedics had already been dispatched and that she needed him to start CPR on his mother. He put the phone down and placed his mouth over her purple lips and expelled the contents of his lungs into hers. "One-one thousand, two-one thousand, three-one thousand, four-one thousand, five," he counted out the compressions as he gave them and tried to breathe life into her. He compressed her chest again. "Oh, God!" he sobbed. "Oh, God, she's not breathing," he announced to the operator.

"Everything's going to be okay," the operator said. "I hear the sirens in the background. Go outside where they can see you."

If it wasn't the first Sunday and she had known that Pastor King wouldn't be looking for her, Charity wouldn't have come to church. She was exhausted. She and Iesha came to an understanding that they both felt okay about what happened with Mr.

Wright. Charity verbally forgave her sister, and was glad that her court hearing had gone well, but feelings of anger kept cropping up. Add that to the minister's meeting that turned into a cat fight, and Emmitt's mother's death, she felt like she had a good reason to stay home.

She couldn't believe that men of God from the church would act the way they did. Reverend Hubbard was so mad he cursed female ministers and threatened to resign. Charity was humiliated. Despite her protest, Pastor King decided that she would call the congregation to worship until the first Sunday of March and that they would all rotate every month.

This morning the tension was so thick in the pastor's study, Charity believed she could cut it with a knife. She excused herself to go to the bathroom and stayed there until she was sure it was time for them to walk into the sanctuary together. The congregation seemed more eager to worship. When she performed the call to worship, she didn't have to admonish the congregation, she simply exalted God, adored His Son, and acknowledged His Spirit. Like sponges soaking up water, the worshippers received every word she spoke.

Church services proceeded as the clerk read the announcements, the hostess recognized the visitors, and the choir sung its selections. But Charity was uncomfortable. She felt like she was being watched. She studied the congregation to see if she could find who was watching her. She did see a man she didn't recognize smiling at her. She tried to ignore the feeling but couldn't. She decided that she would change seats when the tithe and offering appeal went forth. The congregation would then be too distracted to notice her. When the ushers led the congregation pew by pew to the altar to give their gifts, Charity moved to the empty chair beside Pastor King.

The feeling went away. She braced herself for the sermon. She was expecting a blessing today.

After his introductory remarks, Pastor King told the congregation to turn their Bibles to Isaiah 54. That was confirmation for her—that particular chapter was one of her favorites. "When you get there say 'Amen,' if you ain't there, say 'hold up,' and if you don't have a Bible, say 'it don't even matter.'" The sound of laughter and turning pages was melodic. He waited momentarily and instructed the congregation to read verses 16 and 17 along with him. "The subject I want to teach from today is, 'The weapon forged against me is an instrument formed for me.' Turn to your neighbor and look them dead in the eye and say, 'neighbor.'" The crowd parakeeted in unison. "I stopped by to tell you . . . that the weapon forged against you . . . is an instrument formed for you. Now give your neighbor a high five."

Charity listened intently as she jotted notes on the back page of her bulletin. "There's a difference between the words 'forged' and 'formed,' " Pastor King asserted. "When the word 'forge' is used as a noun it refers to an open furnace where metal is heated to be shaped. For example, a blacksmith uses a forge to create weapons. The verb form of 'forge' means to imitate fraudulently, like signing someone else's name to cash a check that doesn't belong to you. Stay with me now, I'm going somewhere with this. The word 'form' means to mold, create, compose, to make or produce. Saints, I stopped by to tell you that the weapon the enemy has forged against you, the one he stayed up all night long putting in and taking out of his forge—is a counterfeit, an imitation. It's a knockoff, it ain't even real." The congregation encouraged him to go on. "Quit getting upset when he throws something at you, quit getting distracted, quit giving up. Next time he come at you, do like you do at the flea market, say 'I ain't buying this, it don't even look real.' What he doesn't realize is that when he throws a weapon at you, he's giving you ammunition to use against him. I can't get no help in here this morning. I said, when he throws a weapon at you, he's giving you an instrument to use against him. Every time he messes with your children, every time he messes with your finances, with your car, with your spouse, with your stuff, and you speak the word out of your mouth, it becomes as sharp as any two-edged sword."

She was pleased that she had received a word of encouragement. She didn't want to talk to anyone; she wanted to go home and anoint and reclaim her house. She realized that she'd been living in fear and expecting something bad to happen knowing that Mr. Wright had briefly taken her keys. She knew her mind was playing tricks because she would swear that things were misplaced in the house. *Xavier could've moved those things for all I know.* She directed her thoughts toward the devil. *You want a fight, you just picked one and I ain't backing down this time.*

After the benediction, Charity gathered her purse, keys, and Bible and was ready to walk in her renewed confidence, when Minister Adams approached her.

"Minister Phillips, I was wondering if you would have dinner with me."

Didn't I just tell this fool . . . "Obviously I didn't make myself clear to you Friday night about where I stand with you." She stepped back when he reached for her hand.

He put his arm on her shoulder and said, "I heard you but I also heard Pastor's sermon today. You are worth fighting for . . ."

She tuned him out, removed his hand, and looked up to see April rolling her eyes and storming out of the sanctuary.

"Oh, God. Look what you did." She ran after April, but the tight pockets of people made her lose sight of her. She made her way toward April's parking space, but by the time she got to the back door, April was speeding out of the parking lot. Defeated, she returned so that she could pick up Xavier from children's church.

"Minister Phillips?" a young woman she didn't know broke her stride.

"Yes?"

"It's good to meet you." She extended her hand toward Charity. "I've heard so much about you." Charity must've looked confused. "My name is Sharon Nelson. I'm Joseph's sister."

Do I know a Joseph? "Joseph?"

"Minister Joseph Nelson? From Kentucky? He's my brother."

"Hi, are you a member here?"

"Oh no, I go to Shiloh. Joseph asked if I would come to meet you. He thought you might feel more comfortable communicating with him if you had some personal contact with someone . . . someone to let you know he's not crazy," she laughed.

Charity half laughed, knowing that Sharon had read her thoughts.

"Well I'm glad you came to visit and I hope you enjoyed the service."

"I did. I always enjoy Pastor King's services. You know, he and my pastor are good friends, but I know him through his wife. I used to sell Mary Kay and she was one of my best customers. She used to throw makeup parties for me, and you know your pastor would be right up in the mix cracking jokes."

"And I know he was. Did you get a chance to say hello to him?"

"No, he looked busy talking to everyone."

The therapist in Charity kicked in, wanting to verify what she'd been told. "I'll take you to him so that you can say hello." Charity led her back to the sanctuary. "Oh, there's First Lady with him."

Before Charity and Sharon could get to Pastor King, his wife saw them coming and started squealing with excitement.

"Sharrrrronnnnn!" Mrs. King hugged Sharon like they were old friends reuniting. "What are you doing here?"

Charity felt relieved to know that Sharon was telling the truth and she listened as they began catching each other up on their lives.

"Where are the girls?" Sharon asked.

"They're around here somewhere. What are you doing these days?"

"I'm in grad school and doing my internship at the county."

Pastor King turned around, after finishing a conversation with one of the church members. "Lord, look who Mary Kay done sent us." He hugged Sharon and then turned to Charity with a puzzled look on his face. "Y'all two know each other?"

"We just met."

"Oh, 'cause you know I have to approve the people you associate with, and I was getting ready to say."

Sharon slapped him on the arm playfully. "Pastor King, don't make me tell Charity them stories from our makeup party days."

"Oh no. Minister Phillips, don't believe anything she says."

Mrs. King turned to Sharon and said, "I wish we could get together for dinner tonight, but we promised the girls to take them shoe shopping. God forbid we renege."

"I'll call you to arrange something so we can get together," Sharon replied. "Minister Phillips, do you want to stop and get a bite to eat? My treat."

"Shoot, if that's the case, First Lady," Pastor King said, "we need to go with them. Sharon's paying."

Charity shook her head at him and answered Sharon, "I've already started cooking so . . . I can't today."

Pastor King put his two cents in, "Sharon, ask her if you can go home with her, Minister Phillips can burn."

Mrs. King chimed in, "Oh yeah, we make sure she brings dishes when there's a church function. What'd you cook for dinner, Minister Phillips?"

Charity smiled, knowing she'd prepared one of their favorites. "Lasagna."

"Honey, you can take the girls to the mall without me," Pastor King joked.

Sharon asked shyly, "Can you feed one more person?"

Since Pastor and Mrs. King approved of Sharon, Charity couldn't find a reason not to. "Sure. You can have dinner with us." *Maybe this is why I didn't feel like having dinner at Momma's today.*

"Please save a doggy bag for me. I know you're going to have leftovers. You cook like you cooking for an army."

Charity let Sharon say her good-byes to the Kings and she excused herself to get Xavier. She was sure that he would be the last child in children's church; everyone was probably long gone. He was eagerly waiting when she picked him up and signed him out.

"Thank you," she said to the youth minister. She joked, "You didn't give him any punch or cookies, did you?" She'd suggested that they offer healthier refreshments. There were some occasions she'd pick Xavier up and he'd be *bouncing off the walls*.

As she walked Xavier toward the sanctuary, she explained to him that they were going to have a guest for dinner. She answered as many of his questions as she could. When she saw Sharon coming from the sanctuary, Charity pointed her out to Xavier.

Xavier ran the short distance to Sharon. "My name's Xavier, what's yours?"

She stooped down and held out her hand for him to shake. "Xavier, it's good to meet you. My name is Sharon."

"Ms. Sharon," Charity corrected.

"Ms. Sharon, are you going to eat dinner with us?"

"Yes, sir. Is that okay with you?"

"Yes. Ummmm, Mommy." He turned to Charity. "What are we eating for dinner?"

"We'll talk about that when we get home, honey. Let's get going." She turned to Sharon. "He'll ask questions all day if you let him."

As Charity drove toward her house, she made sure to use her signal lights and to stop at yellow lights, because Sharon was following them. She was glad that she thought to give her address and cell phone number in case they got separated. She pulled onto her street and drove a little slower. She wanted to make sure that Sharon saw which house she was turning into.

"This is nice," Sharon complimented as she surveyed the house. "Wait until I tell my brother. He is in for a treat. He doesn't know what a blessing you are. Even your street name sounds important—Symphony Woods Lane. I live on Green Street. You can tell the difference, can't you?"

They laughed, and Xavier ushered them up to the house. "Make yourself at home," Charity invited. "You can hang out with Xavier while I get changed and I'll meet you back in the kitchen. Xavier, will you show Ms. Sharon around the house?"

She didn't have to ask twice, he already had Sharon by the hand dragging her to his room.

As fast as she could, Charity changed out of her canary yellow and navy blue suit. She looked for a barrette to secure her hair in a ponytail. She knew there was one in the pocket of her house-coat. She looked all around her room and was annoyed because she couldn't find it. It seemed like her house was swallowing things up—there were lots of small things she couldn't find. *I've told that boy about putting his hands on my things.* She retrieved a rubber band from her vanity and pulled her hair into a ponytail. She began to think about April, then about Sharon and Joseph, and was overwhelmed with her thoughts. "Lord," she prayed. "You know better than I do about what's going on. Open my heart and eyes so that I may see and discern the bigger picture. Also, help me not to be foolish and get ahead of You. Also, Lord, please touch April's heart. In Jesus' name, I pray." Before she went to join Xavier and Sharon, she called April and when she didn't answer, Charity decided to leave a message.

A little more at peace, she went to Xavier's room, where she found Sharon hanging on to Xavier's every word. "And what does this do?" Sharon asked, pointing to the button on the action figure doll he was holding. Charity watched them easily interact and repented for rebuking Emmitt for having their son around Shawanda, someone she didn't know. *Here I am doing the same thing.*

Interrupting her thoughts and their play, Charity joined them. "I take it you guys haven't made it any farther than this room." Xavier made a coy facial expression that his mother loved. He had his father's facial features—drowsy eyes, long eyelashes, and a cute gap-toothed grin. "Thank you for showing Ms. Sharon your room, I'm going to show her the rest of the house."

"I'm going, too." He raced before them to lead.

Charity was nervous about showing off her house. She loved what she had done to it, but Mama Lorraine jokingly called it the *house of many colors*. Every room was a different color. Xavier's room was painted as a sky in electric blue, with white clouds, birds, and butterflies. She even hand-painted a whimsical border below the ceiling. Her room was lavender with a sponged plum overlay, the study was fire engine red, and the kitchen was a bright yellow.

"You should contact *House Beautiful* magazine," Sharon suggested. "I know they would want to put your house in there."

Charity waved the idea off with her hand. "I don't think so." She was impressed to hear that Sharon liked it.

"Is this wallpaper?" Sharon walked into the guest bathroom and touched the forest green and mint julep–striped wall.

"No, I did that myself."

"How did you get the stripes so perfectly even?"

"Measured them with a ruler and taped them off. If you look close enough, you can see the pencil lines in the mint green stripes."

"Girl, Martha Stewart ain't got nothing on you."

"Yes she does. She's got a few million that I don't." They both laughed. "Come on, let's get cooking before I have a whining baby on my hands."

"I'm not a baby."

"That's right," Sharon affirmed. "You're a big boy. Give me five."

Xavier proudly slapped her hand.

They talked like they had known each other for years. It was less than an hour before dinner was ready, and by the time they were done eating Sharon had told Charity everything she knew about her brother. She laughed and cried as she shared the joys and trials of being his younger sister.

"That's why I moved to Charlotte," she confessed. "I was working as a journalist for the Virginia newspaper at the time Joseph was arrested. They were trying to force me to cover the story and I couldn't do it. So I quit. Girl, other journalists and TV broadcasters exaggerated it so bad because he was a police officer that I had to leave Virginia."

Charity was sorry for Sharon and their family. After two years they were still hurting as if the incident happened yesterday. She hated that the night was ending. In some way, Sharon made Joseph more real to her. Everything that he had written about himself and his family, Sharon verified without any prodding from Charity. After Sharon left, Charity prayed with thanksgiving and lifted up Joseph's request for an immediate release. She ended her prayer by asking God for an opportunity to meet Joseph someday.

CHAPTER 20

EVEN THOUGH CHARITY HAD FORGIVEN HER, being back at the office this morning after everything that happened on Friday with Mr. Wright made Iesha feel bad. Every time she tried to do something good, it always backfired in her face. *That's what I get for trying to change. This Christian thing isn't working for me. Life was so much simpler when I was living it my way, doing what I wanted to do.*

She was filing her nails at her desk and reminiscing about the things she missed doing. She could see herself jamming on the dance floor at the Excelsior club, shopping with the girls, and getting her drink on. *I even miss hanging out with Kenny and Nookie. I know I must be desperate now.* Her thoughts switched to Wallace. She cursed herself for dismissing him on Friday night. *I could've had me some, trying to be holy.* She looked at the clock on the computer. He was due to be in his office in a few minutes. She planned to pay him a visit.

There were so many things in the office that rang, she couldn't tell where it was coming from. It wasn't her desk phone. It wasn't the fax. She listened one more time. She snatched her purse from the desk drawer. *My cell phone.*

"Hello?"

"Hey, you."

She forced some enthusiasm into her voice. "Terrence. How are you doing?"

"Disappointed, because I just got your message from Friday night."

"Umph."

"I hate I missed your call. Something told me to stay in Charlotte."

She tried her best to sound interested. "You went out of town?"

"Yes, I went to the beach."

"To the beach?"

"Yep. It's the second week of February, and I went to the beach."

She chuckled. "You're a better man than me."

"That's good to hear. Hey, I was calling to see if I could take you to lunch today. I want to tell you about my beach trip."

What fun, she mocked. "I would love to," she lied. "But I can't today. I have to . . . uhm . . . I have an . . . uhm . . . ." She leaned up to look at her desk calendar for an idea. "I've got something to do." She decided that she didn't have to explain anything to him.

"Either you don't lie very well or you're trying to hide something," he chuckled. "I'm just kidding. I can take a hint. Why don't you give me a call when you're not busy."

"Wallace . . ." Iesha couldn't believe that she blurted out the wrong name.

"On second thought, maybe you shouldn't call me."

"Terrence, I'm sorry. I—"

"Iesha, you don't owe me anything. I'm the one who needs to apologize. I'm sorry I tried to make you want someone you don't want."

She hoped she wouldn't regret this. "No, let me apologize. Right before you called, I was a little down because I messed up big time with my sister on Friday. And I started thinking about how I'm messing up again and that maybe this Christian life ain't for me. So, I was thinking about going back to my old ways and I was thinking about Wallace. But maybe you calling me was a sign from God. You called at the right time." She paused to see if he would respond. When he didn't, she continued. "I can't do lunch with you today." She took a deep breath. "But, I would like it very much if we could meet somewhere for breakfast."

"I would like that, too."

They talked for a few minutes more to arrange to meet at a nearby IHOP. She put a note on Charity's door and left to meet Terrence. It didn't take Iesha long to get there. Since she left right after she hung up from talking to him, she assumed she would beat him there. She lowered her head to pray. "Lord, forgive me. I really don't want to go back where I started. Please help me to continue to move forward. May something be said or done today to let me know I'm on the right track. Thank You. I pray it in Jesus' name."

When she looked up, she saw Terrence waiting. He opened the door when he saw her smile. "I hope you mentioned my name in that prayer."

"My bad." She lowered her head again. "And, Lord, please don't forget to bless Terrence. Amen."

"Amen. I can agree with you on that."

He helped her out of the car and they walked into the restaurant.

She was glad that Terrence broke the silence. "Now that's the advantage of having a late breakfast. They take your order as soon as you sit down."

Iesha agreed. "I hope our food is served just as fast. I'm hungry." Terrence looked her in the eyes. She looked away. "What?"

"I'm just looking. I can look at you, can't I?"

"Yeah, but you making me nervous."

"I'm just admiring you."

"Well, I appreciate it but I thought you wanted to tell me about your beach trip."

"You are something else," he laughed. "The beach trip was

nice. It was so refreshing. It was like being on a secluded island with no one around."

"You went by yourself?"

"Oh yeah. I was feeling like you said you were earlier and I just needed to get away. Just be alone with the Lord."

"Were you ready to give up?"

"No. I have finally surpassed that phase. I was just overwhelmed and needed some direction. I thought I'd heard God wrong on something and I needed to get clarification."

"Did you?"

"Sure enough. But I almost let it go again today."

"Being a Christian ain't no joke. You got to come correct when you walking with God."

"You're right about that."

They stopped talking to receive their food. Terrence asked to hold her hands while he blessed the food.

He took a bite of his country griddle pancakes. "Don't beat yourself up too bad. When you're new in the fold, it's easy to get frustrated with things. Be encouraged, God's going to honor your faith. Don't you dare turn back. Even in the one week that you've been saved, you've come too far to go back where you were."

A feeling washed over her. Her eyes widened. "Terrence, that's just what I was telling God before I came in here. I was just praying about whether I was on the right track. And, He heard my prayer." The realization that God heard and answered her prayer hit her like a ton of bricks. She fought back tears. "My God, He heard me."

He took her hand. "You're saved now. He hears your every prayer. He knows your every thought. And He knows your every desire."

She didn't look away from him this time. "I know. Which is why I'm here with you."

He blushed and dropped his gaze first. "This is going to sound weird, so I understand if you want to run out of here screaming, but I got to tell you. On the day I met you, I knew . . ." He stopped. "Nah, you may not be ready to hear this."

She chewed faster to swallow her pancakes. "I am ready, what is it?"

"You remember saying you were going to call my boss to tell him I was sleeping the day I met you at your office?"

She nodded. "You said you were praying."

"Yes. I was praying because when I saw you, I thought I heard the Spirit say 'that's her.' I was like 'that's her what?' When I realized the Spirit was telling me you were my . . . uhm." He nodded his head toward her to see if she knew what he meant.

"What? Wife?"

He nodded.

She didn't know how to respond. She took another bite of her banana nut pancakes.

"Do you have anything to say about that?"

"I don't know what to say." She shrugged her shoulders. "What do you do when God hasn't spoken to the other person?"

"You wait until He does."

"Okay. Well then we wait." She returned his smile.

"After I talked to you on Friday and learned that you were going out with someone else, I thought I'd heard God wrong, so I took off and drove to the beach. On Saturday I went to this shop and I got this." He reached into his shoulder bag and pulled out a rectangular piece of plastic. "If this wasn't confirmation, I don't know what is." He put it in front of her so that she could read it.

It was a nameplate for her desk.

"Iesha," she read aloud. "Greek origin. Means woman; life; fertile; goddess, literally means female side of God." She looked up at him. "Thank you. All of this time I thought Iesha just meant girl from the 'hood. Now I know what my name means. I wonder how they come up with these things."

"When I asked them to look up your name, it showed this neat diagram of how your name derived from the word 'Jesus.' The male derivatives were Joshua and Isaiah, and Iesha is the female translation. I was floored. My prayer has always been for God to send Himself to me in a woman."

She held her hand up to her heart. "Oh, that's so sweet. And you believe that's me?"

"I believe that."

She laughed and jokingly said, "Boy, you gone make me marry you."

"When?"

"Shoot, I'd marry you tomorrow, if you'd ask." When she saw his expression, she changed her response. "I was just kidding. That was a jokey joke."

"I know." He looked at his watch. "We'd better get finished before you lose your job and I lose my business."

"Your business?"

"Yes." As if he remembered something he said, "Oh that's right, you never looked at the business card I gave you, did you? I own Delivery Direct." He chuckled. "That's why I was encouraging you to call my boss and tell him I was sleeping on the job. I wanted you to call me."

"That's great."

"God has blessed it for four years and counting."

They had to pry themselves away from the table. The only way they could do it was to make plans for dinner.

Charity was glad to find the office empty this morning. She had been meaning to do this ever since she heard the rumor about Present Day closing. She reached in her purse and took out her vial of oil. "Lord," she began to pray. "In the name of Jesus, I consecrate this place to You." With the oil on her fingertip, she drew a cross on the frame of the entry door. "Your name dwells here and Your Word says that if I pray unto You from this place, You will hear and answer me." She moved about the suite anointing whatever she felt inspired to touch. She anointed Iesha's desk and chair, every door, her own office, and finally, Harmony's office. She realized that she had never been in Harmony's office before.

The door was always closed and she never had a reason to visit. "I'll make this real quick," she promised. "Harmony will never know."

Her mouth fell open when she walked in. African woodwork on the walls, a big totem pole in one corner, a yin and yang symbol hanging on the door. She hoped that decorative piece on Harmony's desk was not a real crystal ball. She anointed the desk and the chair. When she went to touch Harmony's bookcase, she noticed books on hypnosis, healing power of meditation, and several self-help books. "Satan, I rebuke you in the name of Jesus. You are a deceiver and a mocker of the power of God. You have been made a spectacle of over two thousand years ago and are disarmed. You have no power. Get out of here, you liar." She prayed in tongues and set her hand to touch the bookcase when she felt someone come into the room. She stopped praying and turned to find Harmony. Even though she was no longer praying, she could feel the flow of prayer still churning within her.

"Did I miss something?" Harmony asked coolly.

"No, I just blessed the whole office suite and your office was last. Everything's all blessed and consecrated."

Harmony walked over to her desk. She took a Kleenex and wiped away the oily cross and set her belongings down. "It was that way before you came in here."

Charity's heart was beating fast but she refused to fear. "Yes, but now that I've been here, God's anointing can flow freely."

"God is love and love is God. There is nothing that can stop the energetic flow of love."

"Harmony, one of the many reasons I recruited you to work with me is because you are one of the wisest women I know. But when Iesha told me that you've been reading horoscopes and New Age books, sanctifying this office became a priority for me. I'm afraid for you, Harmony, because you've allowed Satan to deceive you."

"Perfect love drives out fear, Charity. Since fear is of the devil, I'd say you're the one he's trying to sift."

"That's what I'm talking about. You've never used Scripture out of its context. Something's going on with you, Harmony." She surveyed the office again. "Look at this," she pointed to the African woodwork on the walls. "You don't know what this is, where it came from, and what spirits it has attached to it."

"I use it as a point of contact to bless my ancestors."

"Come on, Harmony, you're smarter than that. I know you got that from one of those self-help books. You know we don't believe in communicating with the dead. Sit down, Harmony, and let's talk this out."

Charity relaxed when Harmony did as she suggested. "Those New Age books twist the Word of God and pervert what we believe in. Karma, energy, reincarnation, mind control . . . all of that mess is perversion of the Gospel."

"Karma is real, Charity. Even the Bible tells you that what you reap, you sow."

"Yes it does, but it doesn't attribute the outcome to energy of the universe. It puts the responsibility solely on us."

"That's right. That's exactly what I've learned through my study of everyday miracles, that we choose our own destinies."

Lord, please help me minister to her. "Harmony, you know that our lives are predestined. God knew us before we were even formed in the womb."

Harmony scratched her head. "Hmmmm."

"You know that's right. This New Age mess takes a little bit of Scripture and twists it. All of their principles sound good and it's easy for a Christian to be drawn into it. Like they teach a lot of mind control. Everything's mind over matter. You're only poor because you think you are or you're so afraid of lack, you close yourself off from the flow of money. They teach that you over- come situations by working to change your attitude and men- tality. That's very close to what the Bible teaches, 'as a man thinketh in his heart, so is he.' The only difference is they attribute psychological success to the individual, promoting self-suffi- ciency. The Word tells us that the only way to renew our minds is by the Word of God, so that when we experience success, we attribute it to God."

Harmony looked like she was still thinking.

"This totem pole, this crystal ball, these yin and yang symbols . . . They make for good decorations, but they're all idols. For some people, these things are their gods and they follow their system of doing things. Our God is not inanimate nor is He energy, He is a Spirit."

Charity could see that Harmony was tearing up.

Charity continued to minister to her. "And we know that He is a forgiving God. So, if you are ready, I will pray with you and ask for His forgiveness."

Harmony nodded.

"Father God, I thank You for the opportunity to minister to my sister and Your daughter, Harmony. Thank You for being a God who is slow to anger and quick to love. Thank You for recognizing we are but clay. Find pleasure in the fact that Harmony wanted to know You in a deeper way, but forgive her for going about it wrongly. Lord, I plead the blood of Jesus over her right now. For the blood blots out transgressions and cleanses from all unrighteousness. Your Word says that You are faithful and just in removing our sins as far as the east is from the west. We thank You for remembering Your promises. Satan, you are rebuked in the name of Jesus. We have on the whole armor of God and are standing strong ready to resist you should you return with this temptation again. You are a defeated foe and a liar. For majesty, power, glory, and victory belong only to the true and living God, forever and ever. It is in Jesus' name we pray this prayer. Amen."

Harmony dried her face with tissues. "Thank you so much. I'm so sorry for—"

"The Bible tells us that there is no condemnation for those who are in Christ Jesus who walk not after the flesh, but after the Spirit," Charity said. "But, Harmony, listen carefully, the only way you can walk after the Spirit is if you are born again. I know you say that you are a Christian, but it's much more than believing in

God. It's having a real relationship with His Son, Jesus Christ. I would like to pray the prayer of salvation with you."

When Harmony nodded, Charity talked with her about 1 John 1:9, saying, "If we confess our sins, He is faithful and just to forgive our sins, and to cleanse us from all unrighteousness." Then, just as she had done with Iesha last Monday, she led Harmony in the prayer of salvation.

"Thank you," Harmony said when Charity finished. Harmony looked around her office. "I see I have some cleaning to do. Do you have time to help me get rid of some stuff?"

CHAPTER 21

JOSEPH CHECKED HIS PHONE CREDITS to see how many calls he could make. He knew he should have about ten, but assuming and knowing were two different things. He sighed in relief to find that he had nine left for the remainder of the month. That was plenty. He'd call his sister tonight, and his mother later in the week. He couldn't wait to find out if his sister went to Minister Charity Phillips's church. He was so excited and anxious that he had to dial the phone number two times to get it right. His excitement went through the roof when he heard his sister's voice on the other end.

"Hey, sis."

"Joseph, are you ready for this?"

"What? You got to meet her?"

"Boy, God is all in this. Do you hear me?"

"Tell me, girl. What?" he laughed with anticipation.

"Minister Charity Phillips is the bomb. Joe, she is beautiful, she is smart, she is so sweet. Everything about her is perfect. You should see her house. Uhhhh, her son is so cute. And church services were off the hook."

"Wow! You went to her house?"

"You're gone have to call me back after this. It's too much to tell in fifteen minutes. Remember I used to sell makeup? Well, her pastor's wife used to host Mary Kay parties for me. So I know them. Anyway, by recommendation of Pastor King, she invited me to dinner at her house. She can cook, too. She is so perfect. She is everything you want in a wife."

"Amen, I receive that. What did you tell her about me?"

"I told her everything. How you had never been in any trouble, how we were raised in a Christian home . . . I told her everything."

"How did she act? Did she say anything?"

"She was mainly listening. I showed her pictures of all of us—Momma, Daddy, everybody. She said you was fine."

He blushed. "She did? Oh man. This is unreal. God, get me out of here."

"He will, He's honoring your faith."

"Lord, I wonder where God is going to send me when I get out. Back to Virginia or Charlotte. I can't wait to see how all of this is going to pan out. Tell me more about my wife. How did she carry herself? What did she have on? What did she smell like? Does she look like that picture in the magazine I sent to you? Give me all the details."

"She looks even better in person. She said that picture in the magazine was two years old. Her hair is longer now. Her skin is so smooth. The girl is flawless. And she's an itty bitty little thing too. She's small and petite, like Jada Pinkett Smith."

"Lord, have mercy."

"She had on this bad bright yellow and navy blue suit, with some navy heels. Smoking! She changed clothes when we got to her house. She just put on a pair of leggings and a shirt. I couldn't believe how down to earth she is."

"I wonder why she ain't married again. Is she dating anyone?"

"I don't know," Sharon whined. "If you believe that she is your wife, you better be glad she ain't married."

"I'm praying that she will visit me. I sent her a visiting form. Oh man, that's our first beep. I'mma call you back. Don't go to bed. You know I have to wait fifteen minutes before I can call you back."

"I'll be up. I got to tell you about her son, Xavier. Joseph, he's so cute. He speaks so properly. He—"

He slammed the phone down after their call was automatically disconnected. What a day it would be when he could enjoy an unlimited phone conversation. His joy could not be contained. He pondered every word Sharon spoke about her. He stuck his chest out and held his head up when he remembered that she said he was fine. He couldn't decide how he wanted to process what had just happened—if he should go to his room and talk to God, or go to the common area and talk to the boys. "God first," he reminded himself. He poured out his heart before God and went back to get a second dose from Sharon.

"Sis, God is so good. I just know that she is my wife. I can feel it."

"Shoot, if I were a man, I'd marry her myself. But let me tell you about Xavier. He is six and he looks just like her. She said he looks like his daddy. Joe, he is soooo cute. He calls me Ms. Sharon."

"I can see him in my spirit. I know we'll get along just fine. You never did tell me how she carries herself."

"I don't know. What do you mean?"

"Like is she ghetto fabulous? Is she prissy?"

"Oh, no. She's . . . both. Like she's very feminine and soft, but she laughs, tells jokes, and she was even sitting on the floor. Now, at church, you can tell she's a minister. She's got that glow about her, but at home, she's a straight-up sistergirl."

"What does she drive? What does her house look like? Girl, you holding out. Give me something I can see."

"She drives a brand-new Explorer. Black. Eddie Bauer edition. And her house is phat. You can tell by the street name— Symphony Woods Lane. It's huge. Every room is a different color, not in a tacky way. It's very creative. Did I tell you she can cook? The girl made some lasagna that was so good, I was licking my fingers."

"This was not supposed to happen."

"What?"

"I was not supposed to fall in love until I was on the other side of the fence."

"Well, God's ways and thoughts are higher than ours. You prayed for a wife and you got one."

"I'm going on about liking her, I wonder if she'll like me?"

"Do you think God would exceed your expectations, and not fulfill hers?"

"Praise God. I called Momma about her last week. She is so excited. She thinks she's an angel."

"She is. I called Momma as soon as I got home to tell her about her. She's praying for y'all. You know how Momma is. She wants to talk to her."

"It's going to happen too."

"Oh, another thing. Joe, she did the opening prayer and tore the church up. The girl is anointed. The whole church was up worshipping God. And she wasn't loud, flashy, or none of that. She was just . . . powerful."

"I can't wait to meet her. Thank you, thank you for going to the church. I realize you didn't have to. I was talking to the boys about it, and they said they wish they could tell their sister or someone in their family to go visit someone for them. They said they would get cussed out. I just want you to know I appreciate you believing in me and sticking by me. You're my favoritest sister."

"And your only sister. You're welcome. I don't know who the blessing was for in meeting her—you or me."

"Well, this phone is getting ready to hang up. I'll call you and Momma next week. I love you."

"I love you, too. Take care of yourself."

• • •

Hankins and Allen were still watching television in the common area when Joseph arrived. He had something for them better than Monday night football. When he started telling them what Sharon had told him, Allen turned off the television just to hear his report. They sat around listening to him like disciples listening to Jesus.

"Brother Word, you getting ready to get out of this place," Allen said.

Hankins agreed. "Sure is. God is doing this too quick to let you stay here. You better start packing your things by faith. You're not going to be here much longer."

When his words penetrated Joseph's heart he became filled with sadness. The life they had helped one another survive was getting ready to change.

CHAPTER 22

EMMITT WISHED THAT THE PHONE WOULD STOP RINGING and people would stop coming by long enough for him to catch up with the speed of life. *Don't people work on Mondays?* Things were happening so fast, it felt as if he were in an uncontrollable dream. The only thing he could do was to go along with the flow, which didn't allow him time enough to feel anything. The people from the funeral home had been by the house, the obituary had been submitted to the newspaper, and arrangements had been made for Greg to attend the funeral the following day.

He sat on the edge of her bed wishing he could reach out to touch her. What he wouldn't give to relive the last twenty-four hours of his life. He would take back all of the hurtful things he said to her. He cursed himself. *I'm sorry, Momma. At a time when you needed me most, I let you down. I killed you. I didn't believe you. Momma, don't leave me like this.* He threw himself onto her bed and beat his fists into her pillows. He grabbed fistfuls of her blanket and squeezed so hard he thought his fingers would go through his hands. *God, where are you now? How could this happen to me?* He cried himself to sleep.

• • •

Iesha was out front calling clients to reschedule their appointments because Charity decided that it would be best to close up for the day. She said that she was emotionally and mentally exhausted after helping Harmony. She'd also told Iesha that Harmony was going home for the day. Iesha wondered what happened back there. She knew it had to be major for Charity to go into Harmony's office, because she had not gone in there in the few days they had been open for business.

Iesha didn't complain because she could use some rest herself. She had a client on the phone when she heard someone yelling and cursing loudly. She placed the client on hold to listen closer. The noise wasn't coming from inside the suite. She followed the raucous sound to the mezzanine, where she could clearly see what was going on. She went back to the caller and asked him to consider another appointment and to call her back later. She ran back to the mezzanine and saw the Humphries trying to prevent a group of people from entering the building. People were coming out of their offices and the food court to find out what was going on. Iesha saw Wallace with the Humphries and decided to see if he could enlighten her.

"Charity! Charity!" she yelled, running back into the suite. "Come here! It's some trouble out front. We need to go down there."

Charity and Harmony both ran up front and followed Iesha's lead. "I wonder who those people are?" Iesha asked, keeping her eyes on the action. "Come on, y'all. Somebody might be trying to blow this place up or something, and we sitting up here. I'm going down there."

By the time the three of them got to the first floor, the crowd had grown monstrous. They pushed their way to the front so they could hear.

"Listen up everyone!" Wallace shouted.

The crowd shushed one another.

"No, let me tell them," Mrs. Humphries pleaded tearfully. "I'm so sorry to have to tell you this. I should have done it sooner but

I just knew God would make a way. Present Day is being fore-closed."

The crowd inhaled together.

"That's right," a white man in a dark, pin-striped suit said. "The owners have had well over ninety days to pay the property taxes they owe. This place will be padlocked on Thursday."

People began shouting and cursing. Someone yelled that they wanted their money back and others followed, making the same demands. Some threatened to sue. Next thing Iesha knew people began throwing food and trash at the two men and woman that the Humphries were trying to keep back.

Iesha felt sorry for her sister. Out of the goodness of her heart, she employed Iesha to show her a better life than welfare could offer. And now, Charity was going to be without work. "You okay, Cherry?"

"I just need to go home," said Charity. "This has been a crazy day and it's not even noon yet. If one more thing happens today, I'm liable to lose it."

Iesha trailed behind Charity and Harmony back to the suite. She returned to the phone to cancel Harmony's last appointment. She was so distracted by the news they had just received that she didn't see the postman enter. She looked up when she felt like she was being watched.

"May I help you, sir?" She covered the phone's mouthpiece with her hand.

"Yes, I have some certified mail for Charity Phillips."

"Hold on a moment." She parked the caller and buzzed Charity's phone to see if she wanted to sign for the delivery. "She'll be right out, sir."

"Thank you."

When Iesha hung up, the gentleman asked her if she had heard about Present Day closing. They talked until Charity arrived. Iesha stepped back and observed while Charity wrote her signature and watched the mailman leave.

"They only send money certified. Girl, I pray that's a check," Iesha joked, trying to cheer up her sister.

Charity forced a half smile. "It's from Emmitt. He said it would arrive today."

"Well, I know that ain't no check. Y'all already divorced, so it ain't no divorce papers. You got the baby. What else could he be sending? And important enough to be certified. Is you gone open it or not?"

"Calm down, Momma number two. Emmitt has changed. He told me he was sending a surprise. And you know his mom just died, so cut him some slack."

"Maybe now he can grow up and be a man."

"Iesha, please." Charity turned over the envelope and neatly severed the flap with her fingernail.

"Cherry, quit acting like that's a Christmas gift and tear that thing open. Dag! You slow as Christmas."

Charity rolled her eyes and took out the second envelope.

"Davis, Watson, and Blalock," she said, reading the return address. "That office is downstairs. Why is he sending me something from them?" She ripped open the envelope.

Iesha's heart was pounding until Charity's scream pierced through. Tears burst from her eyes when she saw that Charity was crying. "What, Cherry? What is it?"

"He's suing me for custody of Xavier, Iesha."

"He can't do that—"

Charity shoved the papers into Iesha's hand. "Obviously he can. It's a court hearing." Charity looked weak in the knees, and Iesha helped her over to a chair in the waiting area.

Harmony came out of her office. "Did y'all hear that scream?" Noticing that they were both crying, she went closer to them. "What's wrong?"

"Her ex-husband is taking her to court for child custody."

"Oh man. I'm sorry to hear that. Is there anything I can do?"

"It's all going to work out. No weapon forged against me shall prosper. I'm going on home."

"No, Cherry, let's go down to that lawyer's office to see what this is about."

"No, don't do that. You're in no shape to do that. If you go down there like this they will use it against you in court," Harmony advised.

Charity wept. "This can't be happening." She stood up and walked to her office.

"Cherry, are you gonna be all right back there?"

"Yes, I'll be right back."

"Harmony, go keep an eye on my sister. I'm getting ready to call that that no-good ex-husband of hers."

Iesha reached for her purse and took out an address book. She had kept Emmitt's mother's phone number in case she needed it one day. She dialed the number, referring back to the listing every few seconds to get the next set of numbers. She grew even angrier with every ring of the phone. *He better be glad he ain't home,* she fumed. She slammed the phone down. She prayed. "Lord, I know You're making a way for me to keep my kids, please see to it that my sister keeps hers."

Charity returned. "I'll call you later. I'm going home." She walked out without turning around.

Iesha called Mama Lorraine. When she heard her mother's voice, she started to cry. "Momma."

"Esha? What's wrong with you, girl?"

"Momma," she sniffled. "Emmitt's taking Cherry to court for custody."

"He's doing what?"

"She got some papers today from his lawyer."

"Where is she?"

"She just left."

"Is she okay?"

Iesha cried harder. "No. Momma, I ain't seen her like this in a long time. On top of that, we found out that Present Day is being shut down. The owners didn't pay their taxes. So she has to close her business. Momma, she put her whole life savings into this center."

"Lord, have mercy. Don't worry, baby. God gone take care of her. And that low-down dog. Didn't his momma just die? And he gone pull some stuff like this. See, God don't like ugly. Did Cherry say where she was going?"

"She said she was going home."

"I'mma meet her over there. I'll call you later."

"I'mma go over there, too. I'll see you there."

Charity could hardly see the road because she was crying so hard. She was doing everything right, how could God allow all of this to happen? *He swears He puts no more on you than you can bear. This is too much. If one more thing happens, I swear I'm going to lose it.* That thought made her cry harder.

She was surprised that she'd made it home safely. With all of the whining she was doing, she was hoping to be killed in a car accident and be taken up to Glory. She was so preoccupied that she didn't remember the drive home. Her car must've been on automatic pilot. She let herself in, locked the door, and looked at the clock on the wall. She had four more hours until the locksmith would come. That was plenty of time for her to take a bath and a nap. Charity rested her head on the bath pillow to collect her thoughts. Before she knew it, she'd drifted to sleep in the tub.

Suddenly, she sat up in the tub, thinking she heard her alarm signal that her door had been opened. She must've been dreaming. She turned on the hot water to reheat the tub. She again thought she heard something, but rebuked spirits of paranoia and fear. She turned off the water and eased her body underneath the water.

"Honey, I'm home."

She shot straight up. "Who's there?" She reached for her robe.

"Where are you, honey?"

"Mr. Wright?" she asked, thinking she recognized the voice. *Oh my God.* She tied her robe and looked around the bathroom for a weapon if she needed it. *Candles, makeup, a mirror. The towel rack, maybe. God, please.*

He appeared in the doorway. He was disheveled and had a flat expression on his face. She knew without a doubt that he wasn't on his medications. "There you are. You're home early from work today. I went by to have lunch with you but you were already gone."

"Mr. Wright. It's me, Charity Phillips, your therapist." She knew it was useless trying to reason with an unmedicated schizophrenic, but it wouldn't hurt to try. "How did you get in here?"

"I used my key."

Think Charity, think. "When's the last time you took your medications?"

"Remember we talked about those medications and agreed I shouldn't take them. They've messed up our sex life. Remember?"

God, please help me. She realized that if she wanted to get out of this mess, she was going to have to play along until she could call for help. Although he was delusional, she was glad that he thought she was his wife, and not someone who was trying to hurt him. "I'm glad you want to have lunch. I'm starving. Go on to the kitchen and make us something to eat. I'll be right there."

"No. I took today off of work to spend time with you. I haven't been a good husband and I want to make it up."

"It'll only take me a minute to get dressed. Why don't you start lunch?"

"But I haven't seen your beautiful body in what seems like an eternity. Can we make love like we used to and then do lunch?"

Lord, please. "I have a good idea." She moved closer to him and gave him a seductive look. "If you go to the kitchen and get us some ice cubes, I'll be dressed in something a little more comfortable by the time you get back. Okay?"

He moved in closer to her. "Now that sounds like a plan."

She turned her cheek when he tried to kiss her. Trying to play it off she said, "Nah ah ah, we need the ice."

His frown turned into a smile. He walked backward out of the bathroom and turned into the bedroom like he knew exactly where he was going.

Charity ran and locked the bedroom door behind him. She dialed 9-1-1 on the phone.

"Hello, I need the police to 1630 Symphony Woods Lane," she whispered. The operator cut her off to ask her questions. "Yes, ma'am. I live here. My name is Charity Phillips. I'm a therapist and one of my clients is an intruder in my home. Please send the police." She was growing impatient with the operator's questions. "He used my key. Maybe when he . . ." She stopped talking when she heard a noise. "Ma'am, I can answer all of these questions when the police arrive. Hurry." She hung up and dialed Iesha's cell phone. Her voice mail picked up on the first ring. She hurriedly dialed Mama Lorraine's cell phone number. There was no answer. Then she heard a light knock on her bedroom door.

"Honey," he called seductively. "I got the ice."

"Just a minute. I'm almost ready."

"Come on now, open the door."

She heard the doorknob turn back and forth. "Why is the door locked?" He turned it again. "Open the door!" He started beating wildly on the door. "My sister's in there!" he yelled. "Stand back, Janice, I'mma get you out of there. Momma! The bathroom's on fire! Momma!"

Charity was too afraid to say anything, but she remembered her first session with him when he alluded to a family secret. She assumed that this was it and he'd become delusional about one of his childhood incidents. She prayed for God to intervene. "Come on, Lord." There was silence, then there was a loud thud. He was trying to kick the door down.

"Get back, Janice!" he yelled.

"Jeffrey, stop!" Charity yelled. "It's not a fire."

"Just get back. I'mma get you out of there."

The sound of the doorbell brought tears to her eyes. "Thank You, Lord, thank You," she sobbed. "Jeffrey, go answer the door."

"No, I don't want you to get hurt again, Janice." He kicked the door so hard this time, it came off the top hinge. He ran to her and held her. "Thank goodness you're safe." He wiped her tears. "It's all right, you're not burned. It's okay, now."

Charity cried all the more because she felt sorry for him. The doorbell rang again and Charity freed herself from his embrace and ran to open the door. She ran outside past the policeman and pointed toward the house. "He's in there."

Just then Mr. Wright appeared in the doorway. Another policeman walked from around the backyard and joined the first one. "What's the problem, ma'am?" he asked her.

Mr. Wright answered. "Sir, there's been a mistake. I didn't hit my wife. I know you've arrested me before on domestic dispute charges. But—"

"Officer, this is not my husband. He is a client of mine and he is psychotic and delusional. He is schizophrenic and I don't know when he's taken his medication last. He thinks I'm his wife. Just a minute ago, he thought I was his sister trapped in a fire."

The policemen looked at each other. "How did he get in your house?"

"I live here. I got in with my own key," Mr. Wright answered, holding up his key chain.

Everyone turned around to see who was pulling in the driveway. Charity was glad to see Mama Lorraine and Iesha both pull up.

"Here's my sister, she works with me in my practice and can attest to what I'm telling you. She wanted to surprise me by having my car detailed. She hired Mr. Wright to do it. I believe he copied my key when she gave him my keys to clean the car."

One officer scratched his head. "Would you like to press charges?"

"No, sir." Her words surprised her. "I'd rather have him involuntarily committed to the hospital for treatment."

Mr. Wright was cooperative as the policeman placed him in handcuffs. Charity could hear Mama Lorraine and Iesha asking questions before they were even near. When Iesha saw Mr. Wright she burst into tears.

"Oh my God. Cherry I'm so sorry."

Mama Lorraine looked confused. "Ya'll gone arrest him? What he do? Break in? He didn't mess with you did he, Cherry?"

Charity shook her head no.

Then Mama Lorraine looked at Mr. Wright. "That's what I thought. You don't mess with a Brown. You look at these girls real good. They're mine. These the last ones you wanna mess with. You hear me? Or you'll have to deal with me. And I'mma tell you in front of the police, next time we have to call them on you, it won't be to pick you up alive."

"All right, ma'am," the policeman said as he whisked Mr. Wright off. "Mrs. Phillips, you still have a right to press charges. I'll see to it that this gentleman is taken to Presbyterian Behavioral Health. Meanwhile, you need to change the locks on your house and your vehicle. If you have any questions, you can call me at any of these numbers." He handed her a business card.

When they could no longer see the police cars, Mama Lorraine and Iesha turned to go into the house. Charity tried to follow them but her feet would not cooperate with her mind. Mama Lorraine looked back and tried to encourage Charity to go toward the house, but the magnitude of everything that happened that day fell on her like a ton of bricks. She collapsed and wailed from the core of her hurt. *How could God allow so much to happen in just one day?* First Harmony, then Emmitt, then Present Day, then this. Charity finally decided that she had had enough of following Jesus.

Chapter 23

TEARS WELLED UP IN HER EYES. She'd tossed and turned all night, tormented by a bout of depression. She awakened Tuesday morning tired from the fight. *I thought joy was supposed to come in the morning.* Charity couldn't believe she was here—again. She hadn't felt this way in three years, since she was with Emmitt. Surely she'd been delivered from this, especially since she gave her life to the Lord the last time it happened. But this time, the voices seemed louder and stronger than ever before.

You might as well end it all, a raspy sounding voice in her head suggested. *You know you're tired of fighting. Tired of pretending. Tired of being on the brink of a breakthrough. Go ahead, Charity, do it.*

"I ought to just kill myself," Charity said out loud as if she thought of the idea herself. She flung back the warm bedsheets and jumped out of bed as if it were on fire. Usually she couldn't stand to touch the hardwood floors first thing in the morning. But she was so intent on getting to the medicine cabinet in her bathroom that she didn't feel the cold floor under her feet. "I'm tired of fighting, tired of pretending, and I'm tired of being on the brink of a breakthrough. I'm tired of doing this alone." Charity licked the moisture that fell to her lip to see if she was really crying. She thought she had cried all of her tears last night. She knew she needed to get her Bible, but she didn't feel like making the effort it took to read and meditate on Scriptures.

All she could meditate on was the fact that she had closed her 401(k) retirement fund to make a $10,000 investment in Horizons, and it was now gone. Even if she wanted to start a new counseling practice, she didn't have the start-up money to do it. She had only about a month's worth of living expenses in her checking and savings account combined. What would she and Xavier do after that? "Protect my son, Lord. He doesn't deserve any of this. He deserves to be happy. Emmitt was right, he's been the better parent all along. I won't fight him anymore. He can do a better job with Xavier than I can." Charity cried even harder.

That's right, the voice validated. *People think you have it all together, but you don't. They think you're perfect at everything. But the truth is that you're a terrible mother, a poor excuse for a minister, a hateful ex-wife, and a trifling therapist. That's why you're going to lose your son, your business, and everything you own.* Charity cried harder. *You've been living a lie. That walking by faith stuff doesn't work for you. You're not doing it right and God is not pleased. Get out while you can, Charity. Do it now.*

"Who am I trying to fool?" she asked herself. "I've been living a lie. I've been pleasing people and disappointing God. I've been so careful to act according to how I thought I should and was supposed to, and this is where I end up. I'm so stupid. I need to get out while I can. I'd rather die than lose my son."

On her way to the bathroom, she caught a glimpse of herself in the tilted oak-framed cheval mirror that sat catercornered in her room. Something about her image disturbed her. She stepped backward to the mirror. Nothing but an overwhelming urge to look into her eyes.

She heard a soft, but firm voice from within her say, *Look into your eyes, Charity . . . Look into your eyes.*

She looked at the mirror and was distracted by smudges and fingerprints. "This mirror is dirty."

The voice sounded more urgent. *Look into your eyes.*

She looked into the mirror and searched her face. It was easier to focus on her premenstrual pimples, chapped lips, and unarched eyebrows than it was for her to hold her own gaze. She wished she could see the things for which people complimented her. She often heard about how beautiful she was, how smooth and even her dark complexion was. A saleswoman at a makeup counter once told her that her skin was the perfect canvas for her large, expressive eyes. Charity figured the woman was just trying to make a sale. She'd been teased so much as a child about having "popeyes" and "platypus" lips that she despised the facial features people complimented most. Her fine shoulder-length tresses were unkempt most mornings but could easily be swept up into a style with her fingertips.

Into your eyes, connect with your spirit.

"Okay, okay." She stepped up and peered into the mirror, fixing her eyes on to themselves.

Greater is He who is within you than he who is of the world . . . In all these things, you are more than a conqueror.

As the voice continued, it began sounding like it was coming from within her. *I can do all things through Christ, who strengthens me. The Lord is my light and my—*

The raspy voice broke in, *But to live is Christ and to die is gain . . . To be absent from the body is to be present with the Lord. Quit thinking about it and do it.*

"Shut up!" she shouted as she dropped her gaze. "I can't take this anymore. God, I'm so sick of this. I can't do this anymore. It's too much. My life is a shambles, where are You?"

She hurriedly walked into the bathroom and opened the oak medicine cabinet that was concealed behind a mirror. She snatched every medication from its place. A half bottle of ibuprofen, a pack of twelve over-the-counter sleeping pills, a bottle of cough syrup, and a pain medication prescribed for occasional migraines. She filled a paper cup with water to drink and went back to her bedroom.

"I'm not taking all of these," she said, dumping the contents on her bed. She put the cup of water on the nightstand and retrieved the phone book from underneath it. "I need to know which one will work."

She found two numbers she thought would be helpful. She hurriedly dialed the first one.

"Poison Control Center, this is Sterling. How may I help you?" the voice answered pleasantly.

"Yes, Sterling," she said matter-of-factly and sat down on the bed. She counted the medication as she laid it out. "I need your help. I have a bottle of prescription pain medications here and I need to know if I have enough to kill myself. I don't want to take these pills and wake up tomorrow. I need this to work. Can you help me?"

"Ma'am, I can hear how frustrated and overwhelmed you are. Please promise me that you won't hurt yourself without first talking about what can be done to help you. Will you do that?"

"Sterling, listen to me. I didn't call you to answer your questions. I called to get you to answer mine. Will you do that?" she mocked. "Because if not—"

"You said you needed my help, right?"

"Yes—"

"Well, the only way I can help you is if you allow me to. Your calling me first was a very positive move. Will you let me help you?"

"The only help I need—"

"Will you let me help you?" he asked, more sternly than the first time.

Hang up on him . . . You don't need him. You have enough pills to do it.

"Ma'am are you there?"

"I really don't need you, I can just start taking what I have now—"

"Ma'am, is anyone there with you?"

"Is thirty-two pills enough, Sterling?"

"I would like to send you some help. What is your address?'

Hang up, Charity. He is trying to trip you up.

"I know what you are trying to do and it is not going to work."
She slammed the phone down and turned to the second number
in the phone book. She dialed it.

"Suicide Hotline," a female answered. Charity almost hung up,
thinking that the voice sounded familiar but she rationalized that
she had heard so many voices this morning that they were all
beginning to sound alike.

"Look, I have thirty-two prescription pain pills here. I just need
to know if I have enough to take to kill myself. Can you—"

"Charity?" the voice asked uncertainly.

*Hang up, stupid. You're so heavenly bound, you're no earthly good.
You can't even kill yourself right.*

She slammed the phone down again. "Oh my God, oh my
God," she panicked. "Where do I know that voice from? That
could be anybody—a church member, a client, a friend. Who? Oh
my God. I've messed up now. Someone knows." She scooped up
the pills in her hand and swallowed as many as she could as fast as
she could.

*MORE, MORE, MORE! You're doing it, Charity. Finally standing
up for yourself. Don't stop now, take the sleeping pills too.*

Disappointed that she did not yet feel anything, she resolved to
take the sleeping pills. She pushed the blue gel capsules through
their foil packaging and swallowed them. She felt the urge to
vomit.

"No, no," she cried. Her voice was fading with each refusal to
eject the poison from her body. "To live is Christ," she said faintly.
"But to die is . . ." Then there was silence.

Chapter 24

As adamant as Iesha was about living a different lifestyle than before, she was glad to not have a job today. "Thank You, Jesus," she sighed. After staying with Charity until after midnight, she was tired. Nevertheless, she refused to complain, because she knew that in the past when the tables were turned, her sister had been right there with her. When she and Mama Lorraine left her last night, Charity had finally fallen asleep after hours of crying and questioning her relationship with God. Iesha was glad that Xavier spent the night at Mama Lorraine's, he didn't need to see Charity like that.

Iesha turned on her bedside lamp, hoping that would wake her up. *The kids have school in less than an hour.*

"Sha-Lai! Quan!" she yelled. "Wake up. It's time to get up."

She knew she needed to get up, too, or else she'd find the kids' still asleep. She dragged herself out of bed and offered a quick prayer on her way to the kids' rooms. "Thank You, Jesus, for waking me up this morning, clothing me in my right mind. Thank You, Lord, for my health and strength, and sparing me from excessive sorrow. In Jesus' name—"

She felt convicted for offering a prayer mindlessly and without reverence. She asked for forgiveness, retrieved her Bible, and knelt in the hallway to pray again. She searched her heart for words to say, and each time her mind wandered she repented and sought all the more to hear from God. Before she knew it, she was praying for Charity. She prayed for everything she could think of—her strength, her salvation, God's protection and provision. She even confessed Psalm 91 over her sister, just like Charity had taught her to do. She refused to get up until she felt God release her. When she went to wake the children, she found them already dressed. Raquan was brushing his hair and Sha-Lai was brushing her teeth.

"Good morning," she greeted.

The kids sang their good morning in unison.

"I oughtta pray every morning if it makes y'all get up and get ready by yourselves. Good job. I'mma go throw something on and we'll be ready to go. We'll get breakfast from Burger King."

She heard Raquan say, "Yes!" before she turned to leave. She went to her room and threw on an old sweatsuit and put her microbraids in a ponytail.

Iesha felt good this morning and she wanted to keep it this way.

Charity had said that if Iesha wanted to be positive, she needed to put positive things into her spirit. Charity also told Iesha that her eyes, ear, and mouth were the gates to her heart and that she needed to guard what she watched, listened to, and read. She thought Charity was crazy for telling her to limit how much she watched the news and Lifetime TV, read the newspapers, and listened to secular music. But she at least agreed that she wouldn't knock it until she tried it.

She tuned her car radio to the AM setting and flipped through the stations.

"Turn it back, Momma," Raquan said when he heard some dance music.

"I'm looking for gospel music, Quan."

"What's gospel music?"

"Music about God." She turned it back to hear the lyrics. She started to turn it when she heard a reggae beat, but she listened to the lyrics about God being an awesome God and recognized them from an older song Mama Lorraine liked.

Iesha sang along as best she could, praising God for reigning with wisdom, power, and love. She looked in her rearview mirror and saw Raquan and Sha-Lai jamming. Raquan was doing the Harlem shakes and only Sha-Lai knew what she was doing. Iesha started dancing too. She enjoyed the clever remix so much she hoped the host would announce the artist's name.

She shushed the kids when the host began talking. "Good morning to you. This is Zoe and Marcus sitting in with you on Morning Joy, helping you to have a terrific Tuesday. That was Kirk Franklin featuring Papa San on 'He Reigns . . .' "

Iesha reached for her cell phone and speed-dialed Charity. She remembered that Charity had played a Kirk Franklin CD at the open house. When she didn't get an answer, she looked at the clock on the dashboard. *Where could she be at 8:00 in the morning?* She hung up when she considered that she could still be sleeping.

She dropped the kids off at school and headed back toward home to do some cleaning. Her cell phone rang. The caller ID displayed Terrence's name and number.

"Hey, you," she greeted him with his own words.

"Hey, sweetie. Have you dropped the kids off yet?"

"Yep, I'm on my way back home."

"I think I have your schedule down pat now. Did you eat breakfast?"

"Sort of."

"Does that mean you'd like to eat with me, or at least watch me eat?"

She looked down at her clothes. "Uh, I don't think I should be out in public with what I have on."

"Please, it's not the clothes that make you look good. You make them look good. I'm sure you're fine. Do we have a date?"

"If you don't mind being with an old Mary J. Blige wannabe," she chuckled.

"Okay, Mary, meet me at Eat Well on Freedom Drive. That's your side of town, right?"

"Yes. How long will it take you to get there?"

"Don't even think about changing clothes. You go straight there. I might get there before you."

After they said their good-byes, she offered up prayers of thanksgiving. God had more than answered her prayers. Not only had He given her a wonderful man, but this man was also fine, financially stable, and fun. Not to mention, saved. She arrived at Eat Well just a few minutes ahead of Terrence. She walked over to his sky-blue Honda Accord.

He kissed her on the cheek. "Girl, Mary J. Blige wishes she looked like you." Iesha blushed and followed him into the restaurant.

"I've got a nine-thirty delivery to make this morning. Will you make the run with me?"

"Well, I was thinking about going to check on my sister this morning."

"How about we do it together after my run?"

Iesha agreed when Terrence gave her a charming look. "Okay, I'll go. But don't make that look no habit. It doesn't work for my kids and it's not gonna work for you."

"I'll have to teach Raquan and Sha-Lai how to do it correctly," he laughed.

She was impressed that he remembered their names. "You have a good memory."

"Only when it comes to what's important."

She just shook her head when she considered how mindful God is of her. She finished her hot chocolate and waited for him to finish his breakfast. Iesha begged to leave the tip while he paid the bill. She'd heard Charity talk about sowing seeds and she wanted to give it a try. When he finished his food, he suggested she leave her car at the restaurant and ride with him.

"If you're delivering something, why aren't you driving your truck?"

"I kept my schedule light today. I just have this nine-thirty and another one later. I let the guys take my load today."

"Oh."

"You think I'm up to something?"

"I don't know. You tell me!"

He smiled. "You didn't tell me you were paranoid. Anything else you think I should know?"

"No that's about it."

"You sure? 'Cause I hate to find out—"

"Oooh oooh, turn that up!" She interrupted when she heard the song that she and the kids were listening to earlier.

Terrence turned up the volume of his CD player. "A Kirk Franklin fan, huh?"

"I heard that song for the first time this morning. I like it."

"Oh, you should hear the whole CD. It's nice. This is my favorite track." He pushed a button a couple of times. "This is called 'My Love, My Life, My All.'"

They rode in silence, listening to the confessions of adoration and praise.

"That is beautiful," Iesha agreed. "I was going to ask my sister if I could borrow her CD. May I borrow yours?"

"Borrow? You can have it. I'll get another one."

Terrence parked the car and walked around to Iesha's door, She observed where they were. She had never been inside of the "gold building" as her friends called it. He went to the trunk to grab his clipboard and a box. He dropped his clipboard. They bumped heads as they both bent down to pick it up.

"I'm sorry," he apologized. "It ain't like this box is heavy."

"You need me to carry something?"

"No, I've got it."

She looked at him crossly. He seemed fidgety and nervous. "This ain't no drug run, is it?"

He laughed. "No. Come on before you call the police on me."

"And you know this."

They rode the elevator to the fourth floor. "I'mma wait for you on the elevator in case something goes down," Iesha joked.

"Come on. I brought you along because I wanted you to know what I do."

"I'll hold the elevator so I can see."

"Girl, come on here." He gently pulled her out and led her to Diamonds Direct.

"Heck no, I ain't going in there," Iesha said, pulling back when she saw a man with a long ponytail in a suit working behind a jewelry counter. "He look like he work for the Mafia. You deliver your package by yourself."

"Iesha," Terrence called her name in a tone she had not heard him use. "Baby, this has nothing to do with my job. I brought you here because I love you and I want to spend my life with you." Even though she was no longer resisting him, she was not quite sure she understood what he was saying. He continued, "You said yesterday that if I asked you to marry me, that you would." He put the box and clipboard down and kneeled on both knees. He took her hands. "Iesha, will you make me an even more blessed man by agreeing to be my wife? Marry me."

She swallowed hard and looked around to see if anyone was watching. "Terrence, you are a wonderful man of God, more than I could ever deserve. But it's just been one week to the day and I have kids that you haven't even met, you don't even know my background, I just lost my job—"

By this time the man with the ponytail was coming out of the store toward them.

"None of those things are relative when God is involved. I believe that you're the woman that He has preserved for me. And I'm more than willing to accept and love everything about you, including Sha-Lai and Raquan. I'll ask you one more time, and if you say no or wait, that's okay. I'm not going anywhere. Are you ready?" She nodded. "Will you marry me?"

She looked into his eyes and saw that he meant every word. She considered what her parents, Charity, the kids, and even her friends would say. She shut out all of their voices and responded, "Yes, I'd be honored to be Mrs. Terrence Davis."

"Congratulations," the man with the ponytail greeted.

But Terrence and Iesha were too entwined in an embrace to pay any attention to him. When they released their lips from the kiss Terrence had initiated, Iesha held his face in the palms of her hands and wiped his tears.

"Congratulations," the man again offered.

They both thanked the man and accepted his handshake. He led them into the store and after about two hours, Iesha selected a wide-band solitaire wedding set.

"I should call my mom," Iesha suggested on the way out.

"That's too impersonal. Let's prepare dinner for her or take her out."

"Okay. But that means we'll have to wait until the weekend to drive up to West Virginia to tell your parents."

"Oh no. We can call them. They already know."

As they walked toward his car, Iesha's cell phone rang. She looked at the caller ID. "Speaking of the devil. It's my mom."

"Momma, I've got some news, are you sitting down?" When she didn't hear a response, she thought they had been disconnected. "Momma, can you hear me?"

"Yes. Esha," she said between sniffles, "Cherry's in the hospital."

"Noooo. Is she all right? What happened?" Iesha could see the concern on Terrence's face. She held her hand over the mouthpiece. "My sister's in the hospital." He slowed their pace and put his arm around her shoulder. "What'chu say, Momma?"

"She tried to kill herself," Mama Lorraine said.

Iesha stopped in her tracks as tears fell. Terrence bowed his head.

"She overdosed on some pills," Mama Lorraine continued. "Pastor King just called."

"Pastor King? How'd he find out before us?"

"Just meet me at the hospital. We'll talk then."

"Is she going to be all right?"

"Right now she's in ICU."

"Oh God. Momma, I'll see you in a little bit."

When they got back to Terrence's car, Iesha told him what her mom had said. She tried to be strong but when he leaned over and laid her head on his chest, she just couldn't hold back the tears.

CHAPTER 25

HE WAS BEING STRONG FOR GRANNY AND AUNT ELISA. He knew that if they saw him crying, they would lose it. Granny and her ex-husband, Emmitt's grandfather, were first in the processional line to the funeral home. Aunt Elisa and her teenage sons were next. Emmitt and Shawanda were behind them. As best as he could, he blocked out the sniffles, coughs, and choking sobs behind him. *I can do this. I can do this.* The closer he got to the champagne-colored casket, the more he felt like a Spike Lee movie character, being rolled onto a set instead of walking. He was glad to see that Granny was composed. She bent down and kissed her restful daughter on the cheek and went to sit on the first row. He watched Aunt Elisa approach and survey her lifeless sister, Elaine. He could tell by her shuddering shoulders that she was crying. *Oh Lord, please don't let her show out.*

It looked like Aunt Elisa was getting ready to kiss her, but the shrill of her scream pierced his heart. "Take me, Lord. Take me now, Jesus! Don't leave me, Elaine."

Emmitt looked back to see how far he was from an exit. The waiting line was too monstrous. Wailing and sobbing could be heard as far back as the line extended. The louder Aunt Elisa got, the louder the crowd became. When he turned around to check on his aunt, three female ushers were wrestling to get her out of the casket.

"Stop! Stop! That's my sister. Stop!"

Granny arose from her seat and walked up to where they were. "Elisa, if you don't get your behind out of that casket, I'mma let them close you up in it. Since you want the Lord to take you too."

Emmitt thought he was going to laugh at how fast his aunt climbed out of the box. But it was his turn to view her body. He felt awkward knowing that all eyes were on him. He blocked out everyone else, looked at his mother, and closed his eyes. He filled his lungs with as much air as he could and exhaled slowly to keep himself calm. He took a red rose from the cascading arrangement atop the closed bottom half of the casket and placed it into one of her hands. He kissed her sweetly on her forehead. When his tears would not allow him to behold her any longer, he started toward his seat. He watched the rest of the processional like he was watching a funeral on a television sitcom. He held the same hope that at the end of the program, his mother would sit up in the casket and they'd laugh at how real it all seemed.

The little comfort he obtained from that thought was extinguished by the sight of two sheriffs coming in with Greg. The sheriffs unshackled him and escorted him to where his mother lay. Emmitt and Granny both stood up to greet and comfort him.

"Mom-ma. Mom-ma," Greg sobbed. "I'm sorry, Momma. Forgive me, Momma, ple-eease!" The church was torn up again. When Greg started hyperventilating and falling to the ground, the sheriffs walked him over to Granny, who was motioning for them to bring him to her. She led him to a seat and let him rest his head on her bosom. "It's all right, baby," Emmitt heard her say. Emmitt leaned over to acknowledge his brother.

Emmitt couldn't take it anymore. He sobbed too. The two of them together on both sides of Granny wailed for the loss of their mother.

After the hour of visitation, the funeral seemed more bearable. A cousin sang "Precious Lord, Take My Hand," and returned later to sing "What a Friend We Have in Jesus." One of Aunt Elisa's boys tearfully read "Why I Must Leave You," a poem that he had written. Emmitt was appreciative of the remarks people made about her. Every now and then, he looked around to see who he recognized. Their father, Greg Sr., was there and so were their two stepfathers. He and his brother acknowledged them all and everyone else who hugged them or spoke to them.

Just as things felt like they were settling down for Emmitt, the funeral director asked him if he wanted to see his mother before the casket closed for the final time.

Greg leaned over Granny. "What he say, man?"

"Do you want to go up there to see her again before they close the casket?"

"You going?"

"Are you?"

"Go on up there," Granny nudged them both.

The officers stood up with Greg and escorted them both. Emmitt wasn't sure what to do. He stood beside Greg and they just watched her, then hugged each other and went back to their seats. The pallbearers escorted the casket out of the funeral home and the flower bearers followed behind. The ushers motioned for the family next and then the others pew by pew. The recessional line came to a standstill at the double doors.

The floral arrangements were so big that Emmitt could barely see what the holdup was. He assumed the pallbearers were having difficulty.

Shawanda was holding Emmitt's hand and was gently rubbing it while they waited. He became distracted as he watched Aunt Elisa pull her eyeshades down and tap Granny to get her attention.

"He better not start no mess, that's all I know," Elisa swore.

Emmitt tapped Aunt Elisa. "Who ya'll talking about?"

She pushed her shades back up. "Nothing, baby. I see an old friend of your momma's."

"Where?"

Aunt Elisa gestured vaguely. "Somewhere over there."

Emmitt scouted the whole area and almost missed the gentleman who was politely smiling at him. When they made eye contact, the man waved. Emmitt thought he looked familiar but couldn't place where he knew him from.

"Don't speak to him," his aunt warned. "He's a lying dog. Your momma couldn't stand him." She snarled up her nose and shooed the man with her hand.

Emmitt looked confused. "Who is he?"

"Come on here," Granny interrupted. "The line is moving."

"Is there a problem?" Shawanda whispered to Emmitt.

"I have no idea."

Once they were outside, mourners came to greet them and offered words of encouragement. It was good to speak with people he had not seen in years. He especially liked their stories of what he was like as a toddler and little boy. If he had collected a dollar for every time someone told him he looked like his mother, he would have well over a hundred dollars by now. He looked around and noticed that Aunt Elisa and Granny were gone.

"Did you see where my aunt and grandma went to?"

Shawanda looked around. "Uhn huhn. They were just right here."

"There they are," Emmitt said, spotting them. "Lord, I hope they ain't starting no trouble. They over there talking to that man."

"Is that your daddy?"

Emmitt looked at her crossly. "No. My dad is here though. I'll show him to you when he comes out."

"Oh, I'm sorry. You look a little like him."

"Stay here. I'mma go see who this man is." Emmitt ignored Shawanda's protest and walked over to Aunt Elisa, Granny, and the man. "Is somebody going to tell me what's going on?"

The man spoke first. "Hello, son." He stretched out his hand for Emmitt to shake. "Your Aunt Elisa is just glad to see me." He glanced at her sideways.

Emmitt shook his hand. "Hey."

"Emmitt, do you know who this is?" Granny asked.

Emmitt looked at the man, embarrassed. "You look familiar but I don't remember where I know you from."

"That's because the last time I seen you, you was this high." The man put his hand out to the side at his waist to demonstrate.

Aunt Elisa pressed his hand down lower. "No, he was that high."

"Elisa, you done embarrassed yourself one time. You sure you want to do it again?" Granny asked.

"That's okay, Willie Ann. I had it coming."

Emmitt looked confused. "Who are you?" he asked.

Aunt Elisa answered before the man could. "Emmitt, you remember the neighbor me and your mom used to always joke about? The one we told you we named you after?"

He nodded impatiently.

"Well, this is him. Your namesake, Emmitt Chambers."

A smile broke across Emmitt's face. "Hey." He reached out to shake the man's hand again. "I thought that was a story they made up to satisfy me. I used to always ask why my little brother was Greg Jr. instead of me. Shoot, as much as they talked about you, youdda thought you were my daddy," he chuckled.

Emmitt saw his Aunt Elisa shoot the man a look so cold that even he stiffened. Emmitt continued, "I'm glad to finally know it ain't a lie."

The man avoided eye contact with Elisa. "Looks like you turned out to be a fine young man. I'm glad we share the name."

"That's the only thing you share," Elisa quipped.

Granny elbowed her in the side. "Lord, Elaine gone turn over in her grave and she ain't been buried yet." She pulled Elisa away, leaving the Emmitts alone to talk.

"You have to ignore my Aunt Elisa. She's just grieving."

"Me, your momma, and your aunt Elisa go way back. Believe me when I say she's always been like that."

They both laughed.

The man attempted to break the silence. "So, is that young lady your wife?"

Emmitt shoved his hands in his pockets. "I'm divorced. My ex has our six-year-old son. That's my girlfriend."

"She's pretty."

"Would you believe she asked me if you were my daddy?" The man didn't answer. "She said I look a little like you."

"Maybe that comes from the name," the man said. "You still love your ex?"

Emmitt shrugged. He didn't know why he didn't say no like he did when James or his mother asked him.

The man moved closer like he was about to whisper a top secret. "Don't make the same mistake I did. If you love her—I don't care who she's with—swallow your pride and get her back. Your son deserves to know you."

Emmitt absorbed the advice. "That's the same thing my best friend said. I don't want my son to be fatherless or raised by another man. I want to . . ." Emmitt stopped talking long enough to notice the man wiping his face and eyes with a handkerchief. "You okay?"

The man hesitated before he spoke. "It just makes me sad to know you're going through the same thing I went through—with your mom."

"With my mom?"

The man rested his hands on both of Emmitt's shoulders. "Yes. I was there when your mom and Greg Sr. were together and she was pregnant with you. We loved each other but she chose Greg over me because she felt he could provide better for the both of you. I begged her to leave him for me but she refused. She made me promise to stay away and I told her I would if she gave you my name."

"You did what you had to do. My situation is a little different. It's easier to walk away when it ain't your kid. But that's my son—"

The man applied pressure to Emmitt's shoulders. "And you are mine."

Emmitt's body posture caved like someone had jabbed him in the chest. He had to catch his breath. "I'm your what? . . . Son?"

"Yes, Emmitt. You are my son."

Emmitt loosed himself from the man's grip. "I . . . you . . . this . . . I gotta go." He raced off toward his car. He ignored the man as he called him back. He even stumbled past Granny, Aunt Elisa, and Shawanda. They were all a bunch of liars and he didn't want to have a thing to do with them. And that included his mother. He drove in the direction of his home, refusing to stay for the burial. How could she, of all people, keep something like this from him?

As he drove, it all began to make sense. He remembered Greg Sr.'s mistreatment of him and the fights it caused when his mother confronted him. That's why his mother felt obligated to bail him out when he got into a bind. Maybe that's why she was so dead set on him getting custody of Xavier. The tears stung his face. What little bit of stability he had left crumbled into pieces.

Assuming that it was Granny, Aunt Elisa, or Shawanda calling him on his cell phone, he started not to answer it. But then he remembered that he forwarded his home phone calls to his cell and the incoming call was from Iesha Brown.

"Hello?" He tried not to sniffle.

"Is this Emmitt?"

"Yes."

"Emmitt, this is Iesha, Charity's sister. Because of the stunt you're pulling, trying to take Xavier from her, she laying up in the hospital in a coma. I can't stand you. If she dies, I'mma personally come to Greensboro and kill your black behind myself." Then she broke down and started crying. "Why are you doing this to her, Emmitt?"

Emmitt's head was swimming. All he heard was Charity and coma. "Did you say Charity is in a coma?"

"Hello? Can you hear? That's exactly what I said."

"Oh man. Is Xavier all right?"

"He doesn't know anything yet."

"Good. I'mma drive up there tonight."

"Man, you ain't slick. You ain't coming nowhere near him."

"I'm not— Do you need anything?"

"Yes, for you to leave us alone."

Emmitt hung up when it was clear that Iesha had ended the call.

Chapter 26

SHE WATCHED THE WOMAN in the sleeveless bright white sundress sit down at a small table. As she looked around, Charity didn't recognize the woman or the place where she was. *A woman at a table in the middle of nowhere, surrounded by trees and flowers. Oh, I get it. I'm dreaming.* She attempted to find out where she was in the dream. She couldn't see herself. *This is weird.* She tried to move her legs to get to the woman, but they wouldn't move. She tried again. She could not lift the weight of her legs. She tried her arms, but they too felt like dead weight. Frustrated, she screamed to get the woman's attention. If she was in her dream, surely she could hear her. She opened her mouth to yell for help but nothing came out. Charity had dreams like this before, and she called them devil's dreams. Just as she would do at any other time, she rebuked him in her mind until he left her. *Satan, I rebuke you in the name of Jesus. I bind you up and loose myself from your grip, you defeated foe. I submit unto God, forgive me, Father. And I resist you, Satan, now flee.*

She began to hear voices. She turned her attention to the woman. She was still at the table and sipping from a teacup. She was talking to someone at the other end of the table but like one of Mama Lorraine's bootlegged videotapes, Charity couldn't see the farther end. All she could see was a hazy white film. She could hear the woman's voice clearly but the other voice was muddled, resounding. Charity heard the woman say, "Yes, I would like to go back and try again." The other voice echoed a response that Charity could not understand. The woman cried, "I promise to remember what you've told me . . . righteousness is a gift, it's not earned. I'll remember, I promise." The echoing voice answered and this time Charity could plainly hear it, "I love you, daughter. You are forgiven." Charity wanted the voice to tell her she was forgiven too. She attempted to lift her leg—she needed to get to the table. This time her leg was lighter than it had been earlier. She kept trying. Though unable to speak, she could hear herself moan. She moaned to see if the woman could hear her. When the woman turned around and Charity saw her own face, she cried out. She was the woman and she could hear her name being called.

"Cherry! Cherry!" she heard someone say. "Go get the doctor, she moved."

Charity moaned, trying to answer.

"Hallelujah! Thank You, Lord! My baby's alive."

She recognized her mother's voice and tried to open her eyes. She was still dreaming and could see herself getting up from the table.

"God, I thank You. God, I worship You." She heard her mother say.

"Where . . . am . . . I?" Charity asked between moans.

She could feel someone grip her hand. She gripped back. She could feel herself being kissed on the face.

"Open your eyes, Cherry. It's Esha. Can you hear me? Open your eyes. Come on."

Charity tried but she could only see herself sadly walking away from the table. With every step, she could feel the distance between herself and the person on the other end.

"Come on, Cherry, open your eyes. Ya'll need to be praying. Daddy, will you come and lay hands on her?"

She heard a man's voice say, "Father, You said lay hands on the sick and they will recover. I know that You honor Your word. Lord, we speak those things that are not as though they were. According to Your Word, Charity is well. She is recovered. The chastisement of her peace was upon Jesus and by His stripes she is healed. Amen."

When Charity felt a cold hand on her forehead, she opened her eyes. "What . . . happened?"

It looked and sounded like pandemonium in the room. Mama Lorraine was running around praising God. Terrence was jumping up and down in place blessing the Lord. And Iesha was on her knees worshipping. Mr. Brown just sat in the recliner crying tears of joy. Only the nurse was available to answer her.

"What happened?" she asked again.

"Today's Friday, February 11, and you just awakened from a three-day coma," the nurse answered.

Charity tried to sit up. Her body still felt heavy.

"Oh no, sweetheart, don't try to get up. Your body's still weak."

Charity looked confused. "A coma?"

"Yes, do you remember what happened?"

She sadly lowered her head and nodded.

The nurse lifted Charity's chin, "Uhn huhn. Hold your head up," she smiled. "You had too many prayers sustaining you for you to be ashamed."

As they could, Mama Lorraine, Mr. Brown, Iesha, and Terrence joined Charity individually to welcome her.

"How are you feeling?" Mama Lorraine asked.

"Tired."

They all laughed. Iesha joked, "You've been asleep for three days, you ought to feel rested."

Charity held her hand to her throat. "I need some water," she requested.

Iesha fetched a cup of water for her. When she handed it to her, Charity noticed her ring. Her throat was too scratchy and dry to talk. She pointed to her finger as she sipped water.

Iesha held out her finger for Charity to inspect her ring. "You like it? Terrence and I are getting married."

"You didn't waste any time, did you? Congratulations!" Charity said in a whisper.

"All right," the nurse warned. "I'mma let you folks visit for a few more minutes then I'mma have to ask you to clear out of here. I need to call for the doctor."

Mama Lorraine was holding her daughter's hand. "How long should we go for?"

"I'd like to see her rest without interruption for the rest of the day and night. When I call the doctor, he's going to order a series of blood tests and a liver panel to check for damage. Hopefully, we won't find any."

"Will we be told the results of the test?"

"Yes, sir," the nurse answered Mr. Brown. "We can let you know those when you come back tomorrow. I've got to take these tubes and things off of her and help get her bathed. Poor thing's going to be poked and prodded for the next couple of hours. She'll need to rest. You folks could use some rest too. You haven't moved in three days. You'd think you were the ones in a coma."

They laughed. Charity could tell that they didn't want to leave her. She made eye contact with her mother. "I'll be fine. Go on home."

Mama Lorraine squeezed her hand and kissed her on the forehead. Charity basked in the love and peace she felt among her family. And vowed to herself that she would let nothing, no matter how devastating, make her want to throw it all away again. "Where's Zavey?"

"In school," Mr. Brown answered, combing his daughter's hair with his fingers. "We can't wait to tell him the good news."

"I was just making sure he wasn't with Emmitt. Does he know what happened?"

Mama Lorraine asked, "Who, Emmitt or the baby?"

"Both."

"Your daddy and I told Xavier you were sick and resting in the hospital. You know we didn't call Emmitt."

"I did," Iesha raised her hand like a shy schoolgirl. "Ha ha," she laughed to play it off when Mama Lorraine gave her one of her deadly looks. "I called to cuss him out Tuesday."

"What did he say?"

"Nothing. Don't start worrying about him, Cherry."

"That's right," her father agreed.

"I just don't want him to use this against me in court."

Terrence spoke, "If our God has made death behave, don't you think He'll show up for you in the courtroom? He can take care of a court case."

"Amen," they all agreed.

Charity was glad to have been moved to a room on a regular floor. It was early Saturday morning, and a doctor had come in with a casually dressed woman. Charity could tell by the identification badge that she was a staff person. "Hello," the doctor greeted. Charity's parents were already there and they both returned his greeting. Mama Lorraine thanked him for his help. She told him that she and her husband had grown to like him over the past three days that he'd worked on Charity. Then she stepped away from the bed to make room for him to speak to Charity.

"Ms. Phillips. I'm Dr. Gellar," he said to Charity. "It's good to see you up."

"It's good to be up."

"The nurse checked your vital signs and everything looks good. No internal damage, your liver is fine. You look good. How're you feeling?"

"Good enough to go home."

"Before that can happen, I have someone here you have to meet." He motioned for the young lady to move closer. "This is Lynette Spence, she's from the Behavioral Health unit and she has to assess you before we can discharge you."

The woman reached out her hand for Charity to shake. Charity accepted her gesture. "What am I being assessed for?"

"To see if you should be admitted to our Behavioral Health unit."

"Oh, I don't need to be. I've learned my lesson."

"What would be a good time for me to come back?"

Charity looked at the clock. "Will you give me an hour to get cleaned up and then come back?"

"Yes, sure." She stepped back.

Dr. Gellar spoke again. "If Ms. Spence finds that you don't need to be admitted there, then I will discharge you this afternoon. If she finds that you should be admitted, then I will transfer you today." He stood up to assure the family that everything was all right. Then, he and Ms. Spence left.

"Lord, now they trying to lock me up on the psycho ward," Charity chuckled.

"Girl, you ain't going nowhere."

"You right about that, Momma."

"Cherry, who is Sharon Nelson?"

Charity thought for a moment. "Oh, the girl I was telling you about that had dinner at the house with us last Sunday. Why?"

"She's the one who called the police and called Pastor King."

"Huh?" Then Charity remembered Sharon telling Mrs. King that she was completing her internship at the county.

"When Pastor King called us, he said she told him she works for the county's suicide line and recognized your voice. God was definitely in it, because she even remembered your address. The paramedics say if they hadn't gotten to you when they did, you would have been dead upon arrival."

Charity shook her head and thanked God.

"She's called the hospital to check on you every day. I have her number if you want to call her later. She seems like a sweet girl."

"Thank you, Momma. I'll get the number later. Has Pastor been by?"

"Every day. You sure he's married? 'Cause I'd swear—"

"Daddy, please."

"I'm serious."

"Baby, you want something to eat?" Mama Lorraine asked.

"No, ma'am. I'm hungry but I don't have an appetite. I don't think my stomach would hold anything. Just the thought of eating makes me sick." She tried to raise herself up higher on the bed. Mama Lorraine helped her. Her body was still weak and the IV pole didn't make it easy for her to move. "I'd like to take a shower."

"I can help you with that."

"Lorraine, you can't do that. Them nurses is gonna have to do that."

"Cherry, where's that nurse's button? I'll ask them myself."

Charity pointed to the red button with a picture of a white nurse's cap on it.

"May I help you?"

"Yes, ma'am. This is Lorraine Brown. I'm the mother of the patient in room 645. She's requesting a bath. Is it all right if I give her one?"

"Oh no, ma'am. She has an IV pole with her. Please let Ms. Phillips know that her nurse will be there as soon as she can."

"I told you."

"Did I ask you anything, Charles?"

It felt good to hear them bicker again. *Thank You, Lord, for sparing my life.*

"Charles, I need you to step outside. I got something I want to talk to Cherry about."

Her father stood up. "Cherry, holler if you need me. You know how your momma is. I'll be right outside the door."

"At least you divorced your troubles," Mama Lorraine joked to Charity. When Mr. Brown left the room, Mama Lorraine sat on the edge of the hospital bed and locked her eyes with her daughter's. "Baby, you have endured many things throughout your life and God has brought you through them all. Rape couldn't take you out, abandonment couldn't, an abusive marriage failed. Ever since we've had you, we've known that God has been good to you. Remember that song we used to sing?"

Charity listened as Mama Lorraine began to sing about how God has been good to her all her life. When she finished, Charity said, "God is so good to me."

They were interrupted by a knock. A nurse peeked in from behind the door. "Are you ready?"

"Yes," Mama Lorraine answered for Charity and squeezed her hand. Mama Lorraine got up off the bed. "I'mma be outside with your daddy." As Mama Lorraine was leaving, Charity heard her humming the rest of the song.

"You ready?" the nurse asked again.

"Yes ma'am."

"Call me Rose, sweetie. I'm not much older than you."

"Okay, Rose. That's a beautiful name and it fits you too."

"Why thank you. That's exactly what it means, *beautiful*. Your name is just as fitting."

"Charity?"

"Yes. Char-i-ty," she enunciated.

"It sounds like a charity case, someone who's needy."

"Oh no, I don't think of it that way. When I learned your name and heard your folks talk about you, I thought of the King James version of the word, meaning love. Someone who walks in love, and always giving to others."

Charity thought about her life. "Yep, that would be true. That's how I wound up here—I was giving so much of myself, I felt empty."

The nurse helped her out from the bed and into the bathroom. "It's not a bad thing to help. That's a gift not given to many people. But it's a terrible thing when your motives are not right. Like giving to gain people's approval or recognition.

"Humph." Charity stiffened.

The nurse must've noticed. "I do this so often I forget how uncomfortable it can be sometimes. Would you like for me to just run your water and step outside while you shower?"

Charity shook her head. "No, it's time I learn to delegate and accept help. Thank you."

Rose eased Charity onto the toilet and adjusted the temperature of the water. "Just be patient with yourself. It's going to take a little while to get back to one hundred percent. What kind of work do you do?"

"I feel like I have three full-time jobs. I'm a therapist, a single mother, and a minister."

"Girl, bless you. I challenge you to change your perception about your roles though. Each of them is a calling and you have been anointed and equipped to handle them all. You can only do it if you rely on your Higher Power's strength and not your own."

"Are you saved?"

Rose started to whisper. "Yes. But we can't talk about religion on the job. It's looked at as imposing our beliefs, so we have to say Higher Power."

"Oh, 'cause I was getting ready to lead you into the sinner's prayer and convert you to Christianity." Charity relaxed as they both laughed.

"Are you ready to get cleaned up?"

Charity nodded and Rose helped her into the shower. Before the shower ended, Charity had told her about Emmitt, Mr. Wright, Harmony, and everything else that led up to the crisis.

"You're a strong woman," Rose encouraged her, and reached for the towel to dry her off. "It has already been taken care of and by the time you go out to face it all, it will all be fixed."

"Praise God. I'm believing for that."

"I think your folks brought you some clean clothes in here."

She walked over to the closet and took out a sweatsuit and under-garments. "These little clothes. How do you stay so small?"

She and Rose laughed. "I know, I know. You stay busy."

Charity got dressed while Rose remade her bed. She helped her to lie back down.

"You go ahead and get some rest. I'mma go check on my other patients."

"Thanks, Rose."

"You're welcome."

"No, thanks for everything."

Rose shooed her and before she closed the door behind her, she said, "You just make sure you remember that righteousness is a gift, and that it can't be earned."

Although Charity understood what she was hearing, she felt that she'd heard it before.

The tap on the door woke her. It was Ms. Spence.

"Did I wake you?"

"Come on in. I've been waiting for you."

She pushed the recliner up to the bed. "This assessment won't take long. Just about fifteen minutes. Okay?"

Charity nodded.

"Again my name is Lynette Spence. I'm a social worker from 7E, the Behavioral Health unit. Our department is called to assess people who feel suicidal, homicidal, or are depressed, or having any other psychiatric issues. I was called to interview you since you were hospitalized for a suicidal gesture. My first question is, are you currently suidical?"

"No, ma'am."

"What happened that you were suicidal?"

"I was overwhelmed with life. I'm a minister, a therapist, and a single mom. Those roles are hard enough, but I take care of myself pretty well. But all in a matter of hours things started snowballing. An employee of mine needed my help, then I found

out the building I rent space from for my practice was in foreclo-
sure, then I received papers from my ex-husband informing me
that he was taking me to court for custody of our six-year-old son,
and when a client of mine stopped taking his medicine and
became psychotic and got into my home, I couldn't take it. I woke
up Tuesday morning and was convinced that I didn't have any
other options."

"That is a lot of stuff happening at one time. Do you feel prepared to return home and handle those things?"

"Oh yes. This little ordeal has taught me that I have been on
the right track, but just doing things the wrong way. I have
learned that nothing is worth my life." She looked the social
worker in the eyes. "Nothing."

"Do you have a therapist? Or need a therapist?"

"No to both of your questions. I have plenty of support, but
I've been too prideful and stubborn to use them. As you can see,
my whole family is close. I have the support of them and my
church family, and I have good friends."

"Do you think you need to be hospitalized?"

"No, I don't need to be hospitalized. I'm not suicidal, or homicidal, or experiencing any other psychiatric problems."

The social worker stopped writing. "All right. We're done."

"What's the next step?"

"You just completed it. I'll write up a report for your doctor, letting him know that I've seen you and that I second his recommendation for discharge. You don't meet criteria for hospitalization."

"Thank you, thank you so much."

The social worker was leaving when Mama Lorraine and the
rest of the entourage walked in. "The prayers of the righteous
availeth much," Charity said. "The doctor should be here shortly
to discharge me."

"Thank the Lord," Iesha said, walking in behind her parents.
"Momma, where'd y'all go?"

"We went to eat. You hungry?"

"I want something, but it has to be light."

Mr. Brown said, "We can stop and get you a baked potato and salad, or soup on the way home."

"I'll try that."

Mama Lorraine didn't look up while she was packing Charity's belongings. "I had a taco salad from downstairs, it was good."

Charity turned up her nose. "That's too heavy. I can't eat that."

"Cherry, I'mma go ask when they think youll be ready to go. Hopefully it'll be in time enough where you can go with Momma and Daddy to pick Zavey up."

"You don't have to go anywhere," Mama Lorraine said. "I like ringing this nurse's button." She pressed the button.

"May I help you?"

"Yes, this is Mrs. Brown. Do you know what time we'll be discharged?"

"Tell Ms. Phillips that we're working on her discharge papers now. I'll say she should be ready to go in less than an hour. Okay?"

"Okay, thank you."

She summoned for her father to help her out of the bed. "Daddy, you're strong."

Iesha laughed. "You only weigh a buck-o-five."

"Watch it, now. You do want to live to get married, don't you? Speaking of which, have ya'll set a date?"

"Not quite. We were waiting until you recovered."

"Well, I'm recovered. When's the wedding?"

"Sometime next year. We've got a lot of learning about each other to do."

"I don't understand how y'all do things these days," Mr. Brown said. "Y'all be engaged for years."

"Me and your daddy got married in a day."

Charity said, "That's because you went to the justice of the peace."

"And we've never looked back," Mr. Brown said, patting his wife on the behind.

"Get a room," Iesha blurted.

They continued talking until the nurse came in with Charity's discharge papers and explained them to her. Her father helped her into the wheelchair and wheeled her out of the hospital. On the way to her father's van, she noticed the wooded lot on the hospital's lawn. There was a single white picnic table in the middle of a landscape of trees. She kept her eyes on the area. It seemed like she'd been there before.

Chapter 27

When Terrence helped Iesha out of the car, she gripped his hand tightly and wrapped his arm around her waist. "Honey, you sure you're ready for this?"

Terrence opened his trench coat and wrapped Iesha in it. "I'm fine," he assured her. "Nervous, but fine." He bent down to kiss her on the lips.

"There's nothing to be nervous about. The kids are going to love you."

"I hope you're right."

"I am right." This time she kissed him fully. "Happy Valentine's Day."

"School's out," he whispered, interrupting the kiss.

Iesha turned around to see children filing out of the building. She turned back to face him, "What are you doing?"

Terrence was using the rearview mirror to smooth his hair, his light beard, and goatee. "Trying to make a good first impression." He smoothed his coat with his hands.

"They're seven and nine, honey. Candy will get you a lot farther than your handsome face."

"You should've told me," he smiled. "I would've stopped by the store."

"Too late." She pointed. "Here they come now."

Iesha took a few steps ahead of Terrence to meet her kids. "Hey, guys. Did you have a good day in school?" They both nodded but their eyes were fixed on Terrence. "Good. I have someone I want you to meet. Remember I told you about Mr. Terrence? He wanted to come and meet you. Say hey."

"Hey," Raquan shyly muttered from where he was.

Sha-Lai was a little more animated as she waved.

"Hello. I bet you're Raquan," Terrence playfully said to Sha-Lai.

"Noooo. Sha-Lai."

"That's a beautiful name for a beautiful young lady." Sha-Lai blushed. Terrence turned to the boy who was practically attached to Iesha's leg. "You must be Raquan?" he asked.

Raquan nodded slowly.

"Give me five, man."

Terrence seemed to relax when Raquan slapped his hand.

"He'll warm up to you," Iesha promised. "He's a little shy."

Iesha was surprised to hear Raquan speak. "You gone marry my momma?"

"Quit asking stupid questions," Sha-Lai scolded. "Momma already told you that."

Terrence bent down to talk with them. "Well, that's what I wanted to talk to you two about. I wanted to know if it was okay with you."

Sha-Lai and Raquan looked at each other and giggled. Sha-Lai shrugged her shoulders. "I don't know. Momma?"

"Guys, Mr. Terrence is so sweet. Look at him, he's cute. He's smart. He loves God. He makes me happy. I want to marry him."

If the sun had shone as bright as the kids' smiles, the temperature would have gone up forty degrees. Terrence knelt before Iesha. "Ms. Iesha Brown, will you take me to be your husband, to love and to cherish?"

"I will," she agreed.

"Sha-Lai, will you take me to be your stepfather?"

She covered her uneven-toothed grin with her hand. "I will."

Even Raquan was eagerly awaiting his turn. "Raquan, will you take me . . . to the skating rink, and fishing, and to the beach?"

Raquan laughed. "Yes."

"And will you take me to be your stepfather?"

"Yes."

"Good, 'cause this cement is cold." Terrence stood up. "Group hug?"

They huddled and hugged.

Iesha began to sing the Barney song about loving and being a family.

"Momma, you're embarrassing," Sha-Lai said, breaking the hug to look around for witnesses.

"Quick, Sha-Lai. Get in the car before anyone sees you." Terrence opened the car door for her to jump in. Raquan slid in behind her.

"Y'all be careful. Don't mess up Mr. Terrence's car."

"Shhhh," Terrence lightly whispered to her. "Leave them alone."

"Okay," she said, getting into the passenger seat. "You remember that."

Iesha could not describe the way she felt if she tried. She was finally participating in the family life she had been observing. In the past, whenever she saw fathers with their children, driving their families, or a man and a woman holding hands, she got overwhelmed with feelings of loneliness; with Terrence, her longing was over.

She stole glances at him as he drove to her house for dinner. This was her best Valentine's Day ever. To show him appreciation, she offered to cook for him her best dish—spaghetti. A part of her was ashamed of her meager governmental housing, especially since Mama Lorraine always called it nasty. But she knew that Terrence would not criticize her.

"Do we need to stop by the store for anything?" Terrence asked, interrupting her thoughts.

"No, I got everything I needed earlier."

Sha-Lai spoke up from the backseat. "I want something from the store."

"Yeah, can we get some bubble gum? Please, Momma. Pul-leeze."

"Don't nobody want no bubble gum, stupid."

Iesha could feel her blood rising. "Come on, guys, that's enough. Sha-Lai, what have I told you about calling your brother names?"

"Sorry," she halfway apologized.

Terrence turned into a convenience store parking lot. "That was nice for you to apologize, Sha-Lai," he said.

"What are you doing?" Iesha asked.

"Going to get some bubble gum and a treat for Sha-Lai for apologizing."

Iesha looked back and saw the smile on Sha-Lai's face. "No, that's what she's supposed to do. She shouldn't have been calling him stupid."

"Well, I'm here now. You can just give it to them later then."

"No, neither of them have done nothing extra special that they should get a treat."

"I don't like going back and forth in front of them," said Terrence. "Maybe we should do this some other time."

"I think that's a good idea because I don't want you to feel like you have to buy their affection."

"I'm not buying their affection, I'm just buying bubble gum."

"Let's just go on to the house, please," said Iesha, trying to be as civilized as she possibly could. She didn't want the drama queen to come out.

"I think we agree that this is not a good time to talk about this," Terrence said.

Iesha just turned her head and looked out the window. *He*

doesn't want to get me started. The rest of the ride was silent. Not even the kids spoke. Iesha wondered what the silence meant. She lied to herself thinking that if he no longer wanted to marry her that she was okay with it. She wanted to let him know that she was okay but being weak was not her style. She rolled her eyes at her thoughts. *I am not going to be a doormat.* She sat reservedly in her seat with her arms crossed until they got to her house.

She got out of the car before Terrence could make it around to open the car door for her.

"Honey, are you okay?"

Iesha opened the door for the kids and without looking at him said, "Uhm hum."

"You sure?"

She did not want to be like this but she didn't know how to act otherwise. "Look, Terrence, I said I was okay." She slammed his car door shut and walked before him to the porch. *Please, God, help me,* she pleaded.

"Let me get that for you," Terrence offered.

She had never noticed how loudly the storm door squealed until he pulled it open for her. It irritated her even more. "What do you think I did before you got here?" she asked him. "I'm not some weak woman who needs rescuing. I take care of my own chaps, I open my own doors, I cook my own food, I cut my own grass, and I can even do my own oil changes. So, if you think I'mma turn into one of those prisses who don't do jack, you got another think coming."

When Terrence didn't respond, she went into the house. With an attitude, she said to him, "Welcome to our humble abode. It's not much, but there are a lot of people living in big, fancy houses and are miserable. But we have a home here and we are happy." Sha-Lai and Raquan were just as quiet as Terrence. Iesha knew she must've been making a fool of herself. "Kids, go to your room. I'll call you when dinner is ready." She did not have to tell them twice, they were gone before she closed her mouth.

"Well?" she asked, trying to provoke a response from Terrence.

"Well, what?"

"Well, aren't you going to talk to me?"

"I want to talk to you but I don't want to argue with you."

"What do you want to talk about?"

"For starters this is the first time I've been inside your house. Are you going to show me around?"

She softened. "There's really nothing to show, but if you want to see it, I'll take you on a grand tour." She knew he must've been glad to see her smile. As quickly as she could, she walked him through the house. She wasn't expecting any compliments since she never received any. They ended up in the kitchen. She washed her hands and pulled the half-baked spaghetti casserole out of the refrigerator. Terrence washed his hands in the sink, too. Together they cut up the ingredients for a salad.

By the way he approached her, she knew he was treading lightly. "Honey, I hope you don't really believe that I think you are a weak woman. Because don't. I open doors for you and pull chairs out for you because that's the way my father taught me. That kind of a lifestyle is a compliment, not an insult. And so is what I want to ask you. This is not meant to demean you in any way. Would you be okay with you and the kids moving into my house?"

Iesha could have jumped for joy but she couldn't let him see that. "Move into your house? Do you have enough room for me and two kids?"

"Honey, this is all predestined by God. I remember when I found my house, I didn't know why I felt led to buy such a big house, but I loved it. And I believe by faith that you will too."

"I can't wait to see it. It seems so weird that we're engaged and I haven't been to your house or met your parents."

"Well, we have had some things happen to slow us down a bit. Do you want this cut up too?"

Iesha looked in the bowl of lettuce, cucumbers, cherry tomatoes, and carrots and decided that they had enough cucumbers. "No, but you can butter that bread over there."

Within a matter of minutes, they were all sitting down for dinner. Iesha was proud of the kids, who were well behaved. They didn't fight. Sha-Lai didn't ask a lot of questions, and Raquan ate like he had some sense. She was impressed with how good Terrence was with them. He didn't tire of their conversation and he balanced his attention among the three of them. She felt an urge to apologize to him and to let him know she appreciated him.

After dinner, Iesha sent the kids to their rooms to get ready for school tomorrow and to take baths. She led Terrence to the living room and they sat on the couch. She flipped through the television channels. "Do you like *The Jamie Foxx Show?*"

"I watch it sometimes."

"There's nothing else really on. Do you want to watch it?"

"Girl, just being in your presence is enough for me."

She blushed and turned toward him. She pulled her legs up on the couch and let them rest behind her. "I need to apologize to you."

"No, you were right. I was trying to buy the kids' affection."

"But that doesn't mean I can talk to you any kind of way. That was disrespectful."

"You gone make me fall in love with you even more."

Iesha could hear the shower running. That meant Sha-Lai was showering. Raquan only took baths. As long as there was a new person in the house, Raquan would stay in his room from shyness. She put her hand on Terrence's chest. "That's what I want you to do." When he did not refuse her touch, she pushed herself up on her knees and eased backward into his lap. She slid her body down on his so that she could rest her head on his neck and shoulder. He cradled her and planted warm kisses on her cheek and neck. Her heart was beating as fast as her breathing rate. She pushed herself up on all fours and turned to face him. She did not care that they were not married, they would soon be. Neither did she care about the kids being in the house. She wanted to know what else God had in store for her. She put her hand under his shirt.

"Baby," Terrence panted. "We can't do this." Iesha tried to kiss him again. He blocked her tongue with his. "I know you love me. You don't have anything to prove. We will not go into our marriage under a curse."

Iesha wasn't sure about what he was talking about, but she rested her head on his chest. "I'm sorry."

"It's okay." He patted her on the head and kissed her forehead. "Just promise that when it's my turn of weakness, you'll be strong enough to stop me."

"You better pray about that one." Iesha scratched her head and said, "So you're really going to make me wait?"

"You're the one who wanted to wait."

"Well, yeah," she admitted. "We have to plan a wedding, reception, honeymoon. I need a dress. We need someone to take pictures. Not to mention bridesmaids and groomsmen."

"Would you be okay with a small, private ceremony? With just family and a few friends?"

"Yeah."

"You just get a dress and, believe me, my mom will handle the rest. She used to do weddings. She still has all the decorating stuff. We'll ask her when we visit this weekend."

"Okay." She laid her head back on his chest.

She noticed a change in Terrence's facial expression. "What?"

"I think we'd better wait that year out."

"Now, you get me all excited and change your mind."

"No, you were just talking about the kind of wedding you wanted and I downsized it. If that's what you want, that's what you should have."

"Ahhh, that's sweet."

"And besides," he said slyly. "We can't get married without premarital counseling."

"I was thinking about that."

"Do you mind if I call my pastor tomorrow and set something up?"

"Oh yes, please do."

This time when she plopped her head on his chest, Terrence said, "Oh, no. I need to go home and take a cold shower." He stood up. "I'll see you tomorrow evening."

As if she was trying to make sure he dreamed about her, she kissed him in a way that he should remember for a long time.

CHAPTER 28

EMMITT WAS GLAD FOR THE PEACE HE FINALLY HAD. The phone had stopped ringing and people had stopped coming by. He needed to clear his mind. It had been a week since his mother's funeral and he was more distracted by his meeting Emmitt Chambers and by Charity's hospitalization than he was about his mother's death. Everything he knew and believed about himself was a lie. He was even lying to himself about Charity. He loved her and he wanted her back. He went to his closet and pulled down a footlocker. He sat opposite the opened chest on the bed.

He remembered the day before Charity left home, she'd come home from work and found him on the back deck cooking on the charcoal grill.

"You're cooking?" she asked. He knew that she was surprised because they had both stopped cooking and weren't even communicating at that time.

"Yeah . . . our wedding pictures."

Charity walked back in the house and momentarily returned with two picture frames. "Oh, you forgot these." She took the photos out of the frame and threw them on the open fire.

He'd tried to stop her, but he didn't want her to discover he was lying. Knowing what time she would be getting home, he set some newspapers on fire and told her that he was burning their wedding photos. Those photos along with their wedding video were stored in the chest he was now looking through. He opened the handmade, white lace–covered photo album. He observed how tenderly he had held her taking their first dance. The picture of them cutting the cake and laughing made him laugh too. He remembered Charity daring him to smear cake in her face. They looked so happy in the pictures. *How did we let it get so bad?*

In the family photos, he recognized that his mother looked happy for them. She proudly stood by his side in some, and lovingly stood by Charity in others. He touched the photo as if he could touch his mother. *Life is too short. You never know when it's your time.* Before he thought about what he was doing, he reached for the phone. He wanted to talk to Charity and he wanted another chance. He dialed her number but hung up before it could ring. Wrestling with his thoughts, he dialed the number again, but hung up before he could get an answer. He almost dropped the phone when it rang in his hand.

"Hello?"

"Emmitt? Were you trying to call me?" He was too startled to speak. "Emmitt?"

"Huhm," he cleared his throat. "I'm here. I was just . . ."

"Are you okay?"

"Charity, we need to talk. There's a whole lot of things I need to tell you—"

"And there's—"

"I know," he said, cutting her off. "I know there's a lot of things you want to say to me. But I think if you let me talk first, you won't need to say half of what you think you want to say. I have some apologizing and explaining to do. I'd like to talk in person."

When she did not respond, he continued. "I know what you're thinking. I'm not up to anything. I'm not trying to pull one over on you. I just want to talk."

"I'm not sure that this is a good time. I've only been recuperating for a few days. I'm not sure I can handle this right now."

"Iesha called and told me about you being in the hospital." He paused. "I feel so responsible for that. Charity, I'm so sorry for all I've done. Can we please talk about this?"

"I can't meet you halfway and I don't feel comfortable having you in my house."

"I know. I know."

"Can't we just talk on the phone?"

"I'd like to see you. I would like for us to talk face to face."

She was silent for a moment. Emmitt wondered what she was thinking. "All right," she said. "You want to talk? We'll talk here. For one hour and that's it. What time will you be here?"

He looked at his watch. "It's four o'clock now. I can be there by six thirty or seven."

"I'll see you then—"

"Thank you, Charity."

"Don't thank me just yet, Xavier will not be here when you get here."

Although Emmitt did not agree, he could understand her limitations. "That's fine, Charity. I just want to talk."

"Good-bye, Emmitt."

"Bye."

He was so excited he felt like thanking God. He knew that Charity's agreeing to meet with him was nothing short of a miracle. He decided he'd leave the praying and talking to God to her. She was the preacher, not him. On the way out, he scanned his CD case and grabbed Brian McKnight's first album. When he got to the car, he slid the CD into the player and selected track seven. "Never Felt This Way" used to be Charity's favorite song. While making their wedding plans, Emmitt had convinced her to walk down the aisle to a traditional here-comes-the-bride piece. But on their wedding day, he surprised her by having his cousin serenade her with a rendition of "Never Felt This Way." He remembered how she stopped in the aisle when she recognized the instrumental chords to the song. Even from the altar where he stood, he could see the ceiling lights reflect her glistening tears. He quieted his thoughts to listen to the words. Emmitt programmed the CD player to repeat the song and he listened to it all the way to Charlotte. He turned down the volume so that he could rehearse what he would say to her.

"Charity, I'm sorry. I love you and I want us to be together again." *That's too simple*, he mused. "Charity. Please forgive me. I apologize for hurting you while we were married and afterward. I've been prideful and selfish. Since Momma died, I realized that life is too short to be unhappy. Unhappiness killed her. I don't want to die that way. I love you and I'd like to work things out." *Charity'll never go for that. I'll just say what's in my heart when I get there.* He smacked his lips out of frustration. It was going to take a miracle and then some for him to pull this off. He was never one to humble himself for risk of appearing weak. He needed some divine intervention and that meant he was going to have to pray.

"Dear God," he said aloud, sounding more like he was writing a letter. "I hate to be coming to You like this, but I need Your help." He looked out the passenger window and saw the driver next to him looking back. He picked up his cell phone and pretended he was dialing a number and he was talking into the phone. "I messed up and I want my ex-wife and my son back, in that order. Since Charity serves You and is raising my boy to do so, I know if I want them in my life, I'm going to have to serve You too. Help me, Lord. Amen."

As he was approaching an intersection, he saw a yellow sign with the word ROSES hand painted in red. He decided to stop and buy a dozen for Charity. He pulled into the lot and drove around to where the Latino couple were selling bouquets. He was impressed with their setup. They had displays of floral arrangements wrapped in plastic, as well as vases of flowers. There were even a few people shopping. Mainly husbands or boyfriends who must've forgotten Valentine's Day and were trying to make up, he guessed.

"Is there such a thing as purple roses?" an older white man asked Emmitt.

"I don't know, man. That would be nice since my wife's favorite color is purple."

The man chuckled. "Yours too?"

They stayed side by side looking through the array of flowers. "You like these?" Emmitt initiated the conversation this time.

"They're put together nice, if that's what you're asking. I have no idea of what to look for. My wife likes to have Valentine's week, not just Valentine's Day."

"Long as you don't tell my wife."

"How long have you been married?"

Emmitt looked away. "We're actually divorced. But I'm in town to see if we can work things out."

When Emmitt made eye contact with him again, the man asked him, "Do you know the Lord?"

"I don't go to church or anything—"

"No, I asked you if you know the Lord. Do you have a relationship with Jesus Christ?"

"No, not really."

"Well, I believe our being here at this place at the same time is a divine appointment. Have you been praying to get to know Him?"

"Yes, I have."

"Well, hallelujah, that confirms it because I pray daily to be put in people's paths so I can lead them to Him."

Right there under the canopy flower stand, the man prayed for Emmitt and his family and led him into a prayer for salvation. Afterward, he talked to him for a few minutes more. "You may not feel different. Salvation is not based on feelings. There may be days you don't feel saved. Salvation is a knowing." He handed Emmitt a tent folded card that he took from his wallet. "This is a card from our church. It has some Bible verses you be sure to read. To get to know who Jesus is, I recommend that you start with the book of John. Get yourself into a Spirit-filled Bible-teaching church. All of this sounds like mumbo-jumbo right now, but just like He did today, God will lead you."

The man paid for his and Emmitt's flowers. Emmitt thanked the man as they walked to their cars. "Now," Emmitt said to himself. "I know there's a God." He arrived at Charity's house a little before 7:00. There was not a nervous bone in his body when he rang her doorbell.

Charity opened the door. "Hello," she greeted stiffly.

"Hey. These are for you." He pulled the roses from behind his back.

Charity's voice was still flat. "Thank you." She stepped away from the door so that he could come in. "Have a seat in the living room. I'll put these in the kitchen."

He felt like he would burst with excitement as he walked into the living room. As far as he was concerned, he and Charity didn't really have to talk, he felt like what he needed to do had already been done at that flower stand. He picked up the big Bible on the coffee table. He wouldn't mind reading the book of John. He wanted to know what it said. He flipped through its pages but couldn't find John. He turned to the front of the book for the table of contents. He then sequentially ended up near the back of the book. *In the beginning was the Word, and the Word was with God, and the Word was God.* When Charity entered the room, he slammed the book shut.

She sat down. "Okay, where should we begin?"

Emmitt placed the Bible back in its place and turned toward Charity. "I want to apologize to you. I am so sorry for all of the pain I caused you." Even though Charity had turned her head, Emmitt kept talking. "You have been right so many times about so many things. I apologize for not listening to you, for not respecting you. I'm sorry I didn't know how to be a husband to you."

"I accept that," Charity said firmly. "But that's not the first apology I want to hear."

Emmitt looked at her with a confused expression on his face.

When he saw the tears fall from her eyes, he froze in place. He didn't know whether to reach out to hold her or to let her cry.

"What about for choking me? Emmitt, you've never admitted or apologized for choking me."

He held his head in his hands and racked his brain to remember the incident she was referring to. He honestly could not remember choking her. He remembered them arguing over the baby. He remembered shouting loudly at her. Either he cornered or pushed her back to the wall. But that's all he remembered. "Charity, I really don't remember. But if I choked you, why didn't you scream?"

She stood up fighting mad. "How could I scream when I couldn't even breathe?"

Emmitt heard wailing but he didn't know that it was coming from him. "Oh God," he moaned in between sobs. "Oh God. I'm sorry. I'm so sorry."

When Charity tried to comfort him, he held her away with his hand. "Emmitt, don't do this. Let me help you," she demanded softly.

"How come I don't remember this? And if I don't remember this, what else have I done that I don't remember?"

He allowed her to sit next to him on the couch.

"I'm not trying to be your therapist, but because I am one I know that there is an explanation for this. I have just never wanted to accept it. It was easier for me to believe that you were lying about not remembering that you choked me." She turned his head toward her. "But it's not uncommon for people to suppress traumatic experiences and to not recall specifics later. Like the time your mother's boyfriend held you at gunpoint. Do you remember all of what happened that day? What about the day of your accident? How much of that do you remember?"

Emmitt shook his head.

"Well, this is comparable to that. Another point of view to consider is the spiritual explanation. I believe this one even more. You were not yourself when your hands were gripping around my throat. Emmitt, you said things you would have never said, to anyone. Do you remember what you said?"

He shook his head again.

"You called me all kinds of names, using choice words I had never heard you say, and you threatened to rip my heart out. You were not yourself," she reiterated. "No one wants to kill me like that, no one but the devil, and what does the devil aim for daily? My heart, the thing that connects me to God." She closed her eyes. "Even while it was happening, all I could see was red, or blood. I don't even remember seeing you. Maybe I was blacking out or something, I don't know. But I truly believe you were possessed, on an assignment from the enemy to take me out. I don't even remember how it ended. Or why you let go. I don't remember that. . . ."

Emmitt considered everything Charity said and as sincerely as he could he asked her forgiveness. "Will you please forgive me for . . ." He looked down and then up again. "For . . . cho—choking you. I would never hurt you in that way. Seeing my mom in and out of abusive relationships and marriages, I have always vowed that I would never hit a woman. And I did. I'm sorry. With God's help, I'll never hurt you again."

She put her arm around his shoulder and said, "Thank you. That's all I've ever wanted to hear you say. But in order to get God's help, you have to be saved. Are you ready for that?"

He wiped his face and smiled lightly. "I am already."

Charity squealed in delight, "What? When? How?"

He was so excited he told her the whole story in about a minute.

"That's great. I'm happy for you. Xavier will be glad to hear that. We've been praying together for you."

He sighed. "Speaking of our son. I want to apologize for this whole court thing. I don't know what I was thinking, or if I was thinking at all. I was feeling sorry for myself about the way my life has turned out and I felt like I needed something to validate me. The only thing I have to show is Xavier. And I guess I wanted to hurt you for leaving me. You told me you'd never leave."

"And you told me you'd never hit me."

"I know." He looked away and then back at her. "I'm dropping the court case. You're a good mother. You're doing a good job. I'm sorry for this whole court thing and for not supporting you financially." He held his head down again. "I was so concerned about what you'd do with the money I should've sent that I could never send it. Again, I was just wanting you to hurt. I know this is not much, but I want to give you this." He pulled his checkbook from his back pocket and tore out a check he had already filled in. "This is just a thousand dollars. I plan to send more after all of Momma's affairs are settled."

"Why are you doing all this? Why now? I mean, getting saved, apologizing, giving me money? Why couldn't you do this two years ago? When I needed you?"

"I don't know. I wanted to. I don't know." He wiped her tears with his hand. "I love you. I know that this is all a shock. But I want to give you seven days to think about something. I don't want you to answer now. You have until next Tuesday to decide."

"What?"

"Please consider remarrying me."

Her tears came too fast for him to wipe her face dry. "What about Shawanda? Don't you two have a daughter together?"

A scowl came across his face. "No! That's her daughter by another man. I was just with her trying to deny the pain I felt for not being with you." He received her when she slid closer to hug him. They sat there in silence and awe for at least a half an hour. When they finally started talking again they talked about the desire they used to share about relocating to New York. They both agreed they needed a new start.

Chapter 29

Charity was still on cloud nine from her meeting with Emmitt when her phone rang. She assumed it was him so she didn't look at the caller ID.

"Hello?" she answered pleasantly.

"Hey, Charity, it's Sharon. I'm so glad to hear your voice."

She'd been meaning to call Sharon but did not know how she would receive her. "It's good to hear from you, too. I've been wanting to call but I didn't know if you'd be comfortable."

"I felt the same way about calling you. I—"

"Sharon, I don't mean to interrupt but I need to thank you. Thank you for saving my life. The paramedics say if you hadn't called when you did, I would have been dead within five minutes."

Sharon sighed. "That was no one but God. I wasn't even supposed to be there that morning. One of the persons who mans the phones on Tuesday mornings called in sick. They called me at the last minute and asked me to man the phone for a few hours. I'm an intern there."

"How did you recognize my voice?"

"I wasn't really sure but it was like something told me who you were before I even recognized it."

"I just thank God through you. Because of y'all I'm doing well.

I'm taking time to think about what I'm going to do. I know you've heard about Present Day closing?"

"That's talk of the town until another tragedy comes along. Are you going to open another practice?"

"I don't know. I'm receiving some unexpected money and I'm considering working in the ministry full-time."

"That's wonderful. Not to change the subject, but besides finding out how you were doing, I wanted to see what your plans are for this weekend. I need a road buddy."

"Where are you going?"

"To Kentucky to see my brother."

Charity didn't know if she should go since she was considering Emmitt's proposal, but she was eager to meet her brother in the Lord. "Uuuuh. I want to go." She paused. "But, I don't know. Does he know about what I did?"

"Oh no, I wouldn't do that."

"Bless you, you're a sweetheart. Anybody else would've told the whole town by now." They both laughed. "I do want to go." Charity looked for an inconvenience, "What time are you leaving?"

"Visiting is Friday, Saturday, and Sunday, from eight in the morning to three. I'm off on Friday so we can travel that morning, rest up that evening, see him on Saturday, and head back home."

"Let's see, today's Saturday. Does he know you're asking me to come?"

"He doesn't even know I'm coming."

"That's even better, count me in. Let me make all of my arrangements and I'll call you back later tonight."

The bags under her eyes were proof of Charity's exhaustion. The seven-hour trip kicked her behind, and if she had known that Kentucky was covered in snow, she wouldn't have come.

"It can't be time to wake up," Sharon said without even rolling over.

Charity stepped away from the mirrored sink and looked back at the clock on the nightstand. "No, it's five ten. I just can't sleep."

"Girl, I'll sleep for the both of us. I'm tired. Get me up at seven."

"Okay," Charity said simply. She wished she could crawl back into bed, but she knew she wouldn't sleep. Her mind was too preoccupied with meeting Joseph. Why was she even here? she wondered. What was he like? What would he think about her? What would they do or talk about from 8:00 to 3:00? She was getting anxious just thinking about it all.

She retrieved her Bible from her duffel bag and went into the bathroom. She closed the lid and sat on the toilet. "Lord," she prayed. "I thank You for this day, and for its mercies. Thank You for going before me today and accomplishing Your will. I will not be anxious or fearful. What can man do to me?" Scripture began to ring up out of her heart. "Fear of a man will prove to be a snare, but my hope is in You. I am fearfully and wonderfully made, and my soul knoweth that full well. Give me wisdom, Father God, to know how to handle every situation. I thank You in advance for hearing and answering my prayer. It is with Jesus' name that I can do all things. Amen." She flipped through the pages of her New International version, desiring to read from the Book of Psalms. She turned through them, passing her favorites but stopped at Psalms 107. She figured she stopped because she was wasting time, but when she got to verse ten, she knew that it was referring to Joseph. "Some sat in darkness and the deepest gloom, prisoners suffering in iron chains, for they had rebelled against the words of God and despised the counsel of the Most High. So He subjected them to bitter labor; they stumbled, and there was no one to help." She reread the passage. "What are you trying to say Holy Spirit?" she asked aloud. She kept reading. "Then they cried to the Lord in their trouble and He saved them from their distress. He brought them out of darkness and the deepest gloom and broke away their chains."

"This is about Joseph, isn't it?" She felt a confirmed yes in her heart. She continued to ask questions about him and learned that Joseph was one of God's favored and that his imprisonment could be used for good and to further God's Kingdom. She also repented for holding him in contempt because of his situation. Although she and Joseph had exchanged only two letters apiece, she felt assured through Scripture that he would be released soon.

Charity didn't know what to do with the "information" she now had. Maybe she and Joseph would work together in the ministry, or maybe God would use her to minister to him, or something. Whatever God had in store for her to do with Joseph, she asked Him to reveal it today during their meeting. She was confident that He would.

By the time Charity finished her shower and left the bathroom, Sharon was already up. "I thought I was going to have to come in there after you," Sharon joked.

"Second to God, the bathroom is my refuge. It's the only place I can go without Xavier."

"He's so cute. I told you he should be on TV or in magazines somewhere modeling."

"You and everyone else. I guess I'm waiting for someone to come up to us and give us a contract."

They laughed. Sharon went into the bathroom, and Charity carried her duffel bag to the bed, where she poured out her toiletries. She put on some deodorant and lotion, and thought of putting on a CD. Sharon had brought *Go Get Your Life Back* by Donald Lawrence and played it for most of the road trip. Charity had fallen in love with the two versions of "Bless Me" ("Prayer of Jabez") and "Seasons." She played Lawrence's solo "Bless Me" track.

While Lawrence repeatedly pleaded for God to enlarge his territory, Charity, clad only in her underwear and pantyhose, found herself kneeling before God with tears in her eyes, and her hands outstretched toward the ceiling. She and Lawrence poured their hearts out together on two more rounds of the same song before she got up to finish getting dressed.

Charity was dressed when Sharon rejoined her in the room. "You like that song don't you?"

"It's beautiful. It's a good worship song."

"You're right about that. 'Seasons' is my favorite though. We sing it at my church."

"I'll play it for you."

They talked and sang as Sharon got dressed and Charity put on her makeup. "You always look so put together," Sharon told her.

"Chile, trying to be perfect and trying to control everything is what landed my behind in that hospital bed. But thank you anyway."

"I understand exactly what you're saying. There's a difference. Sometimes I think we Christians get it all wrong. We're already made in His image, the problem comes when we try to fit into the image, not even knowing we're already there. I forget how I heard this, or where I heard it, but I heard this man say, 'It's not that we are humans trying to learn how to be Christians, but that we're Christians learning to live as humans.' That has always stuck with me. I don't have to be no more than who I am made to be."

"Look at you ministering to me. You better do it, girl."

"It's so much freedom in that perception."

"You're right about that."

"So back to what I was saying. You are so perfect with your little waist. Your complexion is smooth and you look good in your clothes. And I don't know nobody that can wake up with their hair still in place."

"It's called I-have-a-good-hairstylist."

They laughed. Charity accidentally looked at the clock. "Uh, we better hurry up. It's after seven."

"Remind me to get directions to the prison when we go to eat the continental breakfast."

"I will."

• • •

Although the prison was a straight three miles from the hotel, neither Charity nor Sharon spoke a word. Charity's stomach was in knots because she hated the check-in process. That's why she rarely visited her father at the federal prison in Atlanta. It made her feel like a prisoner.

Sharon broke the silence. "You nervous?"

"So nervous I got to pee."

They laughed. "I don't know if I'm more excited about you meeting my brother or me introducing you to him." She clapped her hands in excitement.

They walked into the lobby and stood at the desk behind a few others who were going before them.

"You need to fill out one of those papers," the woman directly in front of them said.

"Thank you."

This was the same form she had to fill out in Atlanta. She suspected that the rest of the process would be the same too. She sighed. It took them a whole forty-five minutes to do nothing but wait. When a guard finally appeared, they thought he was going to give them some bad news.

"All right, let's go," he said, like the people waiting were the holdup.

They all stood and followed him. They stopped at every door and had to have their IDs checked and their hands scanned under a fluorescent light to make sure their hands were still stamped. This was ridiculous, Charity rolled her eyes. The guard let them out of the last set of doors and led them outside. They could see the campus and dormitories from where they were. They walked one hundred feet to the visiting facility. Charity didn't even look up, she just followed the persons in front of her to get her hand scanned and ID checked for the last time. She looked up when she heard Sharon squealing.

"There he is, there he is."

Charity looked in the direction Sharon was pointing to find Joseph, a bronze-colored, broad-shouldered man who was smiling like he had just won a million dollars. The boy was so fine, he made the tan-colored prisoner uniform look like an Armani suit. Charity nervously waved and returned his smile. After they were done at the desk, Sharon walked briskly before her and hugged her brother.

He held her. "Look at you, girl. You look good. Looking like Momma."

"Joseph," Sharon said, "meet Minister Charity Phillips." She had her hands outstretched toward Charity as she stepped forward.

"Look at my wife," he said. "Girl, you are fine!"

Being called his wife made Charity nervous.

"Isn't she beautiful?" Sharon added. "Just perfect. Y'all look good together."

Joseph hugged Charity and then he leaned back to kiss her. She turned her cheek to him. "Thank you," he said. "And you smell good."

He led them to their assigned chairs and sat between them. He didn't appear nervous and he had the same confidence that he wrote with.

"Your picture does you no justice," he told Charity.

"It was an old picture and the only one I could e-mail to the editor of the magazine."

"Wow. I can't believe that just three weeks ago I read your article, felt led to write to you, and now you are here with me. And better yet, you're with my sister. Y'all act like y'all have known each other for years."

Sharon smiled and said, "Joseph, she is so sweet and so down to earth."

"Well, I know who to call when I'm beating myself up," Charity said.

Joseph asked a guard for a Bible and ministered to them about a revelation he had received during Bible study the night before. Sharon listened intently and encouraged him to keep talking, even though Charity felt like he was talking too much. It seemed as if he was trying to prove to her that he was really saved. Charity was embarrassed when prisoners and their visitors would occasionally look back or over at them. Joseph was talking a little too loud. When he finally took a break from speaking, Sharon agreed to find him a soft drink from the vending machines.

He turned to Charity, "Did you notice how people around us stopped what they were doing to look at us and to try to hear what we were talking about?"

She nodded.

"They're attracted to the anointing on me. That always happens to me."

Charity smiled politely. She wished she were bold enough to tell him that people were looking at him because they couldn't hear themselves talk over him. They were trying to let him know that he was getting on their nerves, and hers.

"I've been talking so much, my throat is dry. I need to drink something before my breath start stinking."

Charity smiled. "Bless you," she said softly.

His eyes widened. "What you say?"

"I said 'bless you.' "

"Oh, I thought you said my breath stinks."

Charity shook her head. God was making it clear, all right. This man was arrogant and needed some balance. All he talked about was God and the Bible. *Definitely not my type.* Sharon returned with a Pepsi.

"Did you want anything, Charity?"

"No, I'll wait closer to lunch."

"So, sis, are you dating?"

"Yes, remember I wrote you about Tyree?"

"Oh yeah, yeah. Y'all still together?"

"Yes, we're planning to get married. I think I'm getting a ring soon."

"Oh, that's serious. I know I don't have to ask if he is saved and spirit-filled, right?"

"He is both. I just have one complaint." Sharon leaned over to make eye contact with both her brother and Charity. "Tyree is a fine young man, looks just like Morris Chestnut, on fire for the Lord, soon to be a minister of the Gospel, but the boy has no balance."

Charity thought she would fall out of her seat.

"If it ain't a Christian program, he won't watch it. If they ain't singing about God, he won't listen to it. He doesn't go to the movies, he doesn't do anything. I love him but I get discouraged because I can't figure out if I ain't where I need to be and need to step up to where he is, or if he is just out there in left field."

Joseph spoke first. "Well, I think there needs to be a balance."

Charity pursed her lips to keep them closed.

"Righteousness is not obtained by deeds, it is a gift of grace. We make our walk with God harder than it has to be. All we have to do is receive righteousness, but we get into bondage thinking we have to make ourselves righteous."

"Charity and I were talking about that this morning." Sharon glanced at Charity. "About how trying to please other people and trying to appear a certain way because you are a Christian will run you to an early grave."

Charity looked down, then up again. "And you don't have anything to prove to me," she said to Joseph. "Through prayer, I have learned who you are. I know your character. You don't have to try to impress me."

Sharon stood up. "I'mma go to the little girl's room."

Joseph turned to Charity. "You are so right. I'm sitting here trying to impress you and let you know that I am not an average prisoner. And I want my sister to know that I am doing well in spite of my circumstances. Thank You, Holy Ghost. I apologize."

Now, he had her attention. A man who could recognize when he was wrong and promptly apologize. She took the Gideon Bible out of his hand and said, "I know what's in here." She pointed to his heart. "Tell me what's in there."

He allowed her to ask questions. Sharon returned and helped him fill in the blanks. Charity was intrigued and enjoying the time she spent with him. She learned about his failed marriage, his daughter, and again about how he came to be imprisoned. When she asked if he had heard anything from his former partner, he told her he hadn't, but that he knew he was serving a life sentence. Finally, she listened as he told her about the clemency appeal that he recently submitted to the governor. She shared his excitement and committed to pray for him daily.

The visit was going so well that when the guard gave the final call for visitors to leave, she felt sad. After Joseph stopped trying to impress her, she found him to be funny, attentive, and sincere. She wished he wasn't in prison. Joseph asked Charity if he could pray with her.

"What about me?" Sharon asked playfully.

"Now, you know I'm going to pray for you. Just after I pray for Charity."

Charity allowed Joseph to hold her hands as he prayed. "Daddy, I thank You for blessing me with an opportunity to meet Charity. She is all You said that she would be and then some. Her visit is a testament to Your faithfulness to me. How blessed it is to know that You remember me and that You love me."

Charity listened carefully as he was praying. She was glad to hear him use Scripture in his prayer.

"Where can I go from Your Spirit? Or where can I flee from Your presence? If I ascend into heaven, You are there; if I make my bed in hell, behold You are there. If I take the wings of the morning, and dwell in the uttermost parts of the sea, even there Your hand shall lead me. And Your right hand shall hold me."

By the time Joseph finished praying, Charity had a change of heart. Why wouldn't she want a man with a faith like Joseph's? She didn't hesitate when he asked for her phone number. She helped him commit her number to memory so that he could have it put on his phone list for approval.

During the ride home, she and Sharon talked about Joseph so much, they reached Charlotte sooner than they expected. Charity couldn't believe how fast her heart had changed. *If only Emmitt was as spiritually mature as Joseph, and if Joseph was as available as Emmitt.*

CHAPTER 30

IT WAS JUST TUESDAY and Joseph was more than pleased to have received another letter from Charity today. He walked over to the mailroom counter and without looking at the other pieces of mail, he pushed them to the side. The two pictures she sent had him mesmerized. The woman was breathtaking. In the first picture she was standing behind an executive chair with her hands resting on its back. *She looks presidential*, he giggled. She was wearing a tailored brown blazer with a champagne-colored silk shirt underneath. He studied her big eyes and admired her gracious smile. "Umph, umph, umph. Thank You, Father. You are the bomb!" The other picture revealed Charity and her son, posing beside a sand sculpture that was supposed to be a castle. He turned it over. She had written, "Me and Xavier at Myrtle Beach, summer 2004." He found himself wishing that she didn't have on the white capri pants over her bathing suit. She looked good and was shapely for someone so petite. Xavier looked just like her. He had the same eyes and smile as his mother. He was handsome and he looked like a good boy. He was wearing a white tank top and swimming shorts that matched Charity's navy blue and white swimsuit. When Joseph had his fill of staring at the pictures, he read the card she sent. On the card front, sprinkles of rain were coming down from a cloud and there was an umbrella lying upside down on the ground with water in it. The inside read, "I'm praying a downpour of blessings for you." His smile turned into a blush when he read about how much she enjoyed her visit with him.

He stuffed the card in the envelope and walked back to his dorm. He had a few minutes before he had to go back to work. He wanted to run and tell Allen and Hankins about what he'd received, but he believed they were probably sick of hearing about Charity by now. That's all he had been talking about since the visit. Before he could get to his room, he heard his name being called.

"Nelson, let's go."

He looked at the security guard like he was cross-eyed. This particular officer was always looking for someone to harass. "I'm not going to be here long, officer. I just came to freshen up before I went back to work."

"Where have you been? We've been looking for you. You need to report to your counselor immediately."

He was getting annoyed by now. "Have I done something wrong, officer?"

"No, you're out of here."

Supposing that the officers had finally won their complaints against him and the others who were holding the nightly intercessory prayer meetings, he feared that he was going to be shipped to another facility. He wanted to smack that mocking smile off the guard's face. "Thank you," he replied, and stormed off.

He went to his room and washed his face. He knelt by his bedside and prayed. "God, please be with me when I stand before Officer Johnson. Touch his heart so that when he sees me, he sees You. If their intentions are to have me moved, Lord, send Your ministering angels to mess up their paperwork. The only move I want to make from here, Lord, is to my home. May it be so, in Jesus' name. Amen."

He arose not feeling much different from the way he did when he fell to his knees, but he rested in knowing that God was still in control. When he walked into Officer Johnson's office, the counselor stood up to greet him. He was usually glad to see Joseph, so his greeting did not change Joseph's demeanor. "Hey there, Nelson, are you all packed?"

His heart sank; it was true that they were moving him. Angrily, he snapped, "Where am I going this time?"

"Nelson." The counselor looked at him with raised eyebrows. He picked up a letter from his desk and handed it to him. "Didn't you get your copy of this in the mail today?"

It took everything he had not to snatch the letter out of his hand since everybody wanted to play games with him. He reached for the letter to read it. "Does this mean what I think it means?"

"Well, that depends, do you think it means you're a free man?"

"Please don't play with me." He talked more slowly, "Does this letter . . . mean that I . . . my appeal was granted and I'm immediately released . . . and I can go home?"

Since Joseph was talking to him like he couldn't hear, the guard talked slow and motioned with his hands like he was doing sign language. "By the authority of the Federal Bureau of Prisoners, I decree that you, inmate Joseph Nelson, number 03554-520, are a free man. Your appeal was granted. It looks like the witnesses that testified against you in the first trial had corroborated with your former partner. When they received your appeal hearing notice and were going to have to come back to court, they both turned in statements saying that their testimonies were false. That's all the prosecutor needed to let you go. You're scheduled to leave on the five-thirty-p.m. Greyhound bus heading to Virginia."

Joseph fell to his knees and thanked God for His faithfulness. He was crying like a baby when he went to hug the counselor. "Thanks for everything. Thank you, thank you."

"You better get going, Nelson—I mean, Joseph. I've only got three hours to get you to the bus station."

With that, Joseph ran at lightning speed to the canteen where Allen and Hankins worked. He was out of breath when he reached them. "I'm . . . going . . . home . . . today."

Even though he would confess his immediate release every day, they could tell by the tears streaming down his face that he was really going home. They all shouted with praise and hugged and cried together. The life they'd helped one another get through had already changed. "I only have three hours before my bus leaves, so I have got to get moving. Hankins, I want you to carry on with the intercessory prayer meetings. Don't let no one stop you. Allen, you are an encourager, keep the bros encouraged. You know how I did it, you used to imitate me and play the part, now I want you to be the part." Then, he started crying. "I love you guys so much. Thank you for everything you've done. You've stood by me, tolerated me. You taught me so much. I love you."

Hankins and Allen were crying just as hard. Allen spoke first. "I will do as you've said. You go out there and show them. Don't ever forget me, man."

"Never. We've got business plans, remember?"

"It's busy out there. You make sure you make time to write and send wedding pictures."

"I won't have to. You'll be at the altar with me. I've seen it in the vision and I know it will speak."

"Lord, what are we going to do without Brother Word?" Hankins joked.

By this time everyone in the canteen was crowded around them and rejoicing with them, even the guards.

It became a little easier to depart when he pushed thoughts of what he was leaving behind and thought of where he was going. Joy filled his heart when he envisioned the look of surprise on his family's faces. He fought the urge to call them. He'd rather them be surprised. Once he was on the bus, he enjoyed every minute of his twelve-hour ride. By the time he got to Virginia, he had told the driver his whole life story and talked out his plans to surprise his family and future wife. He arrived in Virginia, just as scheduled, at 5:45 a.m. on the dot. That was perfect timing because his mother is an early bird and was probably already up cooking breakfast for his father.

He used his gateway money and took a cab to the house. He was so excited he couldn't wait for the driver to count out his change. "Just take the whole thang." He grabbed his one box and walked around to the back door, where he saw the light on in the kitchen. He knocked on the door. Through the sheer curtains he could see his mother tiptoe out of the kitchen. *Momma's still the same,* he thought. He knew she was going to get his father. It was too early for anyone to be knocking at their door, and he knew she was not going to answer it.

"Who is it?" his father's voice boomed.

Joseph knocked again without answering.

"Who is it?"

Joseph knocked again. He was about to burst with excitement when he heard the chains being taken off the door. Joseph could hear his father fussing, "Who is this knocking—"

Joseph threw himself into his father's chest. "It's me, Daddy."

"Beverly, Beverly. It's Joseph. Joseph's home."

"Oh my Lord. Hallelujah." She ran into his arms.

"Hey, Momma." The only person's hug that could be sweeter than his mother's was Charity's.

He was sure that all of Virginia was at his home church for Wednesday night Bible study. The news about his homecoming traveled quicker than he did. There were phone calls and visits he had not yet made. He defied the fatigue that was trying to weigh him down since he had been up for twenty-four hours. But there was no way he was going to miss the opportunity to let his church family know that their prayers had been answered. Although people swarmed around him, he couldn't help but wonder about how his friends were doing in the intercessory prayer meeting back in Kentucky.

"I don't know how far we'll get tonight," the preacher's voice broke through the loud buzz of laughter, praise, and conversation. "God has answered a prayer we've lifted up to Him for two years." The congregation went wild. "I know some of us had given up," he said, cutting them off again. "I know there were times I wanted to throw in the towel and stop praying, but God said 'No, I will do this. Hold on to your faith.' And Saints, He has. I want to present to some, and introduce to others, my very own nephew, who is now a minister of the Gospel, Minister Joseph Nelson Jr." He applauded with the rest of the church as Joseph rose to his feet and waved. "Come on up here, son. There's a word of deliverance in your mouth. Tell us your testimony."

When Joseph reached the pulpit, the church's praise was cut off instantaneously like a light with a light switch. He gave honor to God, acknowledged his family, and then his church family. He thanked them all for their prayers and testified how God heard them and how he received his salvation the first day he walked into the prison. He told them everything, from how he used to play one role in the church on Sundays and "live like the devil Monday through Saturday," to how prison had humbled him so much that all he had was the Word of God. He knew that their hearts were being convicted and they were also being encouraged. He ministered to the young and old folks alike. "This walk is not for naught. You keep fighting the good fight of faith, the diligent shall be rewarded."

It was almost eleven o'clock when they got home. He was beyond exhausted. He couldn't even call Charity, and he hoped that Sharon had not called her. No matter how much sleep came upon him, he knelt beside his bed and prayed unto God as he had done nightly for the past two years.

Chapter 31

It was Thursday. Charity was already two days late in responding to Emmitt's proposal. Even though she had prayed for her marriage to be restored, she still thought about Joseph. She could see God's hand in both situations. How else could she explain Emmitt's transformation or the way in which Joseph found her? She truly loved and believed that they could make their remarriage work, but she felt a deeper connection to Joseph. *But I know God wouldn't bring me a man I can't have right now.* She considered asking God for a sign, but knew better than to test God. She laughed at her foolish thoughts. "God, I'm grateful for where You have me. I just want to please You. I will not move until You tell me to. Thank You for clarity, wisdom, and patience. Amen."

Expecting that it was Emmitt on the other end of the ringing phone, she picked it up and answered, "Publishers Clearing House."

"I'm sorry," the voice chuckled. "I have the wrong number."

Charity thought she recognized the voice. "No, I'm sorry. This is the Phillips's residence. May I help you?"

"Charity?"

"Yes?"

"It's me, Joseph."

"Joseph, how are you? I was wondering when you would call, I thought you'd forgotten the number."

"Oh no, it's etched in my heart now. I'll never forget it."

"Oh," she said simply. "Joseph?"

"Yes."

"When my dad calls me from prison I have to go through an automated message. Your calls don't have one?"

"Yes."

"I didn't hear it."

"Wonder why that is?"

She held the phone out in her hand and looked at the caller ID. "This area code is Virginia? You're not in Kentucky? How? . . . When? . . ."

"Whoa! Slow down. I thought surely Sharon would call you and spoil my surprise, but I guess she didn't. I was released on Tuesday."

"And you're just now calling me?"

"My family had me busy. Seemed like the whole city came to church last night and welcomed me back. I didn't get home till late."

"How'd you get out? What happened? Tell me all the details."

"It was your visit and your prayers that did it."

Charity hoped she wasn't being modest. "It wasn't anything I did. I can't take credit for any of this."

"I'll tell you all about it when I see you in person."

"When will that be?" she asked. She couldn't believe she was just thinking about Emmitt and now she was wondering when she would see Joseph.

"This weekend?"

"Friday or Saturday?"

"Saturday."

She felt her heart drop. "Saturday might not work because my sister's having her engagement party here at my house. She's getting married. I won't be available Saturday at all."

"How about Sunday?"

"Actually, I guess you can tag along on Saturday but I have to warn you, I'll have another man with me." Sensing that he was not catching her joke, she added, "I'm talking about Xavier."

"Girl, don't play with me like that."

They laughed. "Two more days before I can see you, huh?"

"Since being in prison, I don't even go by time anymore. What seemed like a two-year impossibility happened in just the twinkling of an eye Tuesday."

"You're right about that," Charity said.

"Well, I'm going to call you back later tonight, and definitely tomorrow. I have to get ready to go and face my ex to see my daughter."

"Okay. I'll lift you up in prayer."

"Please, it's going to take that and then some," Joseph said.

Charity hung up and danced all around the house. God was not playing. He was meaning business and she made sure she let Him know she was in agreement with what He was doing. She stopped dancing when she thought about Emmitt. *What do I tell him? How do I tell him? This is going to break his heart. Oh man, I'm going to have to tell him no.* She prayed, "Please, God, don't let him use this to turn his back on You."

She wished she had her best friend to talk to. April would know exactly what to do, but Charity hadn't talked to April since their misunderstanding about Minister Adams. Charity made up her mind to call her. She knew April was at work and considered leaving a message for her at home. "No, I want to talk to her and get this over with." She dialed her work number.

"This is April."

"April, are you busy?"

"Not really. Is everything all right?"

"Yes. I'm talking fast because I can't talk long. Iesha's having her engagement party at my house on Saturday and I have to go and help her get some things ready today."

"She is?"

Charity tried to say everything in one breath. "Yes. We haven't talked in over two weeks, you won't believe all that's happened. Iesha is saved and has a saved husband-to-be. Anyway, I need to apologize to you. I'm sorry that you and I fell out. I never meant to let anything come between us. You are my best friend and I love you. If I had known that Minister Adams liked me, I would not have gone to that ceremony with him—"

"I know, Charity. I was just beside myself, and too prideful to call you sooner than I did. It's water under the bridge. Let's just pick up where we left off."

"You think you were beside yourself. I was beside myself. You see where I ended up? Mom told me you visited."

"Yes, she called me after it happened and asked me to come to the hospital," April said. "I was there on the first two days but you were out of it. I stopped coming, it was hard to see you like that. You were hooked up to all of those machines. I'm just glad you're alive and well."

"I'd been trying to reach you beforehand. Did you get my messages?"

"Yes, but I was so angry it was good that you didn't catch me."

"You forgive me?"

"Already done . . . nailed to the cross . . . dead and stanking."

"I have so much to tell you. I know you know my business closed, but you don't know that Emmitt was suing me for child custody." She kept talking over April's sighs and "you lyings." "Emmitt's mother died, he got saved, and last week asked me to remarry him. But before you start shouting, Minister Joseph Nelson from Kentucky—"

"The one in jail."

"Yes, he has been released and will be here Saturday."

"Girl, this is too much. I got to excuse myself so I can go get my shout on in the bathroom. Call me later tonight. Oh, how's my godson?"

"Missing his godmother."

"Kiss my baby for me. I'll see you later."

That was easier than Charity thought. She had feared April

would still be upset, but now she was glad that she called her. She had missed two Sundays of church and hadn't seen or heard from Minister Adams, even though his phone number was on her caller ID.

She changed into some better clothes than the ones she threw on to take Xavier to school. She was running a little late and was supposed to be at Iesha's house within fifteen minutes. She knew that it was Iesha on the other end of the phone calling to curse her out.

"Yes," she answered.

"Hey. I've been trying to reach you."

"Hi, Minister Adams. I'm sure you've heard that I've been in the hospital."

"Yes, Pastor announced it to the congregation. Are you doing okay?"

"Yes, I'm fine. Thank you." There was a moment of silence, "So, how can I help you?"

"I just wanted to clear the air between us."

"It's clear. And I just talked to April for the first time in two weeks."

"I'm sorry to hear that you and April had a falling-out."

"Well, there were things you and I both didn't know."

"Like?"

"Like, you didn't know she liked you, and I didn't know you liked me. Had we known those things from the beginning, the ending would have been different." She glanced at her watch. "Uhhh, Minister Adams, I really have to be going. I'm supposed to be at my sister's. She is running on nervous energy and I do not want to be cursed out."

"Okay, I just wanted to let you know that I'll be leaving at the end of the month, next week."

"Oh. Where are you going?"

"I've been offered a church to pastor in Indiana."

"Congratulations," she offered.

"Thank you, I'm very excited. Well, I know you have to go. I'll leave you with all of my contact information. Hopefully, we can keep in touch."

"That shouldn't be a problem."

"I'd feel even better if I could pack you up with me."

"Sorry, that can't happen."

"It could if we married."

This man doesn't know when to quit. The silence was deafening, but she broke through it. "Let me go before you get yourself in some trouble. I'll see you at church on Sunday."

She sped out to her car and over to Iesha's. *Just last week,* she thought to herself, *I couldn't get a man, and in one week alone, I've gotten one proposal, one semi-proposal, and a man that I could fall in love with. What in the world is going on?*

Charity was in her bedroom, between helping Iesha and looking out the door every five minutes to see the guests who were arriving. The engagement party was due to start in less than an hour and she and Iesha were both nervous.

"How are you going to be the matron of honor and you're more nervous than Iesha is?" April asked Charity. "Get away from that door and help her finish getting dressed so I can start with her makeup please."

"Okay, First Lady." Charity helped Iesha put on a formal, plum, halter-necked, beaded gown with a faux two-piece fitted bottom. "Ooooh, Iesha, this color looks good on you. You should get married in this gown."

Iesha hugged her. "The way y'all acting, it's like this is the wedding day. Ya'll making me nervous. Am I doing the right thing?"

"Do you have peace?"

"Yes, I'm just scared. What if—"

Charity didn't have to answer because April knew exactly what she was going to say. She quoted 2 Timothy 1:7 in a question, "For God hath not given us the spirit of what . . . ?"

Charity and Iesha both answered, "Fear."

"But, He gave us the Spirit of what?"

"Love, power, and self-control."

"Amen."

They were interrupted by a knock on the door. "Iesha, get back in the corner so no one will see you." April and Iesha moved to an inconspicuous spot and April continued applying her makeup.

"Who is it?" Charity answered the door.

"Delivery for Iesha."

Charity cracked the door. Terrence had sent his best friend over with a card and a single red rose to give to her.

"Ooooh, that's sweet. Tell him we said thanks and she'll be out in about thirty minutes."

Before she could close the door, Mama Lorraine barged her way in to shoot some pictures. "Oh, Esha, you look so beautiful. Smile . . ." She took a picture of them. "I just got through with the men, the kids, and the house. Can I get some pictures of y'all?"

Mama Lorraine took several pictures. "All of the food is ready. Your aunties are down there preparing the tables. We should be ready to roll soon. Y'all need to hurry up. People starting to show up."

"Yes, Momma," Iesha whined.

They were sure that the knock on the door was their exodus notice.

Charity answered the door. "We're ready."

"And you look it, too."

"Joseph!"

He kissed her softly on the lips. She didn't protest.

"Hey, Sharon," Charity greeted. "Your memory is remarkable. I can't believe you found your way back here."

"I can see you're busy, I'll go mingle with some people," Joseph said. "See if I can find your folks. I just wanted you to know I was here."

She was grinning so hard she couldn't kiss him back when he

planted his lips on hers a second time. Charity closed the door and fell against it. She pretended to fan herself.

"That's him?" April asked. "He's fine. We gotta talk."

Charity laughed.

Iesha agreed. "He is fine, Cherry."

As if this were a mock wedding, Charity and April escorted Iesha out to the family and living room, where the party was being held. Traci and Mercedes greeted Iesha. Charity was glad that they were acting civilized. She waved back at Sharon and Joseph as she passed them. She noticed how happy Terrence looked as he eagerly waited for Iesha to be brought to him. He winked at Charity as she turned to stand beside them. Charity surveyed the crowd of people, looked over at how happy Iesha seemed, and fought back her tears. This was a moment she wouldn't have wanted to miss for the world.

Chapter 32

Some time later . . .

CHARITY THOUGHT SHE WOULD NEVER get used to living in a different state. Although she missed her family, friends, and church, she was enjoying her new life.

"Momma." Xavier leaned over and whispered to her, "I know what this says." He held up the church bulletin for her to see.

"I bet you do," she said, lowering the folded program in his hand. "Let's read this later, we should be listening to Daddy preach."

"Okay, but it says 'The Good-ness of God Min-i-stries,' " he enunciated.

"Good job. Let's see if you can listen as well as you can read."

Charity sat proudly in the first pew encouraging her husband by nodding her head when he made eye contact with her. Joseph was preaching his heart out about Jonah being in the belly of a fish. "But he prayed. I said, he prayed," he sang climatically. "I'm telling you, church, you could be one night away from your miracle. Keep praying, keep praying. He slept in the fish's belly on the first night, slept in the fish's belly on the second night, and slept in its belly on the third night, but early, ear-ly, I said early the next morning, he found himself on the sandy shore of freedom. Your situation might look impossible right now, but if you keep on praying, God will answer."

Charity was glad to see the small congregation receiving him. They were saying, "Amen" and urging him to "preach, Pastor, preach." She looked around and noticed that their families were enjoying this just as much as she was. An outsider would have thought he was Mama Lorraine and Mr. Brown's son the way they were beaming. Even his parents wore a smile brighter than the sunlight shining through the stained-glass windows. When Iesha and Terrence weren't fighting with Sha-Lai and Raquan over their new baby daughter, Tyesha, they were paying attention. Sharon and her fiancé, Tyree, had made it, as did April. The icing on the cake was the card Emmitt sent to her by Mama Lorraine, blessing her marriage. The letter he'd enclosed told her that he'd always love her, which reminded her of the gentleman he was when they first married. She almost laughed out loud when she remembered the part where he wrote he'd try hard not to ask Xavier any personal questions about her during their visits. She prayed silently that God would take care of him and bless him with a deserving wife.

Then, she directed her attention back to her husband when she heard him ending his sermon. He likened his two-year imprisonment to being in a fish's belly and how God used the situations to change both his and Jonah's heart. "Before I take my seat, I just want you to know that if God can do it for me, I know," he sang, "He can do it for you."

Charity, along with the whole church, was up on her feet, applauding him. The church's trustee placed a glass of water on the podium for him. He winked at his wife as he sipped from the glass. He gave an altar call and six people received their salvation; and three joined the church. Pastor King approached the podium so that he could install Joseph as the new pastor of the church.

"Well, church," Pastor King said. "I believe Kentucky is in for a revival." The church applauded. "Pastor Nelson, you be encouraged. You're going to do well up here in the mountains." He turned to the church. "I hear it gets cold up here in these parts. Y'all make sure to take care of your pastor. Help keep him warm." He looked at Joseph again. "You'll do well as long as you keep the fire of the Holy Spirit burning in your spirit. The Lord has given you a very fine first lady, Charity, my daughter in Christ. And He's given you a fine church to shepherd. I'm excited for you. You're going to do well." Pastor King performed the traditions of the installation services and went to his seat.

Joseph took the microphone to give the benediction. "Before I close the service, I want to thank my wife, Mrs. Charity Nelson." She smiled and gave him a look that only he could translate. "Stand up, honey. Let everybody know who you are." Charity stood up and shyly waved. "Ain't she fine? Make me wanna sop her up with a biscuit." The church laughed. "I would also like to thank my parents and my family for coming today. Momma, y'all stand so the church can see you. I thank the Browns, my in-laws, for being here. Pastor King, thank you so much. I want to thank my friends, Brother Jay Allen and Eric Hankins. Ya'll stand. Church, these are brothers that God also turned around in prison. Give God a hand-clap of praise. Bless you, bros. Last but not least, I want to thank the late Chaplain Nesbit, the former pastor of this church and my everlasting friend, for not giving up on me. If it weren't for him allowing God to use him, this would have never been made possible." When his voice started to crack, he went into the benediction. "Now to Him who is able to keep us from falling, bless us all with grace, peace, mercy. Amen."

Reading Group Guide

Prologue
"I'm ready . . ." Joseph declared impatiently to the chaplain—and to God. When have you experienced that sense of I'm-ready-what's-the-holdup during your waiting times with God? What kind of emotions rush through you? What Scriptures encourage, restrain, or challenge you? Why do you think God gives prophecies and visions—only to make us wait for their fulfillment?

Chapter 1
Charity was told that an all-black counseling center wasn't necessary—that the world has enough separation and segregation. What do you think—pros and cons? What are the values of racially (or ethnically) specialized services? What are the risks?

Chapter 2
"Where in the Bible does it say we can't buy bootleg tapes?" In response, Iesha quotes, "Thou shalt not steal." How would you respond? How do you reconcile decisions such as Mama Lorraine's with your faith?

Chapter 3
Does Emmitt sound like an abusive husband? What kind of behavior do you characterize as abusive between spouses? Does your definition encompass physical, emotional, and psychological abuse? Why or why not? What faithful response should the Christian church (and/or believing spouse) have to an abusive marriage?

Chapter 4
Charity's pastor talked about times of transition and change. In terms of women in leadership and the privilege of age versus youth in leadership, how does your church handle change? Why? How do you handle differences of opinion on such issues with your church leadership?

Chapter 5
Mama Lorraine called a sort of family meeting to discuss issues raised by her earlier conversation with Iesha. How does your family handle conflict—or issues with the potential for sparking conflict? Was the Brown family discussion an example of healthy and effective conflict resolution? Why or why not?

Chapter 6
Loneliness is a burden for all of us at some time or another. Brother Lee found some comfort in his work; Joseph recommends fellowship with the believers—but admits to himself that the fellowship was hardly a cure-all in his own lonely life. How do you deal with loneliness in your own journey? What comforts you? What chases away at least part of the lonely feeling?

Chapter 7
"Thy maker is thine husband . . ." What does that text in **Isaiah 54** mean to you as a woman? How has the meaning changed if you have made the transition(s) from single woman to parent and/or spouse?

Chapter 8

"I don't want to talk Bible right now," Charity told her friend. "I just want to be straight up." Can you empathize with that feeling? Why or why not? In what ways do church, Scripture, and religion prevent us from being real—in good ways and in not-so-good ways?

Chapter 9

How were you disciplined as a child? How do you (or would you) discipline children of your own? How does Scripture guide you? How do social and cultural values influence you? How do you distinguish between effective discipline and abuse (neither of which is always physical)?

Chapter 10

Iesha is awed by the sense of being given a second chance. When has God given you one? What does it mean to you to serve a Lord who has been called the God of second chances?

Chapter 11

Joseph reads Charity's article and sees her photo—and senses that God has chosen her for his wife. His friends think he's crazy. What about you? The author clearly affirms such divine methods. (Charity's pastor had a similar experience with his wife.) Do you think God really works that way? Why or why not? How would you feel about identifying your life partner in that way—and why?

Chapter 12

Harmony's particular flavor of faith is a bit unorthodox. Terrence particularly challenges the appropriateness of Christians consulting horoscopes. How do you feel about such issues and why? How do you relate to others whose views differ from yours?

Chapter 13

Emmitt's relationship with his mother is unhealthy, agreed? How have the relationships between mothers and sons been particularly significant in the black family? What is your experience with mother-son relationships, whether as a mother, as a sibling, or as an in-law? What mother-son models does Scripture offer us, and what insights can we gain from them?

Chapter 14

If you received a letter from an inmate such as Charity's from Joseph, what would be your reaction? How would you respond, if at all? Why?

Chapter 15

What do *you* do when your past comes knocking on your door? How does your faith or Scripture guide you?

Chapter 16

"Even when you didn't get what you were expecting, you're satisfied with what you got," the mailroom employee marveled to Joseph. Could the same be said of you? Why or why not? What spiritual quality or character trait is required to reach that level of satisfaction?

Chapter 17

This chapter might be titled, "Adventures in Dating" . . . Iesha and Wallace, Iesha and Terrence, Charity and Michael, and then Mr. Wright. What kind of adventures have you had? How has faith in God affected those adventures?

Chapter 18

Charity struggles with decisions concerning dancing, especially to secular or worldly music. More than once in the novel, the question of "balance" arises. How do you achieve the balance of being "in the world but not of it"? How do you test your own spirit's vulnerability to the spirits around you?

Chapter 19

"The weapon forged against me is the instrument formed for me," the minister declares. How have you experienced that scriptural (and spiritual) dynamic in your life? In other words, what weapons forged by your enemies have become (or might still become) tools or instruments used for good—your own or others'?

Chapter 20

Has a guy ever said to you, in one way or another, "God told me you're the one"? How did you (or would you) react? Consider Iesha's cautious response: "What do you do when God hasn't spoken to the other person?" In general, how cautious are you about accepting other people's pronouncement of God's will or vision for your life? Why?

Chapter 21

How important do you think the respective families are to a couple's relationship? How do you balance the scriptural "leave and cleave" principle (see **Genesis 2:24**) with the truism that you don't just marry each other; you marry each other's family?

Chapter 22

Scripture *does* say that God will never tempt us beyond what we can handle. It seems reasonable to extend that principle to the concept of God won't burden us beyond what we can bear. However, don't we all have days when, like Charity, we feel like this is too much? How do you handle days like that? How do you minister to others who are having such days?

Chapter 23

Suicide. Has it ever touched you? In what way(s)? What motivates people to attempt it? How do family and friends respond? How do you think God responds? How can we minister to one another in the church—when suicide is contemplated, threatened, attempted, or accomplished?

Chapter 24
Iesha raises the issue of needing more time with Terrence—time to explore other aspects of who they are in terms of children, background, careers. He responds, in effect, by saying, "None of those things are relevant when God is involved." Do you agree or disagree—why and to what extent?

Chapter 25
Funerals are occasions that evoke complex emotions and a range of reactions. How does your experience of a funeral differ depending on how the relationship you, the family, or the deceased have had with God? How does your faith help you navigate the complicated maze of grief—publicly and privately?

Chapter 26
When God observed in **Genesis 2** that it wasn't good for the first human being to be alone—that the man needed a suitable helper (in KJV, "help meet")—God wasn't only thinking about a marriage partner. We all need help from other human beings sometimes (see **Ecclesiastes 4:9–12**). What kind of support system do you have? How willing are you to admit that you need their help? Why?

Chapter 27
"She did not want to be like this but she didn't know how to act otherwise." Iesha's inner struggle is reminiscent of Paul's (see **Romans 7:15–25**). When have you experienced that same wrestling? How do you achieve victory in the struggle?

Chapter 28
Charity prayed long and hard for a restored marriage. Now it seems her prayer has been answered. What do you think? What would you say—and why?

Chapter 29

"I don't have to be no more than who I am made to be." "We're Christians learning to live as humans." What do you make of those statements? What do you think they mean? What might one or both mean to *you*?

Chapter 30

How have you experienced the difference between claiming a thing in faith—and actually receiving it? What does that difference say about the nature of our faith claims? To put it another way, if there *wasn't* a difference, does that suggest that we are taking God's answer to our prayers for granted? Why or why not?

Chapter 31

In just one week, Charity received one proposal, one semi-proposal, and met a man she thinks she could fall in love with. How would you discern which apparently open door to walk through? Is there only one right door—or might God's hand be present in each of those situations? Why or why not?

Chapter 32

"Keep praying," Joseph exhorted the congregation. What are you praying on? How is God answering that prayer? What encourages you to keep on praying?

Glory Girls™

Reading Groups for African American
Christian Women Who Love God and Like to Read.

BE A PART OF
GLORY GIRLS READING GROUPS!

**THESE EXCITING BI-MONTHLY READING GROUPS ARE
FOR THOSE SEEKING FELLOWSHIP WITH OTHER WOMEN
WHO ALSO LOVE GOD AND ENJOY READING.**

For more information about GLORY GIRLS, to connect with an established group in your area, or to become a group facilitator, go to our Web site at **www.glorygirlsread.net** or click on the Praising Sisters logo at **www.walkworthypress.net.**

WHO WE ARE

GLORY GIRLS is a national organization made up of primarily African American Christian women, yet it welcomes the participation of anyone who loves the God of the Bible and likes to read.

OUR PURPOSE IS SIMPLE

- To honor the Lord with <u>what we read</u>—and have a good time doing it!

- To provide an atmosphere where readers can seek fellowship with other book lovers while encouraging them in the choices they make in Godly reading materials.

- To offer readers fresh, contemporary, and entertaining yet scripturally sound fiction and nonfiction by talented Christian authors.

- To assist believers and nonbelievers in discovering the relevancy of the Bible in our contemporary, everyday lives.